MEGIDDO'S
SHADOW

MEGIDDO'S SHADOW

ARTHUR SLADE

WENDY
LAMB
BOOKS

Published by Wendy Lamb Books
an imprint of Random House Children's Books
a division of Random House, Inc.
New York

WENDY LAMB BOOKS and colophon are trademarks of Random House, Inc.

www.randomhouse.com/teens

Educators and librarians, for a variety of teaching tools, visit us at
www.randomhouse.com/teachers

Library of Congress Cataloging-in-Publication Data
Slade, Arthur G. (Arthur Gregory)
Megiddo's shadow / Arthur Slade. — 1st ed.
p. cm.
Summary: After the death of his beloved older brother Hector in World War I, sixteen-year-old Edward leaves the family farm in Canada to enlist in Hector's batallion, where he attempts to come to terms with what has happened.
ISBN-13: 978-0-385-74701-1 (alk. paper)
ISBN-13: 978-0-385-90945-7 (glb. : alk. paper)
ISBN-10: 0-385-74701-2 (alk. paper)
ISBN-10: 0-385-90945-4 (glb. : alk. paper)
1. World War, 1914–1918—Juvenile fiction.
[1. World War, 1914–1918—Fiction. 2. Brothers—Fiction.] I. Title.
PZ7.S628835Meg 2006
[Fic]—dc22   2006011494

Printed in the United States of America

10 9 8 7 6 5 4 3 2 1

First Edition

This novel is dedicated to the memory of:

Corporal Edmund Hercules Slade, 1867–1949
Trooper Cecil Henry Edmund Slade, 1891–1949
Lance Corporal Arthur Hercules Slade, 1893–1975
Trooper Herbert George Slade, 1894–1962
Private Percy James Slade, 1897–1918 (KIA)

And to all those who fought in the Great War in all armies.

Author's Note

The names of locations used in this book are as they appear on British military maps from the time period. Many of the names have changed since that time.

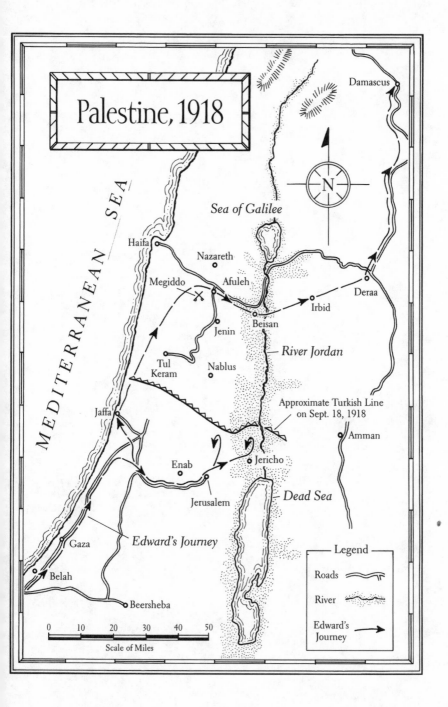

MEGIDDO'S
SHADOW

BOOK ONE

Oh! we don't want to lose you
But we think you ought to go,
For your King and your Country
Both need you so.
We shall want you and miss you,
But with all our might and main
We shall cheer you, thank you, kiss you
When you come home again.

"Your King and Country Want You"
Lyrics by Paul Rubens

1

The letter was stained with mud from France, but there was a British army stamp in the corner, and the handwriting looked fancy and official. Maybe Hector had won a medal! He'd finally given the Huns a good, hard punch on the nose.

I left the general store, nearly tripping on the sidewalk planks as I searched the envelope for clues about its contents. I wanted to rip it open, but it had been addressed to Dad. My breath turned to frost in the October air. Hector must've jumped out of the trenches and taken a machine-gun nest, or perhaps he'd captured a bunch of Germans. He'd joined up in 1916, so he'd been over there for more than a year; lots of time to do something heroic. I jogged the half mile to our farm, watching for our white and green house to appear on the other side of the hill, with the rolling prairie spread out beyond it.

Maybe Hector would be getting a Victoria Cross pinned to his chest. He would make the papers all across Canada.

I stopped in my tracks. I fingered the thin envelope, my mouth dry. *What if it's not a medal. What if* . . . I wouldn't let myself think the words.

If he'd fallen in France I'd surely have felt something deep in my heart, even thousands of miles away here in Saskatchewan.

Such dark thoughts had made my legs numb. I leaned against our sign that said BATHE FAMILY FARM. Father had carved it to put a name to the fields he'd cut out of the prairie. Land he intended to pass on to us boys.

No Hun bullet would ever kill Hector, but perhaps he'd been so badly wounded that he couldn't even pick up a pen.

My hand shook as I flicked open my pocketknife and slit the envelope. I'd tell Dad I just couldn't wait to read the good news.

I scanned the first few lines.

R.S. Major
27/09/17
15th Canadian Batt
B.E.F.

Dear Mr. Wilfred Bathe,

You will no doubt wonder who this is writing to you. I will try to explain as well as I can; I am the regimental sergeant major of the above battalion. I have a very painful duty to perform in—

My heart stopped. It wasn't just a "painful duty," but a "*very* painful duty," and I knew what had to follow. I sucked in a rattling breath. And another. *Oh, God. Oh, no.*

I forced myself to move toward the house. It was an eternity before I got there. I opened the door, the squeaking hinge unusually loud. I passed through the empty hall and up the worn stairs, glancing at the Union Jack that hung on the wall. I pulled myself up with the rail. I'd gone from sixteen to a hundred years old.

At the top of the landing I stopped to wipe my icy, sweaty palms on my overalls. I glanced at the oval photograph of Dad in his dragoons uniform, medals from the South African war glittering on his chest. Hung next to him was the picture of Mother in her Sunday best, and the thought of her made my legs go weak. It was a blessing God had taken her; today would have broken Mom's heart. Beside her was a photograph of Hector and me, when he was fourteen and I was twelve. I looked away and tried to swallow the lump in my throat.

Maybe he'd just been terribly wounded, his bright green eyes blinded by gas. That was why he couldn't write. Or perhaps his arm had been blown off. If so, when he got home he would still be able to fork hay with one hand. I'd help him. I would.

I knocked and entered the master bedroom. The stink of pee and old sweat hung in the air, a sign of how weak Dad was now. He lay sleeping, sheets pulled up to his neck, cheekbones sticking out of his long, pale face as though he were starving. His once proud and bushy mustache was limp and stringy.

5

I sat on the wooden chair and waited, my hands still trembling. Dad had been bedridden for seven months, leaving me to seed, harvest, and do the chores. In March, on the anniversary of Mom's death, he stayed in bed all day, as prickly as a cactus. He didn't get up the next day, or the next. In fact, he didn't get up at all. He gave up on everything. The man I'd seen flip and pin a calf in a heartbeat couldn't even pull himself out of bed.

It wasn't the first time he'd been bedridden. Once or twice a year he'd go all dour and stay in bed. Mom would give him a day or two before she grabbed his work clothes and boots and goaded him to his feet. After her funeral he spent three days in bed. On the fourth day Hector set Dad's work clothes and boots on the end of the bed. Dad was out to the barn within an hour, not saying a word.

This time, I'd tried the same trick after the first week, but no luck. When it came to Dad, Hector had the magic touch; it'd always been that way. All I could do was call Dr. Fusil, an old man with sharp eyes. This was, of course, against Father's wishes.

"Wilfred's body is fine," Dr. Fusil said out on the front porch after the visit. He slowly pulled on his coat. "His mind, though, is troubled. If his condition worsens and he refuses all food and water, there's a sanitarium in Regina I could recommend. That'd leave you with a heavy load, though."

I'm already doing all the work! I felt like shouting. But instead, I only shrugged, and the doctor putted away in his Model T.

Now, I sat back in the chair, making it creak.

"What's in your hand, Edward?" Father asked.

His gray eyes searched mine. I could see every long day he'd worked.

"It's a letter from Hector's major."

Father closed his eyes. Several moments passed before he rasped, "Read it, will you?"

I unfolded the letter. The writing was perfect; not even a smear. I had to swallow several times to ensure my voice wouldn't crack.

R.S. Major
27/09/17
15th Canadian Batt
B.E.F.

Dear Mr. Wilfred Bathe,

You will no doubt wonder who this is writing to you. I will try to explain as well as I can; I am the regimental sergeant major of the above battalion. I have a very painful duty to perform in telling you of the death of your son Hector. He was my batman, as no doubt he will have previously told you in his letters home. He spoke very highly of you and asked me to write should the worst come to pass.

We went into the attack on the 26th day of this month, and Hector was killed by a rifle bullet that struck him right through the heart. Death was instantaneous. This happened just as we were approaching the German front lines. You have my most sincere and deep sympathy for the loss of your brave

lad; no one knows better than I of his qualities as a
soldier. Believe me, I feel the loss very much. I gave him
instructions to stay behind and come up after the
attack and his reply was "Major, wherever you go I am
going too." He was made of the right stuff. You will be
officially notified as to the location of his grave and I
am sure if there is any more information I can give you
I shall only be too pleased if it is in my power.

> *Yours sincerely,*
> *F. Gledhill*

My throat was dry and my body numb. I'd become hard-ened clay. No, not quite. My hand was still shaking.

A tear slid down into the wrinkles on my father's face. I'd never seen him cry, not even when he'd split his hand open chopping wood. Not even at Mom's funeral.

We should have had a telegram, but someone had forgot-ten us. Hector had died almost two weeks earlier. All this time I'd thought he was alive.

I squeezed the arm of the chair and nearly ripped it off. It wasn't right! My father was broken and my brother dead. "I'll join up, the moment I'm eighteen," I'd promised Hec-tor. "I have to keep you out of trouble!" But now I wouldn't wait until I was eighteen; the Huns could be pissing on his grave as I sat here waiting for Dad to speak.

What if we lost the war? Then Hector's sacrifice would be for nothing. "I have to enlist," I whispered. Dad stared into space, not hearing me. "I have to enlist," I repeated, louder.

His eyes grew cold. "You're fifteen years old—that's far too young!"

"I'm sixteen! All you have to do is sign the permission papers."

"I would never sign them. Don't even think of it." He coughed and cleared his throat. "Hector's gone. He's . . . gone. You're all I have left, Edward."

"It's my duty."

"No." Though his voice and body were shaking, he managed to sit up. "Now, you listen to me, Edward! It's *not* your duty. Duty is what kills young men. I knew what he was getting into. I should have made him stay home."

"We're at war! He didn't have a choice, and neither do I."

"You'll stay here."

I wanted to shout *No, I won't!* but I bit my tongue and spoke as calmly as I could. "All the grain is in. Only our cows need to be fed, and the Somnerses will help with that. If I'm not back by spring we can rent our land to Mr. Sparrow."

"I don't rent my land."

"Well, why don't you get out of bed and do the work yourself, then? I've been doing it all on my own for seven months."

I thought he was going to leap up and strike me. I waited, shouting silently—*Get up! Get up! Hit me! What do I care?* But he slumped back.

"Never speak to me that way again." His voice was hoarse. "I am your father. You aren't going anywhere. I forbid it."

Then he closed his eyes.

*　*　*

I couldn't stay in the house. I stomped around the yard, not bothering with my overcoat because I wanted to freeze right to the bone. I stood in the stubble of the nearest field and stared across the rolling land at the sinking sun. In the spring our home quarter looked beautiful and green, but now it was dead and cold.

I wiped my eyes and the sun blurred.

"God made the sun," Mom had told me when I was little, holding my hand. "God made the sky and the earth and the animals, all out of nothing. And then he made men the keepers of the earth." It was such a simple revelation: all of the world made by one hand and entrusted to the care of mankind. And who was a better keeper of the earth than the British Empire? From Australia to India to South Africa to Canada, we were putting everything in order, taming all the savage lands.

But now the dirty Huns were wrecking it all. They'd invaded Belgium and France, raping women, crucifying soldiers, even tossing babies onto bayonets.

I clenched my jaw and looked skyward. *Dear God*, I prayed, *why did you let the Germans kill him?* No, that wasn't what I wanted to ask. They had done the deed. What I really wanted to know was when could I take an eye for an eye? When could I do my duty? I waited for an answer, but all that moved in the heavens were a few red-tinged clouds.

There were still chores to do, so I trudged into the barn, the last rays of the sun shining through the far window. I stabbed the fork into the hay and first fed Abigail, Dad's horse.

Caesar, Hector's horse, followed me to his trough, nudging my side. All along I'd been feeding and brushing him carefully, waiting for the day Hector would return and tell me I'd done a good job.

"Hector's dead," I whispered to Caesar. He turned back his ears. The words made no sense. "He used to ride you and now he's dead."

Caesar looked at me and I leaned against him and stroked his mane. "He's dead, dead, dead." After a moment, I pushed myself away. Caesar would be mine now. The thought made me sick.

Hector had taught me how to snare gophers. We'd swing them by the neck and hang them on the fence, pretending they were Boers. I'd do the same to the Germans.

"Hector is your North," Mom used to say. "Whichever way he goes, you go, too." It was true; I followed him like a dog, chased cattle through creeks with him, went on long rides into the Cypress Hills looking for Red Indians or bears. He punched me when I got on his nerves, passed on words of encouragement when I learned to skate, and passed down his clothes to me when he'd outgrown them. I touched my chest. My overalls had once been his. I bit my lip. My body was shaking in the cold.

I could hear his voice reading bits of the newspaper to me, articles describing how Canada had bravely declared war alongside England.

"I'm gonna go," he told me a few weeks before his eighteenth birthday. "I wanted to tell you first. I'll break it to Dad tonight. You'll have to pick up the slack around here, but you're plenty strong enough to do that."

11

He signed up in Moose Jaw and wrote a letter home nearly every week. I'd memorized them all.

There'd be no more letters now. I grabbed the pitchfork and jabbed a seed sack, imagining it was a German. Hector was in the ground. Taken away from me. I stabbed the sack again and again, then slammed the fork against the wall.

Hector was dead and the war was still going on. This wasn't a time to lie around reading about it in *Boy's Own Paper*. I knew what I had to do.

2

At two in the morning I crept past the dark rectory to the church, my rucksack slung over my shoulder. I slowly opened the front door. The full moon shone through the windows, casting shadows across empty pews. A stained-glass Mary watched as I walked down the aisle. And Jesus, too, dressed in white robes, hugging a lamb, his eyes full of forgiveness.

I set my rucksack on the front pew and let out my breath. I reached into the bag, pulled out the letter I'd just composed, and walked toward the altar. Christ's eyes followed me. He'd been a good son, doing everything his father had asked. Jesus knew his duty. He had sacrificed his life to save mankind from sin. I would have to be just as brave as him.

I set the letter on the altar where Reverend Ashford would find it in the morning.

The polished-wood smell of the church was soothing and

familiar. I stood where I'd been confirmed four years earlier, when I was twelve. Back then Mom had pressed the collar of my white shirt so stiff my neck had been rubbed raw. A year later I wore that same shirt to her funeral. She'd caught galloping consumption, and though I asked God to save her, she had suffered a horrible death, coughing up so much blood she drowned in it. Sometimes God has his own, mysterious plans.

She was in heaven now, at least. With Hector by her side.

I climbed the two steps into the choir loft, my favorite place in the church. People came from miles away to enjoy my voice: a gift passed down from my mother; from God. Pride is the Devil's work, but I really was good. Mother and I had sung together several times, bringing the congregation to tears.

Singing was the one thing Hector couldn't do. I reminded him of that by waking him up with a loud song every harvest morning. He'd cover his head and shout, "Get the gun, Dad, there's a giant canary in the house!"

But once, after Mom had left us, I'd sung solo at a wedding, and Hector had later told me, "You've got a glorious gift, Edward. Keep singing. It reminds me so much of Mom."

I leaned against the loft rail, closed my eyes, and quietly sang:

"There is a happy land, far, far away,
Where saints in glory stand, bright, bright as day.
Oh, how they sweetly sing, worthy is our Savior King,
Loud let his praises ring, praise, praise for aye."

It was my favorite hymn. When I sang it, I felt God reaching down from heaven to lift me up. Maybe Mom and Hector could hear me.

"Practicing for Sunday, are you, Edward?"

My eyes snapped open. Reverend Ashford stood at the end of the aisle, a bear-sized man with a priest's collar.

I moved to the altar, snatched up the envelope, and held it at my side.

He walked down the aisle, the hardwood floor creaking. "Can't sleep, eh? Me neither. Too many grumbling bones." He stepped into the loft and looked down at me. In the moonlight, the ragged scar on his right cheek shone. "This time of night is when I do my heavy thinking, but it's kind of late for you—those morning chores have to be done regardless of how much shut-eye you get."

I felt a stab of guilt.

"What's that in your hand?"

"A letter," I said.

"I assume it's for me. May I have a look?"

I handed it to him and he began to read. He glanced at me, then finished the letter. Sweat dripped from my underarms.

"You sound as if you've made up your mind," he finally said. "Have you?"

I nodded.

"You want to join up with Hector?"

"He's dead. Killed." I hesitated. "A bullet through the heart."

Reverend Ashford's shoulders slumped. "Dear Lord, terrible, terrible news! Our Hector? My boy, my boy, I can only

15

imagine how you must feel right now." He put his hand on my shoulder. I looked away. I wouldn't cry. "Hector," he said softly, "he was so full of life. It's hard to believe. Dear God. Such a waste."

"He wasn't wasted! He did his duty."

"Yes, he did, Edward. But there was just so much more he'd have done here—farming, marriage, children. I know he served well, but . . . Hector." His name echoed in the church. "How's your father?"

"Still won't get out of bed. Won't do anything."

"Is that why you're going? To do something?"

"I have to go. Everyone else is. Even the Americans are there now."

He watched me, expecting more.

"Hector would want me to. I know it. And . . . and the songs, that's another reason."

"Songs?"

"The ones they sing at the dance hall. About Tipperary and King and Country. They . . . they're telling me to go."

Ashford was silent; then he sighed. "I was in the Boer war, did you know that?"

"Yes. Dad fought in South Africa, too."

"That's right. Hard to believe it's been fifteen years. England asked us to go, so we went. Killing doesn't ever leave you." The scar on Ashford's face could have been made by a saber. "I assume your father doesn't know you're gone. How do you think he'll feel?"

"He'll be angry. But he doesn't understand!"

"Perhaps he understands only too well."

I shrugged. Dad might have given up on everything, but

16

I couldn't give up. Ever. Hector would never have surrendered. "Wherever you go, I'll go, too," he'd said to his major.

"Reverend, I belong there."

"I don't think you're making the right decision, Edward. You've just suffered a great loss. Wait a few weeks before you decide."

Wait? I couldn't do that. They needed my help now. "I'm going."

Reverend Ashford shook his head. "I can't stop you, Edward. You have to make your own choices and live with them." He paused. "I'll do my best for Wilfred, and I'm sure the Daughters of the Empire will take him meals. They'll see it as part of their goal to help the war effort. And I'll ask Wilfred what arrangements he wants to make for the farm. You never know . . . he may get up and get to work."

"Thank you. I appreciate your help."

"It's why I'm here." He lifted my rucksack and handed it across. "You're important to me, Edward. To the people of Tompkins, too. Don't ever forget that." He set his hand on my head and I felt a lick of panic. Would he grab me and hold me back?

But his eyes were closed. I shut mine and he whispered, "Dear Lord, please watch over Edward. Give him courage and steadfast faith, good judgment, good leaders, and true friends, and bring him home to his family." He didn't remove his hand, so I opened my eyes. "And you bloody well better keep your head down over there!" he said, looking me straight in the eye.

I nodded, we shook hands, and I marched out of the church without looking back. I walked down Second Street, past the Cypress Hotel and the Binter General Store. My footsteps echoed on the wooden sidewalk, a sound like knocking on a coffin.

I had everything I needed inside the rucksack: a change of clothes, Dad's spare razor, my pocket Bible, a few other books, and a pencil.

I hummed "Onward, Christian Soldiers" and followed the main road heading east. Someone would come along at sunrise and give me a ride. In the meantime, I could use the fresh air.

3

Several hours and three rides later, I stood under the shadow of City Hall in downtown Moose Jaw. The tower clock read half past three. I was exhausted, having only slept an hour here and there, and my stomach began to grumble because I hadn't eaten since the night before. I wondered if the Empire ladies were feeding Dad, and pictured him chowing down on ham and fried potatoes like a king. I barked out a bitter laugh—Father hadn't sat up to eat for months; all his meals were delivered to his bedside, where they were mostly ignored.

I dodged a streetcar and made a beeline for the railway station. I'd already worked out my plan: I'd go to the recruiting office and say I was eighteen. I didn't have any certificates, but I knew one of Hector's underage friends had signed up without them. Besides, I'd be seventeen in December. I wasn't that far from being old enough.

The army office was located inside a railcar decorated with the Union Jack and the Canadian Red Ensign, both hanging limp in the air. One white and black banner proclaimed FREE TRIP TO EUROPE: STEP ABOARD. A second said: YOUR CHUMS ARE FIGHTING, WHY AREN'T YOU?

Four men were lined up at the door. The man at the end, dressed in a suit and long coat, nodded. By the time I'd nodded back he'd already turned away.

This platform was the last place I'd seen Hector. That had been a year earlier, and Dad had been with me, dressed splendidly in his Royal Dragoons uniform and beaming with pride in his eldest son. We'd watched as Hector and his fellow soldiers paraded past. My brother was near the front, marching perfectly while a band played "God Save the King."

After the parade, we'd said our good-byes amid a crush of people. Children waved the Union Jack; soldiers kissed girls; mothers cried; fathers smoked cigars and patted their sons on the back.

I stared at Hector. When I was a kid he'd always been the champion of King of the Castle. Now he was more like a god. His hair had been cut short, the buttons on his uniform glittered, and he seemed to have sprouted up an inch or two. When I tried to shake his hand he yanked me into a bear hug and mussed my hair, his green eyes sparkling. "You keep away from them Morris girls, you hear? Or at least leave one for me. And make sure she's a looker." His gaze was like a spotlight on me. I stood there, dumbfounded, unsure what to say. I didn't know when I'd see him again.

"Hey, buck up!" He slipped his arm around my shoulder.

"I'll be back in no time, I promise. And I'll bring you a Hun helmet for your shelf."

That was a lifetime ago. Standing in line, I felt as though I might cry like a child. My tears were a weakness Hector had often threatened to beat out of me. I bit the inside of my lip.

The man at the head of the line burst into laughter. Another shouted, *"Blam!"* while holding a finger to his friend's head.

"They're drunk," the guy in front of me whispered. "Them boys were at the Empress finding courage at the bottom of a glass." He held out his hand. "Paul Oster." His dark hair was curly, and he had a closely trimmed mustache tracing his upper lip.

"Edward," I said, shaking his hand. "Edward Bathe."

"Where you from?"

"A farm near Tompkins. Harvest is done, so I thought I'd join up."

"I'm running away from my wife." Paul grinned, flashing bright teeth. "Kidding, of course; she's an angel. I own a shoe shop on River Street—Oster's Shoes. She and my brother'll look after it now. He's got a crippled hand, otherwise he'd be here, too. You know anyone over there?"

"Yes, some pals and my brother." I drew a sharp breath. For a moment I'd forgotten he was dead.

"Well, I chummed with lots of the Bull Moose Boys—even sold them some fine boots. Told them to kick the Germans' arses with 'em." He chuckled, stroking his mustache. Without thinking, I touched my lip, too.

"How long have you been waiting?" I asked.

He pulled a gold watch out of his suit pocket. "About

forty minutes. They don't seem to be in a hurry to sign us up—maybe the recruiters were at the Empress, too. A year ago the line was halfway down the block. Guess the war is old news now."

The three drunks shouted as the door to the recruiting car opened. A man stumbled inside. The others moved closer to the door. One by one they entered until finally it was Paul's turn. "Good luck," he said, and disappeared into the carriage.

Lord Kitchener stared down from a poster, his large mustache a dark slash across his face. Just under him was written THE EMPIRE NEEDS YOU. He'd been the greatest British general since Wellington; the perfect war minister. More than a year earlier, his ship had struck a mine and he'd been lost. How could someone so powerful die, just like that?

Kitchener looked almost exactly like Major Nixon Hilts, my father's friend from the First Royal Dragoons. Dad and Major Hilts had fought side by side in South Africa. A picture of Hilts on his charger, saber held high, was proudly displayed on our mantelpiece, and I'd grown up staring at it. He'd stayed in the army after Father and would write from India, Egypt, or other exotic places. His letters described how the world needed Britain to be strong.

The major had visited us when I was ten, bringing spears from Africa as gifts for Hector and me. He'd insisted we call him Uncle Nix and patted our backs, telling us we were upstanding young men with glorious futures.

That night Hector nudged me awake and pulled me out onto the landing, where we pressed our heads against the stair rail to listen. Father and Hilts were in the kitchen sharing loud stories of troopers they'd known, horses that'd shied at the sight of waving flags, and battles all across the dry lands of South Africa. The smell of pipe smoke and brandy and the sound of laughter drifted up. I coughed, and a heartbeat later Mom was shooing us off to bed.

Standing in the cold, I could have used a good shot of brandy myself. The train car door opened and a gruff voice shouted, "Next!" I climbed up into the car, which was thick with the stench of a cigar. Behind a desk was a bulky sergeant, his tight uniform threatening to fire several buttons across the room. A cigar was squeezed between two sausage-like fingers. "Close the door!"

I did, blinking smoke out of my eyes.

"What's your name, son?"

"E-Edward Bathe, sir."

"Sir? I'm not a fancy-pants officer! It's 'Yes, Sergeant' to you."

"Yes, Sergeant," I said.

"You catch on quick. Are you of sound mind?"

"I beg your pardon?"

"Have you been drinking? Any mental ailments?"

I thought of Father, resigned to his bed. "No!"

"Good. How old are you?"

"Eight—" My voice cracked. "Eighteen, Sergeant."

"When were you born?" He looked up, watching my reaction.

I'd already worked this out. "In 1899, Sergeant. September nineteenth."

"Good show for popping by so soon. You gonna poke him, Doc? Doc?"

A bald man in a white coat, whom I hadn't even noticed, put his book down, unfolded grasshopper-thin legs, and stood up.

"Open your jacket and shirt." His breath stank of alcohol. He jammed a cold stethoscope against my rib cage. Maybe he'd be able to tell how old I was just by hearing my heart. "Heart's good. Now cough."

I did.

"Stick out your tongue."

He inspected it.

"Read that eye chart for me."

The chart hung on the far wall. I squinted in the smoke but was able to read everything aloud, including the bottom line.

"He's fit," the doctor pronounced, extending his hand to shake mine. "Congratulations, son."

The sergeant shoved several long papers into my hands. "You sign where I've marked the X, then fill out the rest." I read a little of the form. "I'd like those done today," he added.

As I finished, the doctor pulled out a tape measure. "Put your hands in the air."

I lifted my arms and he wrapped the tape around me. "Chest—thirty-four inches." He held the tape up to my head and let it drop to the floor. "Five foot five. No distinguishing facial marks. Any tattoos?"

"No."

The sergeant tapped ashes into an ivory elephant ashtray and picked up a Bible.

"Place your hand on the Bible."

I did, my palm sweaty.

"Edward Bathe, do you swear to be faithful and bear true allegiance to His Majesty King George the Fifth, His Heirs and Successors and to be duty bound to honestly and faithfully defend His Majesty, His Heirs and Successors and observe and obey all orders of His Majesty, His Heirs and Successors and of all the Generals and Officers set over you, so help you God?"

My mind boggled.

"Well?"

"Uh—I do. By God, I do."

"Good lad." He dropped the Bible on his desk and gave my hand a quick shake. "Welcome to the army. Your regimental number is 811683. Don't forget it. Leave through the back door there and report to the armory on North Hill tomorrow morning at oh-seven-hundred hours."

As I climbed out of the car I felt light-headed—I'd been holding my breath. I stepped to the ground and sucked in some cool air. I'd made it! I wanted to jump around and shout like a schoolboy. Thank God!

"You get in?" Paul was leaning against a railcar, smoking a cigarette.

"Of course!"

"Guess we'll be tromping around France in no time! Let's get a celebratory drink."

"That'd be great!" I exclaimed, a little too loud. I wondered if I had enough money for a shot of brandy.

Paul flicked his cigarette to the ground and stepped on it. "My wife hates me smoking these coffin nails. She won't be nagging me about them for a while now, anyway."

As we rounded the end of a railcar we came upon the three drunks standing near the back of the station. One was spewing vomit onto the ground. The other two winked at us and began to sing "Another Little Drink Won't Do Us Any Harm."

Paul and I laughed. "I'll buy," he said. "As long as you don't drink as much as them."

4

The next morning, I stamped my feet to keep warm, look-ing up at the Union Jack flapping on the parapets of the brick armory. The recruiters had made a good haul—there were about a hundred men out front, though some seemed a little old to be soldiers and several were even shorter than me.

"Do you think they'll have a pot of coffee on?" Paul asked. "Maybe eggs and bacon?"

"Yes." I blew on my hands. "And apple pie, cheese, and ice cream."

Paul chuckled. "Well, let me eat it all and you can roll me right over the Germans."

A large wooden door swung open and a tall sergeant with a white handlebar mustache strode out. "Welcome to the One Hundred and Twenty-eighth Battalion! I'm Sergeant Billings!" His voice boomed, inspiring me to stand straighter.

This was the same man who'd trained Hector. In his letters, he'd called him Sergeant St. Nick because of his white hair and mustache. "You're good men for signing up. You've done the right thing, and today you'll take your first glorious step toward becoming Bull Moose Boys, ready to strike a blow for freedom! Now follow me!"

I was the first inside the armory and at the front of the line for uniforms. A corporal reached into the pile and handed me a pair of khaki pants, long woolies, and a dark brown shirt. I clutched the uniform to my chest, squeezing out a mothball stink. The corporal tossed me a new pair of boots, a kit bag, a shaving kit, a greatcoat, and my identity tags.

A few minutes later I was dressed. The trousers fit perfectly, but the shirt was too large. I'd grow into it. I strained to look at the dark blue shoulder straps—the symbol of the infantry. I touched the metal CANADA bar sewn to my left shoulder. It was cold.

I slipped the metal identity disks over my head and under my uniform. If I was killed the green one would stay with my body and the red one would be sent to my family. Hector's was likely on its way home now. I blinked back tears.

I grabbed the two rolls of green wool strips—puttees—from the kit bag and got busy trying to wrap one smoothly around my lower left leg. It was impossible; I looked like an unraveling mummy.

A shadow fell across me. "I suppose your mother dresses you every morning." Sergeant Billings had his hands on his hips.

28

"She's dead, Sergeant."

"Don't be smart with me, Private." But he saw the look on my face. "Well, she probably died of embarrassment." He took a strip and knelt down. "You're all children! You wrap them clockwise, as if you're binding a wound. Start at the ankle, go over your boot, and then tie them off at the knee. They keep the mud out." He wrapped up my left leg. The sight of the sergeant kneeling down reminded me of my dad tying my skates, and a stab of sadness surprised me. I missed him.

The sergeant stood. "You do the other one." He turned an angry red as the puttees kept coming undone. "Clockwise, lad. Get it right! That's better, now pull both ends tight. Good job." Billings clapped me on the shoulder.

"Thank you, Sergeant."

"You'll do well, Bathe. Just like your brother."

I felt as if I'd been hit in the guts. "You remember Hector?"

"Of course. You look like him. He was an excellent soldier."

"He was murdered by the Huns, Sergeant."

He nodded sadly. "I know. I read the casualty lists. I've got a son buried in Flanders. Don't worry, we'll get our pound of flesh from the Germans." He looked me in the eye, adjusted his uniform, turned, and began shouting at another recruit about his puttees.

Wait! I wanted to call out. I needed to know more about Hector. What did he do to be such a good soldier?

I examined my cap. Front and center was a metal badge

embossed with the image of a moose head, and below it the phrase *128th Overseas Moose Jaw Battalion*. I slipped the hat on. If only Mom could see me now, she'd be so proud, and maybe Dad, too. And Hector, of course.

Paul walked over to me, his uniform fitting neatly. "Pretty good! You'll break a few hearts."

I grinned. "You look swell. For an old guy."

"Old?" He pretended to spar, then reached out and adjusted my cap. "That's better."

It was something Hector would have done.

"Company D! Form a line!" Sergeant Billings was standing outside in the courtyard next to a large wooden crate. He held a rifle, its polished wood gleaming, the barrel straight and perfect.

"Look at that beauty!" Paul said.

My fingers tingled to hold one.

"Form a line!"

I ended up near the back and worried that they would run out of guns. When my turn came it was as though I'd stepped onto a stage. The sun was brighter as the sergeant reached deep into the crate to pull out a gleaming Lee Enfield. I took it in both hands and felt its powerful weight. "Use it well, Private."

The sergeant stood in front of us, still holding his rifle. "When you're outside this armory, consider yourself to be on the field of battle," he said. He spoke about musketry care, but I studied my Enfield, the smell of fresh oil filling my nostrils. It was more beautiful than paintings in museums, and more useful. I swung it around, watching the sun sparkle on the barrel. It felt like Christmas.

"Keep it still, Private Bathe!" Billings shouted. "It isn't a peashooter!"

"Yes, Sergeant!" I said, saluting.

His eyes narrowed. "Never salute an officer in the field! Ever! You'd be sentencing him to death if a sniper were in the area."

"I'm sorry, Sergeant . . . sorry."

"And you don't have to salute a noncommissioned officer, either." Billings stepped back a pace and shouted, "Company D! Form ranks!"

We gathered in front of him like curious sheep. "Those aren't ranks! Form into five lines, six men deep." He yanked us into place, the corporals helping him. "Straighten up those backs, you cripples! Now, I want you marching as a unit, eyes forward! Follow me!" We marched around the armory. The two corporals set the pace on either side of the group. I tried to walk just like them.

Billings led us north onto roads and open farmland until Moose Jaw was well behind us. "Looks like we aren't even going to get breakfast," Paul moaned quietly.

From a clump of trees near the road a girl watched us, her brown hair tied in a ponytail, both hands clinging to a feed pail. She looked my age. My heart sped up as we marched toward her. I stuck out my chest and stared straight ahead until the last possible moment, then glanced at her.

She smiled, her doe eyes full of wonder. She winked and I stumbled.

"Eyes front!" the sergeant commanded.

I found my place, dared to turn and steal one last glance. The girl was covering her mouth, laughing, cheeks red. The

31

column marched half a mile down the road, did an about-face and passed the farm again, but by then she was gone. My heart sank.

After another hour we finally stumbled into the armory grounds. The moment the sergeant commanded, "Company D! At ease!" everyone exhaled, and our heads drooped. "Don't lean on your guns!"

We gobbled our lunch and spent the afternoon on an assault course next to the armory, poking straw dummies with bayonets. I was sure I'd have nightmares about the sergeant shouting, "Put on your killing face and kill the baby-killing Huns!"

After dinner I was too tired to move. We plunked ourselves down on straw-filled palliases and watched the sun set outside the windows. Some men lit their first cigarette of the day.

"It's gonna be over before we get there," said one.

"My brother fought at Vimy Ridge. He said the Huns had bathtubs in their bunkers. Bathtubs!"

"You can't smoke on the front because the snipers'll get you."

I listened quietly, trying to gather tidbits that might help me understand what was happening in France—or anything that would make me a better soldier.

Paul was stumbling around, doing his impression of the Kaiser, when he sat on something large covered with a tarp. It made a musical *choing*.

"I'll be damned!" Paul ripped off the tarp, revealing an old piano. He pulled up a chair and pretended to adjust invisible coattails, then began playing slowly with one finger.

He jumped from scales to a jaunty song that had us singing along and stamping our feet hard enough to shake the armory. He winked at me once when I hit a high note bang on, then turned and played with his back to the piano. I whistled encouragement. His song hit a crescendo and he planted his hand on the keyboard, flipped upward, and did a handstand, managing to bang out the final chords. I gasped. Paul waved with one hand, his face tomato red, then teetered and collapsed. I jumped to help him, but he shot to his feet, brushed himself off, and bowed.

"More! We want more!" we shouted.

Paul played several songs, including "Motherland" and "River Shannon." We sang along, a brave, deep bass choir. Some of the men were almost in tune. Paul plunged into "Mademoiselle from Armentières," which I'd heard before, but not with the lyrics he sang; I was shocked that a married man would sing so many dirty words out loud.

Paul stopped and put his hand to his ear. "Does anyone hear a songbird out there?"

He crept around as though stalking an animal, then clapped me on the shoulder. "Hey, it's right here!" He yanked me to my feet, whispering, "You're a born singer."

I faced a hundred and some pairs of staring eyes.

"What's the lady gonna sing?" someone shouted from the back.

"Don't be afraid," Paul said quietly. "Show 'em your God-given talent."

I blinked.

"Sing, you bastard!" yelled a recruit who was sitting right in front of me.

I hummed a note to find my pitch, then thought of a song Mother had taught me:

"Oh, Danny boy, the pipes, the pipes, are calling
From glen to glen, and down the mountainside.
The summer's gone, and all the flowers are dying.
'Tis you, 'tis you must go and I must bide."

The men fell still. By the next verse several voices harmonized with me.

"And if you come, when all the flowers are dying,
And I am dead, as dead I well may be,
You'll come and find the place where I am lying
And kneel and say an 'Ave' there for me."

I finished, pouring everything I had into the last note. A long silence followed, then a roar of clapping. I smiled, but my eyes were wet. That song had been Hector's favorite.

Later, I picked a bed and climbed under the sheets, my skin turning to gooseflesh in the cold. Other men near me had chests matted with hair. What I wouldn't give to have half that amount.

By the time I'd whispered the Lord's Prayer, several recruits were already snoring. I breathed deeply and tried counting sheep. Instead, all I thought of was the farm girl. Her face had been burned into my memory: her big eyes and ruddy cheeks, the way her white hand was lifted to cover her giggling mouth. I was perplexed by the fluttery feeling in my gut. I wondered if she were sleeping now, looking like one of those ceramic Christmas angels. Was she thinking of me? I lay back on my pillow, smiling.

34

The smile left my face when it dawned on me that Hector might have lain in this very spot. I imagined, clearly, the bullet shooting through his heart, the blood spattering his uniform. He'd been so handsome and so sure of himself; to think that one measly bullet had been enough to kill him. I clutched the pillow and felt tears coming down. A sob got stuck in my throat. I bit my cheek.

"Edward," Paul whispered. "Are you feeling all right?"

I slowly let out my breath. Oh, God, I didn't want to cry, not in a room full of men. I hoped it was dark enough to hide my shame.

"Edward? Pal?"

"I'm fine," I said, working to keep my voice steady. "Just a tickle in my throat."

I clenched my teeth and held completely still, not daring to move in case I sobbed again. Sleep eventually, mercifully, snuck up on me.

5

Three weeks later we marched out of the armory to a band playing "The Maple Leaf Forever." We formed a tight column of 125 Bull Moose Boys, following Sergeant Billings down North Hill in perfect step, cutting a line through a skiff of snow. We'd chosen to pack our greatcoats and brave the chill in our uniforms.

Streetcars rolled by, faces pressed to the windows. A few people lined the sidewalks of Main Street and waved Union Jacks from balconies, but it wasn't nearly as crowded as Hector's send-off had been.

We stopped at the train platform and held ourselves rigid as rods. Flashbulbs went off. We'd make the front page of the *Moose Jaw Times*, that was for sure. I hoped Dad would see it and take at least a little pride in what I was doing.

Sergeant Billings marched across the platform and faced

us. "Company D! Atten*shun*!" The musicians fell silent. His face was stern, but his eyes showed a hint of sadness. "I am completely confident that you will perform your duty and bring honor to your regiment and your country. You are brave. You are strong. You are the Bull Moose Boys. I have only one final order. . . ." He paused. "Give 'em hell, gentlemen!"

"Yes, Sergeant!" we shouted in perfect unison.

I stood alone while other soldiers fanned out into the crowd. It seemed everyone had someone to see him off. I wished Father were here. It had been nearly a month; he could have pulled himself together enough to get out of bed. I searched the crowd for his face, but I was being harebrained. There was no way he could have known about this send-off.

"Hey, Edward!" Paul shouted. "Come meet my wife."

I made my way over, jostled at every step. Paul was holding his daughter. His wife, a small brunette with an elegant face, stood as if she were bracing against a stiff wind. "This is Andrea."

"Pleased to meet you," I said, nodding to her. A boy clung to her dress and stared up at Paul as though he were looking at a hero. I smiled down.

"We don't have much time." Still holding his daughter, Paul put one arm around his wife and pulled her close. "Every day I'll think about you, my love. You're everything to me. Absolutely everything." This was meant to be private, but the crowd kept pushing me closer into them. The children hugged Paul and cried.

I shouldered my way toward the station. Girls stared and

I smiled. Mother had always said I cleaned up well. I turned and drew in a deep breath. The girl from the farm was right in front of me. She was even more beautiful up close—hair braided, skin white as milk, her dark deer eyes freezing me in place. She was wrapped in an oversized fur coat.

She came to me, stood on tip-toe, and kissed my cheek. I almost fell over. I breathed in: she smelled of freshly turned soil. She pressed a ribbon into my cold hand. "Go kill those bastards," she whispered harshly, revealing large, molasses black teeth. "Kill every last stinkin' one." She stepped back, turned, and vanished into the crowd.

I stared, shocked by her kiss, her words, and her rotting teeth. I clutched the red ribbon tightly in my fist. What did it mean? Was she my girl? Had she lost someone in the war?

A trumpet called us to the train, releasing me from her spell.

"You look older," a man said.

Reverend Ashford's buffalo skin coat made him look like a bear in the center of the crowd. I grinned from ear to ear.

"I feel older." I laughed and stuffed the ribbon into the pocket of my trousers. "I didn't expect to see you here."

"Someone had to see you off. It wasn't hard to figure out where you'd be training. How did it go?"

"Great! We learned a lot, and we're in top fighting form."

He nodded. "They do look fit."

"We'll get the rest of our training in England. I can't wait! I want to see the Tower of London and Buckingham Palace and maybe Lincolnshire, too. That's where my ancestors came from. Anyway . . . uh . . . how's Dad?"

"The truth? He's a stubborn, bitter man. He forbade me to talk about you. He feels betrayed."

My stomach sank. "I hoped he'd change. Maybe if he saw me now with all these men, he'd understand that I belong here. It's what I have to do."

"You two will have to sort that out between you. I've done what I can. The Somnerses have moved your livestock to their pasture and promised it'll all be in perfect shape when you get back. And the Daughters of the Empire are bringing meals to Wilfred. They assume he has pneumonia. All their clucking might just scare him out of bed."

Dad had never been a good patient.

"I brought you something." Ashford handed me a folded handkerchief. My mother's tartan was stitched in a corner. This was one of her favorite keepsakes: it had belonged to her father. I held it gently.

"I stole it," Reverend Ashford said. "Not a very good man of the cloth, am I? But you'll need a lucky charm, something that'll bring you home."

"Thank you . . . thank you. I'll carry it with me everywhere." The trumpet crowed again. "I'd better go."

We shook hands. "Take care. Remember to pray. And remember where you come from. We'll all be praying for you, Edward. God bless you."

I nodded and followed my fellow soldiers into the train. They leaned out the windows to shake hands and get one last kiss. I found a seat next to Paul and waved to the crowd. There was no sign of the Reverend. The departure bell sounded, the doors closed, and the train chugged away. Soon

Moose Jaw had disappeared, and the flat prairie stretched to the horizon.

Paul stared out the window. "It better be worth it," he whispered.

It would be. All the training and the exercises, the skill with a rifle, it would all come in handy. The Germans were tough, but I imagined thousands of us coming from every corner of the British Empire—Canadians, Australians, Indians—even the Americans were joining in. The Huns were hanging on by their fingernails.

I tried to picture the girl's face again, but all I could see were her brown teeth. If she hadn't spoken I would have had the perfect memory of her. I searched my pockets for her ribbon, but it was gone. Bad luck to lose something like that!

At least I had Mom's handkerchief. I took it out and smoothed it across my knee, all the time wondering if it really would bring me home.

6

I lost count of the number of times I got seasick on the voyage over. The moment I saw the port of Liverpool from the front deck of the *Olympia*, I thanked God a thousand times. I never wanted to sail again.

Within hours we were on a train chugging toward our camp. England was like a painting by an artist who only had several shades of green. I'd never seen so much green in December. Paul and I gawked from our train car window at the hills dotted with tiny cottages. I was in the motherland of the Empire, the land of my father, and the country where I was born. I kept looking for something familiar.

We detrained in Milford and marched four miles through misty rain. I still didn't have my land legs back. The sky leaned on me; this was nothing like home, where you could see far into the distance. We dragged ourselves to the gates of Camp Witley and stood there, sweaty and dog tired, our puttees caked with mud. No one had told the brass that we were coming, so there was a wagonload of paperwork that had to be done. We could only stare at the warm huts, smoke puffing from their chimneys.

"Makes me wonder if some deranged, dotty idiot is in charge," Paul said.

His words made me think of Dad.

"Are you Hector Bathe?" a man asked.

Hector? I spun around. Lord Kitchener glared down at me, his medals glittering. He had no need for a greatcoat; the biting cold didn't dare bite him. As I snapped a salute it occurred to me that Kitchener was dead. But the officer was so familiar. A few feet away, his orderly waited like a guard dog.

"Well, are you Hector Bathe or not?"

"N-no, sir, I'm not."

"Well, I'll be—you're the spittin' image of Hector, lad. He's a Canadian, too."

"He's my brother, sir." Again, I'd spoken as though Hector were still alive.

"You're Wilfred Bathe's son?"

"Yes! Yes, I am. Edward Bathe."

"Edward! How you've grown. It's your old uncle."

Uncle? He motioned for me to move out of line. A grin of recognition crossed my face just as he said, "It's Uncle Nix! Nixon Hilts. But I supposed you'd better call me Colonel Hilts while you're in uniform."

"I will, sir. I remember your visit and all your letters. Oh, and the African spear you gave me is still on my wall. It's so great to see you!"

"I've been meaning to write Wilfred for ages, but you know . . ." He motioned toward France. "How is your dear old father?"

"I'm afraid he's bedridden these days with . . . with . . . consumption."

"Consumption? Bloody bad luck. We need steely men like him. Where did you train?"

"Moose Jaw, sir."

"Never heard of it. What did they teach you?"

"Infantry."

"Infantry! A man with your pedigree? What a bloody waste."

I didn't know what to say to that. Instead, I asked the first thing that came to mind. "Colonel, did—did you ever run into Hector?"

"Yes, last winter. I see most everyone who goes through here, keep my eyes open for the good ones. We had a fine chat. How is he?"

When I took too long to respond, the joy in his eyes faded. Finally, I said, "He's dead. A bullet in the heart."

"I'm so sorry to hear it, Edward. Your father . . . Lord. He must have taken the loss very hard." Hilts set his hand on my shoulder. "It's a terrible price we have to pay, Edward. Terrible. He was from fine stock; I'm sure he made a good show of it."

"I'm sure he did, sir."

"Of course!" He patted my back. "The Kaiser will be punished for every death he's caused, I can guarantee you that."

"I'll give him a smack on the nose myself, sir."

Hilts laughed. "We need more colonial pluck like that!" He looked me up and down. "You're about the same size as your father. I trust you're a horseman?"

"I ride every day."

"I bet you're an excellent rider." He pulled on his waxed mustache. "I have a plan for you, Edward. Report to Sergeant Byng tomorrow. You'll find his office on Victory Street. I'll make sure he's expecting you."

"I'll be there, sir." I wanted to ask why but knew it wasn't my place.

"Good piece of luck that I bumped into you, Edward. Say hello to your father when you write home. Now you'd better get in line; the bean counters want to count their beans."

I watched as the colonel and his orderly strode toward camp. Several soldiers, noting his rank, saluted. I couldn't believe I'd just seen Uncle Nix. He was a colonel now! To think Dad could have been as high in rank as his friend by now if he'd stayed in.

"That was your uncle?" Paul asked.

"We just call him that. He's a really good pal of my father's."

"I'm sticking with you, kid." Paul punched my shoulder. "You've got friends in high places."

It seemed more than chance that I'd met Uncle Nix; it was as if God had chosen to send him to me.

After signing in, we had stew and bread and bunked down for the night on mattresses that leaked straw. The tent was cold, but the brazier burning in the center gave enough warmth.

The tent was so threadbare I could see the stars; it was a different sky than at home.

Reveille sounded at five a.m. I poked my nose outside to see trucks rolling down the gravel streets, cooks hauling steaming water, and a column of mud-stained soldiers returning from night training. They looked bone tired.

We found the mess hall and I sat at a bench and washed my porridge down with a cup of weak tea. A group of Canadian soldiers burst into the room, laughing and confident, their uniforms sharp.

"Where you green buggers from?" one asked.

"Moose Jaw," Paul answered. "We're with the One Twenty-eighth."

"The One Twenty-eighth? They were busted up last week and sent every which way but home."

All of us Bull Moose Boys froze, spoons halfway to our mouths.

"Busted up!" I said. "Why?"

"Attrition. Have to fill the ranks of the battalions already in the field. You're not the only ones; we got our marching orders yesterday. At least we're getting to the front."

If we weren't going to join our battalion, I wouldn't have much chance of finding anyone who knew Hector.

"This is awful," Paul said. "We'll be fighting beside strangers." He threw an arm around my shoulder. "The brass won't bust you and me up—we're a team! With my playing and your singing, we could spend the entire war entertaining the troops."

"Now, that'd be quite the lark!" I'd often thought about how good it had felt to sing for the company. My back was still sore from all the pats I'd received. I turned to Paul with a smile. "But I didn't come all this way to sing."

He grinned. "Your singing could mesmerize the Huns and then I'd pick 'em off."

I laughed.

When breakfast was done, I searched for Sergeant Byng's office, the words "busted up" still bouncing through my head. I wondered what Uncle Nix could possibly have planned. I dared to imagine he'd make me a lance corporal, just like that.

Camp Witley was a labyrinth of huts and tents. I passed several stables and turned a corner. A cavalry squadron trotted by, horses snorting, steam rising from their flanks. The troopers held their lances steady, their faces stern, helmets shiny. They looked so powerful; it was a *Boy's Own Paper* illustration come to life.

I located Victory Street. Each building was numbered, but I had no idea which one housed Sergeant Byng, so I stopped in front of a corporal seated on a bench, reading a book. His uniform was British; the red flannel on his cap showed he was part of the military police.

"Is that poetry, Corporal?" I hoped he was the kind who could take a bit of kidding.

The man squinted at my shoulder insignia, then squeezed his face even tighter, as though a foul stink had arrived. "No, it's a military law manual, Private." He stuck his nose back in his book.

One good smack would show him. "Could you direct me to Sergeant Byng?" I asked through gritted teeth.

The corporal pointed without raising his head. "Number seventy-four."

He had no right to be so snotty; he wasn't risking his life—just arresting drunk soldiers and kissing officers' bums. I pictured giving him a few pokes with a bayonet.

I stomped away and found Byng in a hut marked LOGISTICS AND SUPPLY. He was a potbellied man, sitting near a potbellied stove. "What do you want?"

"Colonel Hilts ordered me to report to you, Sergeant. My name is Edward Bathe."

"Here are your papers." He scribbled on a few pages and pushed them across the desk.

"What's this?"

"A transfer to the remount department."

I dropped the paper on the desk. "I didn't sign up to train horses!"

The sergeant slid the paper back. "Colonel Hilts is short of breakers. He can second whomever he pleases."

"But I didn't ask for it."

"And I didn't *ask* to fill out papers day in and day out, Private! Colonel Hilts has spoken, and one doesn't argue with the Iron Colonel. Just sign the papers, then apply for a transfer back to your battalion after a few months."

"Months?"

Byng held out the pen. "They need you in Remount. You'll be a great aid to the war effort there."

I blinked. Fingers numb, I signed the papers.

"Welcome to the British army, Bathe. Get your gear; the train to Grimsby departs at half past eleven. Here's your pass. Ask your CO to sign these documents and have a runner return them. And leave your gun with your outfit."

I took the pass, along with a packet of other papers.

"You're dismissed." The sergeant went back to his work.

I stumbled out, shielding my eyes from bright daylight. I tromped past the corporal, who was still reading, and narrowly missed his foot.

"Damn! Damn it!" I wished I'd never seen Hilts. What right did he have to send me to Remount!

When I found the Bull Moose Boys, Paul had just pulled a crate from the back of a truck, a cigarette dangling from his lips.

"Perfect timing! You missed all the work."

"I'm leaving for Grimsby; going to the east coast."

He set down the crate. "You're what?"

"I've been transferred to Remount. Uncle . . . Colonel Hilts sent me."

"Just like that?"

"Yes! I'll be breaking horses, of all things! I might as well be back on the farm."

"This is so quick, I'm a little dumbfounded. Now who'll laugh at my jokes?" He grinned and slapped my back. "Don't take it hard, pal. You'll see this whole ragtag gang again. And I'll write. What's the unit?"

I looked at my papers. "The Fifth Imperial Remount."

"Easy enough to remember. I'll keep you up on all the gory details. I'm sure you'll be able to transfer back when they're done with you."

"I hope so. I really do. You and I should fight side by side."

He shook my hand. "Don't be so down, Edward. Next time we meet you'll have a girl on each arm and twenty medals on your chest."

I tried to smile. There'd be no way to win girls or medals in Remount.

7

When I was just a few stops from Grimsby I stared out the window with renewed interest. The train could be passing the spot where Dad had grown up, where Hector and I had been born, but I had no idea what the farm looked like.

An old farmer working on his stone fence stood and turned toward the train. He could've been Dad's twin. I immediately wanted to jump off and talk to him.

I wondered what Paul and the rest of the Bull Moose Boys were doing. Now I'd only be meeting Brits; I hoped they'd treat me well.

I arrived at Remount Depot Number Five after dark, reported in, and was told, "Corporal Grimes is out back." I wandered through rows of corrals and tin-roofed stables lit by electric lamps. Horses neighed hello, but I couldn't find a single breaker. I peered into one of the larger stables.

"Are you Bathe?" a gruff voice asked.

I turned to see a short man with a barrel chest. His nose had been broken and healed so that it seemed to be lying on its side.

"Yes, I was told to report—"

"To me. I know. Rip off those regimental badges; you're Remount now. You'll get new ones tomorrow. I'm not sure why HQ fobbed you off on us, but I expect you to carry your weight. Your cot is in barracks B." He cleared his throat and spat, the gob landing near my feet. "I mean it. I don't want to see those badges again. Go settle in."

Inside the barracks, I closed the door, glad the room was empty. It slept twelve breakers. I was the thirteenth, and my cot had been jammed into a corner. I sat on it.

I was nearly in tears. I slapped my forehead, hoping the pain would snap me out of my funk. I was infantry, and I hadn't come a thousand miles just to break down because of loudmouthed Corporal Grimes.

This had all been an awful mistake! I was supposed to be training for the front, but Uncle Nix had said he had a plan. Breaking horses? That wasn't a plan; that was punishment.

My fingers were cold as I unhooked my Bull Moose cap and collar badges and placed them in a tin box. Removing the CANADA shoulder titles from my uniform felt so wrong. I placed them alongside my collar badges and infantry stripes, snapped the lid closed, and stashed the box in the bottom of my kit bag. I vowed I'd wear them all again one day soon.

Uncle Nix and his fellow officers saw the big picture—maybe this was just the first step. I should have faith.

My section would soon be here. Should I be reading my

pocket Bible when they came in? No, they might think I was a prude. I sat still, feeling naked without my badges.

Someone swore outside so loudly I jumped. The door banged open and a squat, bulky man stomped in. He sniffed the air. "Oo's bin sleepin' in my bed?" he slurred, glancing at me. "Wassit you, Goldilocks?"

"No."

Several other breakers stumbled in, their uniforms torn and stained. They gathered around me like a pack of mangy dogs that had swum through whisky.

"Well! Well!" said a slim man. "Grimes was right, there's someone from the colonies here. I thought they'd all be at home sucking on their mamas' tits."

I bit my tongue.

"What you doin' here, bantam?" a squat man asked.

"I was sent. I don't want to be here."

"Why not?"

"Because I'm trained for infantry. For fighting."

"And we're not? Eh, lads, I think bugle boy just insulted us." He cracked his knuckles. "I'd better teach you a lesson."

"Let 'im be, Guller," the thin breaker said.

"Shut yer gob! We can't have a chitty-faced weakling in Remount."

"I don't want to fight." My voice cracked.

"Thought you were trained to fight." Guller grinned. Half of his teeth were missing. "I'm not a bleedin' savage. Come arm wrestle me; it'll be all civilized and proper. Or are you fritten?"

Frightened? "No, I'm not!"

"Well then, show me what yer made of."

52

Dad had warned me that men always tested each other this way. "Never back down," he'd said, "even if you lose, you'll at least win respect." I sat across from Guller at a small table. He smelled as if he were sweating rum.

He set his right elbow on the table and I grabbed his meaty hand. "Do the 'onors, Bixby," Guller commanded.

Bixby, the thin breaker, plopped his cold hand on top of ours. "When I lift my hand you go like hell."

Guller glared, a burning cigarette jammed in the corner of his mouth. I gripped the table with my left hand for leverage; I'd learned that much from arm wrestling with hockey players back home.

Bixby pulled his hand away and I pushed hard, trying to budge Guller. No luck. He pushed back and I was able to hold him; all that time digging postholes was paying off. A bead of sweat trickled down his forehead. He grimaced and the cigarette dropped, bounced off the table to the floor, still burning. Bixby stepped on it.

Just as I thought he was tiring, Guller grunted like a hog, snapped my wrist back, and banged it into the table. Pain shot up my forearm, but I clenched my teeth, careful to not make a peep. Guller held my arm down. "Good try." His voice was hoarse. "Good try, lad."

He let go and I went back to my cot, opened Kipling's *Kim*, and stared at the words, unable to read. Even holding the book hurt my wrist.

The breakers ignored me, and soon the lights were out. Snuffles and snores filled the room, as if I were sleeping in a pig barn. *Thanks a lot, Uncle Nix.*

What would Hector have done? None of this, because

he'd been in the infantry. I was no longer following him; Hilts had sent me on a different path. Now I'd never know what Hector had experienced.

Our Father, who art in heaven, I began. I said the Lord's Prayer in my head several times, and that brought me some comfort, but by midnight my arm throbbed so painfully I was unable to sleep.

In the morning I checked the tension on my puttees and made certain my buttons were shining. My wrist had swollen up—I hoped it was only a sprain.

Outside, I passed rows of stables. The *ting ting* of ferrier hammers echoed through the yard, and the stench of dung woke me up once and for all. Horses neighed: colts searching out their mothers, geldings calling their brothers.

Corporal Grimes waited at the training corrals, a pack of breakers around him. "Bathe, be more punctual. Now, we've got an easy job for you, this being your first day and all." He grinned, pointing at a horse tied to a snubbing post, struggling to break its reins. "Give number fifty-eight a ride."

Another test. The young gelding was at least fifteen hands high, sable black with a white star in the center of his forehead. I nodded, climbed the fence, and approached the horse from the side so that he could see me. He glared, his ears back. His flanks were sweaty, so they'd already given him a workout.

I untied the reins and the gelding jerked back. With a sharp tug down I showed him who was master and pain shot up my arm. I switched the reins to my left hand and led fifty-eight around the corral, letting him get used to me. "Hey,

54

boy," I whispered. "Hey there, pal." Dad said horses were like women: they liked lots of talking. Fifty-eight snorted and showed his teeth. He could be a biter.

"Get on with it!" Grimes commanded. The breakers were halfway up the fence to get a better view.

I ran my hand across the horse's mane, and he shook as if he'd been stung by a hornet. I stroked his neck. "Good boy. I'm your pal, fifty-eight. I'm your pal." I launched myself onto the horse's back, automatically grabbing the rein with my right hand and sending a jolt of pain up my arm. The gelding threw his rear high in the air, landed hard, then lunged side to side, jumping up and crashing down, kicking away clods of dirt.

My grip weakened. My eyes blurred and I lost track of where I was in the corral, but was aware I could get brained here. The men hooted and hollered—cheering for me or the horse? Then fifty-eight bucked so hard I was tossed heavenward. I threw out my hands and hung in the air for a moment, then crashed to the ground. I collapsed on my right arm when I hit, and bashed my nose.

I rolled over, tasting my blood. The horse reared up and stomped just inches from my leg. Guller jumped in, grabbed the reins, and yanked fifty-eight away. I forced myself to get up, my forearms scraped and bleeding. I wiped my nose with the back of my left hand, looked disdainfully at the blood. My uniform would need a good soaking.

"You did well," Grimes said, "Bixby didn't even stay on him that long yesterday, did ya?"

"He was more tired today," Bixby said. The breakers guffawed.

Their laughter got under my skin. These men chose breaking horses over killing Huns. Most of them were young and healthy enough to fight.

"You're a bleedin' mess," the corporal said. "Wash up at the barn, and if you need stitches visit the regimental aid post."

I spat and turned toward the horse. Guller was leading him to the snubbing post.

"Wash up, breaker," the corporal repeated. "Did you hear me?"

I ran after Guller, grabbed the reins from his hand. The gelding had a wild look and neighed angrily, snorting a spray of snot. I swung onto him and the wild ride began again, but this time I heard my father's voice: "Always move with the horse; never fight against it." I held tight and let my shoulders relax, waiting for fifty-eight to tire. The corrals were a blur; the men on the fence were silent. Soon the swirling slowed and the bucking stopped.

I slid off the horse and patted his head. There was still fire in his eyes, but he was too tired to snort.

The blood on my face had dried and I must have looked half mad. Perhaps I was. I threw the reins to Guller, stumbled to the barn, and washed myself off.

My wrist was already purple and black.

8

Shielding my arm, I pushed open the door to the regimental aid post. There were three other men in the cramped waiting area: one breaker who couldn't stop coughing, another with a cut hand, and a third man, a moaning yeomanry trooper. He was in the worst shape, his foot wrapped in blood-soaked bandages. He looked drunk. "Shot 'imself," the sick breaker rasped as I sat down. "Dumb bugger." He coughed again, bringing up a wagonload of phlegm.

I held my breath, not wanting to catch anything. The throbbing in my arm was unbearable. *God, just make it go away*, I thought. Then I worried that I'd said it out loud. I closed my eyes. The ache seemed to be filling the room.

"Edward," a woman said, and an image of Mom flashed behind my eyelids. When I opened them a young, dark-haired nurse was in the doorway.

"Edward Bathe, come along now. Can you stand?"

"Of course." I got up too fast, my dizziness adding to the general fog I was in. She guided me to a small examining room with curtains for walls.

"Sit down." I sat on the cot. "My name is Emily Waters."

"Oh, uh, I'm Edward."

She gave a slight smile. "I know. Now, what have you done to your arm?"

"Sprained my wrist. At least, I think it's just a sprain."

Her fingers were ghostly against my skin. She turned my wrist slightly and I winced. "How did you injure it?"

"I was bucked off a horse."

"They don't call you breakers for nothing." Even through the haze of pain I noticed she had green eyes. "You gave your nose a good smack, too. Doesn't appear to be broken, but you'll have a swollen sniffer for the next week. Are you usually this clumsy?"

"It was a wild horse!"

"Then why'd you get on it?"

"It's my job," I grunted.

She patted my good arm. "Don't get all wound up; I'm teasing. Your wrist is probably fractured."

"What? It can't be."

"Why? Are you made of steel?"

She was pretty, but she was getting on my nerves.

"Shouldn't the doctor look at it?" I asked.

"Don't you trust me?"

"It's just that . . ."

Emily laughed. "Everyone wants to see Dr. Purves. It

58

makes them feel better. But today you're out of luck. There was an accident with a Mills Bomb; apparently they aren't meant to be juggled. Purves is in surgery trying to save a trooper's arm. Should I fetch him?"

"Of course not!"

"Good. We don't have an X-ray machine, so Dr. Purves would just be guessing anyway."

She lifted my arm and I winced, then blushed, ashamed that I'd shown such weakness. She gave me a kind look as she wrapped my wrist with gauze. "Stubborn, aren't you? And I know how this works. I ask you to watch your arm and you carry on using it until it falls off. I'd like to put you on sick leave, but only Major Purves can do that. So I'll tell you what—I'll show you how to wrap and unwrap it yourself. Keep the bandages tight and don't do any heavy work. Understand?"

"Yes."

She removed the wrapping and bound my arm again. I hadn't been this close to a girl since the one from Moose Jaw had kissed me. She'd had an earthy scent, but Emily smelled like a flower. Was she nineteen? Twenty? She certainly was headstrong.

"The gauze won't be much protection," she explained. "It's really there to remind you not to use your arm." She scribbled on my chart. "I'll write it up as a severely bruised wrist." She handed me a small bottle of aspirin tablets. "Take two of these twice a day and come back tomorrow afternoon. I want to see if the bruising gets worse or if any bones poke out."

"Thanks," I said, searching my brain for something more clever to say.

On the way back to Remount, I kept rubbing my arm where her hands had touched me.

"We're breaking her flight instinct," Grimes said, standing over a mare. She was on her side, eyes wide with fear, each leg bound, while breakers yanked on the ropes, using fence posts for leverage. "She's to learn we're not wolves. We're her masters."

The mare lifted her head, foam specks flying from her mouth. Guller smacked her on the side of the neck with a cricket bat. "Stay down!" he yelled, and whacked her several more times. Each thud made me wince. We never hit our horses back home. Dad would have tanned our hides.

"You're cringing, Bathe. None of us like it, but it's the only way to crack the hard nuts. There's no permanent damage." The mare kicked and the breakers grunted and tightened the leg ropes. "She'll lose her fight soon."

"Did you do this to fifty-eight?"

"Ha! We got tired before he did." Grimes spat in the straw. "I was tempted to send him to the sausage factory, but we hobbled him; worked him to the bone, and that did the trick. You're the only one that's actually ridden him. You're a natural."

A compliment? Or was he setting me up for a fall?

Another smack echoed through the barn. The horse made a gurgling noise as though the rope was choking it.

"You should have washed up when I ordered you to. It wasn't a direct order, but you will do *what* I tell you *when* I tell you. We've some pigheaded breakers, but every last one of them does what he's told. Understand?"

"Yes, Corporal."

"Good." He whistled sharply and Guller looked up at us. "Bathe is going to take a turn."

Guller, sweat on his brow, held out the cricket bat.

"Get to it, Bathe," Grimes said.

I crossed the straw, my feet heavy. The mare was still trying to raise her head. I took the bat and held it with both hands to protect my wrist. The worst I'd ever done to a horse was shout or give the reins a good yank. Dad had told me long before, "Hitting a horse will put fear in its heart, and then you can never trust it."

"Discipline the horse, Bathe."

But I was in Remount now, and Father wasn't here. I swung the heavy bat and hit the mare's flank. Agony shot up my arm. "Harder, Bathe!" Grimes barked. "Harder! She has to know who's boss."

I hit her again.

"Harder!"

I swung, striking her neck, her sides; gritting my teeth to overcome my own pain. "Stay down!" I hissed. "Stay down, damn you! Stay down!"

The breakers held their ropes tight, sweating and swearing. "Stay down!"

Eventually, she did.

"We'll have to do the same thing tomorrow," Corporal Grimes said. "Then maybe we'll be able to get a saddle on her."

It wasn't until later that I checked my arm. I undid the

bandage to find that my wrist had darkened, but I could make a fist. I figured that was a good sign. I bandaged it again, tightly. It was just like wrapping my puttees.

The following morning I faced fifty-eight again. He shook off my every attempt to slip on a halter. "You're the king," I said, and he seemed to like it. "You're the king of horses." With kind words and a handful of oats, I was able to halter him, then get the bridle on him. I spent most of the morning leading him around the snubbing post. I even sang a bit to soothe him.

He was such a beautiful horse; so perfectly muscled and strong, as though he'd been chipped out of marble. God had had a good day when he designed fifty-eight.

After the midday meal I went to the barracks and changed into a clean uniform. I combed my hair and squinted in the mirror. I could pass for twenty, especially now that my nose was swollen. I smiled and was reminded of how much I looked like my mother and Hector. Perhaps they were watching me.

"Lucky me," I whispered. "I'm going to see a girl."

I hummed all the way to the regimental aid post. Two yeomanry troopers sat inside. Both seemed healthy. While I was breaking horses, these men trained with guns, lances, and sabers, learning to be mounted infantry.

"Isn't that grand news about Jerusalem?" I asked. The announcement that the British army had liberated the Holy City from the Turks had been in the paper the day before.

"It's splendid, breaker," a trooper replied. "Maybe one of your horses is over there."

Was he making fun of me? I wanted to explain I was really an infantryman, but I kept my mouth shut.

Emily strolled down the hall and said, "This way, Breaker Bathe." I followed her to the examination room. The sash around her hips showed off her slimness, and her ankles appeared and disappeared under the skirt of her dress. She turned suddenly and I looked at the wall. "Have a seat, Mr. Bathe." She gently unwrapped my arm and examined it, a pleasant, painful feeling. "Well, it didn't fall off!"

"It did, but I jammed it back on."

She laughed. "Any sharp pains?"

Only in my heart, I thought, but then said, "No. I've been very careful, just like you ordered."

"I bet. Do you know what the most common breaker injury is?"

"No."

"Bruised pride. When he gets tossed off a horse."

I smiled.

"Well, your wrist isn't any worse, but be careful for the next few weeks. If you reinjure it, don't wait until it's completely black to come back." She bound my wrist again, pulling the gauze until it pinched.

"I'm free to go?"

"Yes," she said, but neither of us moved. The corners of her lovely lips turned up. "I'm about to take a break. Will you join me?"

"Yes, yes, of course." I sounded too eager. "I've a bit of spare time."

She led me farther down the hall and we passed several

cots. On one lay a naked man, his back plastered by bandages. Why wasn't he covered in front of the nurses? An old urine smell reminded me of Dad's room.

Outside, a few wicker chairs had been set in the sun. Two other nurses wearing thick sweaters chatted with the yeomanry troopers.

Emily seemed to have pulled a cigarette out of thin air. In one movement she struck a match with her long thumbnail and lit the cigarette.

"Gasper?" She held the packet out to me. It had the card of a Victoria Cross hero inside. I wanted to see who the hero was. I shook my head and she slid the cigarettes into her cardigan pocket.

"Well, Edward, where'd you get that accent?"

"Canada. The prairies."

"A farm boy? I could've guessed."

"What's that supposed to mean?"

She let out a ring of smoke. "You've got the *eau de farm* about you." She giggled, though I didn't see what was so funny. "Tell me about your prairies."

"Well, there used to be buffalo everywhere, but most of them are dead now." Why'd I pick that to talk about?

"Buffalo? Red Indians, too?"

"Some, but I was born here in England at Aylesby. My father had a farm."

"Aylesby? It's a cozy place. Have you gone to see your old home?"

"I only just arrived."

"It's a short jaunt. I wouldn't mind visiting the village again."

Then why don't we go together? I wanted to say.

Emily stared as if trying to memorize my face.

"Why are you looking at me like that?"

"You're seventeen, aren't you. Maybe younger."

"No." I coughed. "I'm of age. I'm eighteen."

She laughed. "No, you aren't. They used to make the young ones the bugle boys, but the ranks have to be filled. The recruiters see someone old enough to hold a gun, but I see . . . I don't know . . . such innocence."

"I'm not innocent."

"Have you ever had relations with a woman?"

I blushed, not knowing what to say. The fact was, I'd never even kissed a girl.

"Sorry. I'm being cruel. It's just refreshing to meet someone so pure; you're pure as the Canadian snow." She snorted at her own joke.

"Did you ask me out here just to make a fool of me?"

"No! In fact, we're very much alike, Edward. I grew up on a dairy farm near Cleethorpes. I've milked my share of cows. See?" She showed me her palms. They were callused and muscular, not the dainty hands of a society girl. "Still," she went on, "I can't imagine what it's like where you come from. So wide open. It must be breathtakingly beautiful! Why'd you ever leave?"

"The King asked."

"Have you met the King?"

"No, of course not."

Emily nodded, as though she'd proven a point. She certainly had her opinions about things, but the more I looked at her, the more I liked her. She took a drag of her cigarette

65

and stared out across the misty hills. "I don't feel like I'm doing enough. I should transfer closer to the front; the men there really need help."

She blew another perfect smoke ring. The ghostly O floated through the air and vanished. She dropped the cigarette and stepped on it. "I'd better go to my station. Thanks for the chat. You take care of that arm, Breaker Bathe."

"I will." She disappeared inside the aid post. All the way back to Remount I pictured her lips in the shape of an O. It was the most beautiful thing I'd ever seen.

9

Every morning I helped work on the newest shipment of horses and every afternoon I returned to number fifty-eight. Soon I knew exactly how he thought, what he feared, and what to whisper to calm him down. He'd even nuzzle against me, like Caesar did at the farm. Dad would surely be proud if he could see me now. I wanted to name the horse, but he'd just be renamed by the yeomanry.

My arm gradually healed, though I wished for another injury, maybe even one requiring stitches, so I'd have an excuse to see Emily.

In the evenings the breakers played cards at the mess, arm wrestled in the barracks, or headed into Grimsby to the pubs. I preferred to be alone. I'd walk out into the fields; I missed working on our farm. I wrote a short letter to Dad, telling him where I was and not much more. I didn't expect a reply.

Often I'd pass by the regimental aid post, staring, willing

Emily to step out. I dreamed my way through hundreds of chats with her, in which I was witty and she laughed and looked longingly at me, but I couldn't find the courage to walk in and ask to see her.

On December 15 I went alone to a Grimsby pub and bought a stew pie, the closest thing I could find to a roast beef dinner. I finished with a slice of carrot cake layered with white icing, the kind of cake Mom would make for birthdays, hiding pennies inside. Hector and I would fight over who got the first piece.

The icing at the pub tasted like butter. At first I was going to complain, but it dawned on me that sugar was rationed. Besides, why complain? It was a special day. I'd just turned seventeen.

A few days after that the post corporal arrived as I was leaving for the stables. "Bathe, this has been waiting for you." He tossed a letter to me. "Check your mail at least once a week. It's not my duty to hand deliver it."

I flipped the envelope over. It was from someone named Paul Oster, postmarked from France. Paul! News of the Bull Moose Boys. And it had taken only two days to get to me.

Dec. 16, 1917

Dear Edward,

Well, we're here because we're here because we're here! We shipped out on the 8th. We didn't even have time to say good-bye to the other chaps. In the blink of an eye they stuck us on a transport and sent us to

France. I guess they decided we were trained well enough, or that we would learn as we go.

We joined the 46th. It has a very inspiring nickname: the Suicide Battalion. Doesn't that just warm your heart? Anyway, there's lots of Moose Jaw boys, so I caught them up on the news from home.

Nothing prepares you for this. The racket from the bombardments is terrible, and it makes it very hard to sleep never knowing when a shell will land. The Scots we relieved were ragged. Hope we don't look like them when we're done. The Huns are really putting on the pressure. We get the "stand to" command every twenty minutes or so. We stare across no-man's-land, and no man—or Hun—crosses it. But they will, soon, I bet. They can't be shelling us just for pleasure.

We play cards in between. I've won a comb, two eggs, and a can of tobacco. I'm rich! Saw my first Hun yesterday. He was out clipping the wires. I took a pot shot at him, and boy, did he run scared. I also received a nice packet of sweet biscuits and fruitcake from home. God bless my wife! Suddenly everyone was my best friend. Wish I could have saved you some.

Anyway, it's a mess in the trenches, but we make our home as best we can. We know our duty.

Funny thing, you're on the east coast, right? All you'd need to do to visit is hop a boat. I make a fine cup of tea these days.

> Hoping all is well,
> Your friend,
> Paul

I stared at the letter. Paul wasn't training horses, piling stacks of hay, or shoveling horse dung. I folded the letter and stuffed it in my kit bag.

I shivered in my greatcoat as I walked to the horse barn. My infantry skills were rotting away. I went inside and discovered that fifty-eight's stall was empty.

I hunted down Corporal Grimes. "Where's fifty-eight?" I asked.

"You're supposed to be feeding and watering right now."

"But my horse—the horse— Fifty-eight is gone."

"I sent him and four other geldings to yeomanry last night. They'll knock his stubborn streak right out of him."

"But I . . ."

"But what, Breaker?"

I shook my head. "I should return to my duties, Corporal."

"Exactly."

Back at the stable I stabbed the hay with my fork, filling the troughs. I wished I could have said good-bye. My friend was at the front and my horse was gone. What had been the point of signing up in the first place? I might just as well stayed at home and looked after livestock.

That evening I went to the regimental sergeant major.

"What are you here for, Bathe?" he asked. He was a small, turtle-like man. I was surprised he remembered my name.

"I want a transfer back to my old unit, Major."

"Corporal Grimes says you're a fine breaker."

"That's kind of him, Major, but I could be of more use at the front."

"You're needed here, Breaker." The words echoed in my ears as I walked back to my hut.

I lay on my cot and tried to picture Hector, but all I could get was a bit of an impression of his face, as though he was fading from my memory. Every day was taking me farther away from him. I wanted to know what he'd said over here, what he'd done, who he'd chummed with. I reread the letter from his regimental sergeant major. Since Hector had been his batman, he'd have known him the best.

I pulled out my pen, ink, and paper and wrote:

Dec. 23, 1917

Dear Regimental Sergeant Major Gledhill,

I am writing because I am Hector Bathe's younger brother. He spoke very highly of you in his letters home. Thank you for your thoughtful letter about his death. It was hard news, but my father and I were comforted by your words about his attention to duty.

I know you are very busy with your work, but if you do find a moment I would like to know about Hector's time in your battalion and about his final hours. He was a very good brother, as you can imagine, and I miss him terribly. You can write to me at the address on the envelope. I am in Remount right now but hope to be back with the infantry soon.

Thank you for your consideration.
Sincerely,
Edward Bathe

I took the envelope to the mailbag, all the time wondering if Gledhill was still alive.

I collapsed on my cot, and as the other breakers snored, I closed my eyes, imagined Christ's face, and prayed, *Please let me do my job.*

10

Christmas Day was hard. The officers sent a turkey for us breakers, which we quickly devoured; then most everyone slipped into town to see family or friends. I stayed alone in the hut. The previous Christmas had just been Dad and me. We hadn't even decorated. This Christmas all I could think of was how much I missed Hector. I hoped Dad was getting some turkey.

On Boxing Day, I decided if I couldn't be bold at the front, at least I could be bold at home. I'd walk up to Emily and sweep her off her feet. I hadn't figured out exactly how, but I had faith that the right words would just pop into my head.

Halfway to the aid post the roar of motors cut through the darkness and lights flashed everywhere. Someone began shouting orders. It wasn't a zeppelin attack because bells and bugles weren't calling us to our stations.

When I reached the post, a truck and four ambulances were parked outside, orderlies and nurses unloading stretchers. A man with a crutch leaned up against the back door, smoking a cigarette and staring at the stars. His left arm was a bloody, bandaged stump.

"You there!" A tall, gangly corporal pointed at me, spectacles tight against his eyes. "Grab the other end of this!"

He yanked a stretcher out of the ambulance and I leaned in to grip the handles. The cab was dark and stank of urine, blood, and antiseptic. A man groaned; another coughed. How many were stacked inside?

I held on tight and looked down. Gauze was wrapped several times around the wounded man's head, leaving a hole for his mouth, another for just one eye. He glared at me and I stumbled.

"Watch your step! These boys have been through seven kinds of hell."

"Wash yur step," the wounded man slurred, still glaring.

"Where are they from?" I asked.

"Across the pond somewhere. Guess Fritzie decided to give us a poke. These are the lucky ones; they survived the trip home. Hospitals all along the coast are filled up. They're bringing the overflow here."

Enough wounded to fill all the hospitals in the south? Really. We lugged our man into the waiting room. Cots lined the walls, most of them full. We set our stretcher on one. "Twist your end." The wounded man slid into place without a grunt. His eye remained fixed on me.

"There's plenty more," the corporal said. "Hope you didn't have plans."

74

Our next patient had left both arms back in France. He'd obviously been hit by a shell and was out cold. He'd be in for a shock when he woke up. Just one look at the man's burned skin told me he'd be in pain for years. At least Hector had been spared anything so horrible.

For the next half hour we hauled the wounded inside. The waiting room looked like a slaughterhouse. Some men were awake and able to stand or sit up; others were unconscious, their bandages red with blood. When the cots were full we lowered the wounded onto the floor, slipping a rolled blanket under their heads.

"Thanks, chap." The corporal clapped me on the shoulder. "I'm heading back to the hospital ship. I hope it's empty." He climbed into an ambulance and it motored away.

Inside the aid post Emily stood in the middle of the room, surrounded by bodies. She looked exhausted, her hair slipping out of her bun.

"I'm glad you're here." She handed me a pile of blankets. "We're trying to deal with the worst cases first, so in the meantime, cover the others. Talk to the ones who are awake. They need to hear a kind voice."

"What do I say?"

"Tell them they're looking well." She stepped over an unconscious man and walked down the hall.

A soldier lay unconscious at my feet, his face torn as though he'd been dragged headfirst through barbed wire. I unfolded a blanket, leaned down, and pulled it up to his neck. I could tell by his stink that he'd dirtied himself. I wanted to throw up, but I kept moving. The next patient was shivering, so I spread a blanket over him, and his eyelids snapped open. "Who are you?" he barked.

"Edward. You're home. In England."

His eyes darted left and right. "Why is it so cold?"

"You're doing well." I gave him a second blanket. "The doctor'll be here soon."

The room was a choir of coughs and moans. I wished I could stuff cotton in my ears, as some of the screams were horrific. But worse was the smell: antiseptic, rotting flesh, and urine. My dinner bubbled in my guts. I'd never seen or heard men in such agony.

"My arm! My arm! Give it back!" a man screamed from the surgery ward.

God help them, I thought. It was horrible. All these soldiers, broken, as if some giant machine had ground them up and spat them out. I prayed for them. How could anyone have stood by and watched Christ as he was crucified? Surely he would have experienced something as terrible as these fine men.

The next man I covered had his eyes closed. A bullet had caught him near the heart, judging by where the blood stained his dressing. Just like Hector. And maybe this man was dead, too, his skin was so waxy and pale. But his chest slowly rose. *Good.* I carefully laid the blanket up to his wound, then noticed a glint at his collar. Two maple leaves. He was Canadian.

"Edward," came a hoarse whisper from behind me. "Edward."

I turned and looked down at the next cot. A man stared

up, a bandage over his left eye. His face was one big bruise, his lips swollen and cracked.

"How do you know my name?"

"It's me," he coughed, "Paul."

"Paul?" The voice was familiar. "Paul Oster?"

His bloated lips attempted to smile. "Yes, that Paul."

"My Lord, what happened?"

"A shell. Got the sergeant beside me, blew off his legs and took two pals. I'd just gone to piss. Didn't ever think that'd save my life. Mom always said I was lucky."

I had trouble believing it was Paul. I'd just received a letter from him, for heaven's sake. "You're not hurt real bad, are you? I mean, just a rest and you'll be back at it, right?"

Paul made a crackly noise, a kind of laughter. "Yes, yes, I'm gonna live. But they'll be calling me One-Eyed Hopping Paul from now on."

"Hopping?"

He motioned with a bandaged hand toward his feet.

My eyes followed his gesture to the bottom of the blanket. "What?"

"Don't be stupid, Edward," he rasped. "My right foot was blown off. A shoe salesman with only one foot. That's the punch line to a bad joke."

I felt my guts twisting into a giant knot and I bent down to say, "The doctor'll do something for you really soon, I'm sure."

Paul, suddenly strong, clutched my collar and pulled me close. His breath reeked of blood. "They lied to us, Edward. We're all fighting for mud and piss."

"You don't know what you're saying."

"A man isn't worth anything there. We're just meat, ravens picking at our eyes, rats feasting on our flesh. Good men are shooting themselves in the foot or the arm just to get out." I tried to pull myself away but he held on tight, his mangled lips only a few inches from my face. Two of his teeth were missing. "Don't go to France. Break your leg or crush your trigger finger. Use a hammer, or better yet, a gun to shoot it off. Make it look like an accident."

"I can't do that!" I pried at Paul's fingers, loosening them one at a time. "You're in too much pain. You're . . . angry."

"I mean it, Edward."

I pried away the last finger and pushed his hand back onto his chest. "You'll be all right," I whispered. "Hang on, pal. The doctor'll be along soon. He's a good doctor."

Paul wheezed laughter.

I slowly backed away from him and bumped into a cot. The soldier in the cot released an angry moan. I had to get away from Paul's laughter and the smell of death. I stumbled over a patient and pushed my way out the door and into the open.

The stink followed me, clinging to my clothes and my skin. I threw up again and again, until I was exhausted.

What I needed was sleep. Then I'd go back. I staggered toward Remount.

11

I shot out of bed to the realization that everyone from my section was gone, their cots neatly made. I'd slept through reveille! I scrambled to find my pocket watch. Six forty-five!

I dressed clumsily, my limbs numb. I pulled on my shirt and caught a whiff of antiseptic and blood. I broke into a cold sweat and vomited, leaning against the bed.

"Mom. Mother," I whispered; I had no control over what I was saying. "I'm sick, I'm so sick."

I recalled my dream quite suddenly. The wounded had moaned and grabbed at me, trying to drag me into a wet, muddy hole, their broken limbs scratching me like branches. Somehow Hector was there, but Paul's face was clearer, shattered and bruised.

I shook my head. Such weakness! I'd always known people

lost limbs and died in war. The Huns could smash our bodies, but not our spirits.

Except for Paul. "Don't go to France. Break your leg or crush your trigger finger. . . . Make it look like an accident." His desperate breath had reeked and he was missing teeth. What would his wife think when she saw him? His kids?

I wiped up the vomit with an old sheet, something I couldn't have done if I were missing a hand.

No more! I told myself. I'd be up for field punishment if I was late. There was no time to eat, so I went straight to the stables and started forking hay. The more I sweated, the more my uniform stank of death.

I became weaker as the hours passed. At noon I could swallow only a couple of mouthfuls of stew. I clutched my cup of tea in shaky hands, taking advantage of every ounce of warmth.

In the evening when I closed my eyes I still saw the inside of the aid post. Would the images ever go away? Was this like what my father saw every night after Mom spent her last terrible hours coughing out the final bits of her life? Would I become just like him, my will defeated?

The next day I dragged myself around the depot, limbs still heavy, sickness and dread eating a hole in my guts. I accidentally hammered my fingers twice while fixing the fence and later wrapped the reins around my hand and nearly had my arm ripped off by a gelding. Dad had told me never to tie reins around my hand. What was I thinking?

I should have visited Paul, but I couldn't look at him

while he was missing so much of himself. Maybe the following day I'd go. There wouldn't be time that afternoon.

I was lucky, maybe, that my transfer had been refused. To think such a thing made me feel like a traitor.

A few days later I began to feel better. When I passed by the HQ hut, the post corporal darted out, shoved a telegram in my hand, and walked back inside. *Your presence is requested at 1900 hours on the fourth day of January 1918 at the residence of Colonel Nixon Hilts, Hilts Estate, Laceby.*

I stared at it. Uncle Nix wanted to dine with me. I read the date again. Today! It was today!

With pass in hand I walked to Grimsby and hailed a taxi, an electric brougham two-seater driven by an old man in a moth-eaten greatcoat. His white hair poked out the bottom of his cap. I climbed in, and the two of us sat shoulder to shoulder.

"The Hilts Estate, please."

"I know it well, lad," he said, putting the car in gear. Soon we were bouncing down the streets, the vehicle surprisingly swift and the motor nearly silent. Grimsby and its dead-fish smell was behind us as we rolled down a country lane. The grass was a soft green, a light mist blanketing the hills.

We passed several dairy farms, and I thought of Emily. I ached to think that some yeomanry trooper might sweep her off her feet. She might even become engaged; marriage happened fast these days. I hadn't had the chance to see her since the night all the wounded had arrived, because I still hadn't mustered the courage to visit Paul. I was a rotten pal, but every time I thought of him my guts pinched.

The driver stopped at a set of iron gates. No one appeared to be at the guard station, so I pushed the gates open and entered the courtyard to find a majestic three-story stone house, with lights on in several rooms. Vines trailed up the sides and around the windows.

As I stood at the front door I wondered if Dad had ever been in this very spot to lift the brass knocker.

A well-dressed servant opened the door—an Indian, like Gunga Din. His eyes were steady. "I presume you are Monsieur Bathe." He had an accent I didn't recognize. Perhaps he had been raised in France.

"Yes, that's me."

"Monsieur Hilts is expecting you."

The man took my greatcoat and, limping slightly, led me into the study. Rows of books filled oak shelves, and a large ticking clock showed the time to be 7:12. Above it was a black bear's head, mounted with its mouth open in a roar, flanked by a wolf and a tiger. A tiger!

A banner hung over the fireplace with the image of a lion standing firmly on a crown, below which was a ribbon with the words THE ROYAL DRAGOONS and the motto SPECTEMUR AGENDO. My father had once translated it for me: "Let us be judged by our actions." He had charged into battle with those words on his lips.

"Ah, the old glorious regimental flag."

I spun around. Colonel Hilts stood there in his uniform. Even though I'd spent extra time shining my buttons and badges, the colonel outshone me. "Once a dragoon, always a dragoon. How are you keeping, Edward?"

"Good, sir. You have a grand house."

"Thank you. It's been in the family for years. Would you like some brandy? I know it's traditionally an evening drink, but I find it invigorates me before a meal."

"Yes, I'd appreciate having some." I hoped I sounded mature.

The servant appeared with two snifters and poured us each a drink.

"Thank you, Kulbir." Hilts raised his glass. "To the King." I mirrored the gesture, then sipped the brandy, startled by its burning sweetness. The smell reminded me of the time Hector and I had crouched in the stairwell, listening to Dad and Hilts. A hundred years earlier.

Kulbir replaced the lid on the carafe and limped away.

"Kulbir is the heart of this household. He was my batman; one of the greatest Gurkha fighters ever."

"He's a Gurkha?" I whispered. They were the deadliest soldiers in the British Indian army.

"He had the necessary killer instinct and was a great horseman, too, until a saber severed his foot. He has a wooden one now. We used it to smuggle papers out of Syria."

"Really!" This was the kind of derring-do I'd read about in *Boy's Own Paper*. Perhaps Paul could get himself a wooden foot. If an Indian could overcome such a loss, Paul could, too.

"Ah, it was all in a day's work." Hilts waved his hand. "So, what are your impressions of England?"

"I quite like it, sir."

"Please, Edward, don't call me sir, call me Uncle. I'd appreciate it, and I'm sure your father would, too."

"I will, uh . . . Uncle Nix."

"Thank you." He smiled. "So what do you think of the war effort so far?"

"According to the papers we're doing well."

"Hard to separate fact from fiction, isn't it? The newspaper lords are doing their bit with their heroic stories. My favorite headline is still *The Great and Glorious Retreat from Gallipoli.* When can a retreat be called great? The navy botched the operation from the beginning. And the army should have known that the Turks would be tough nuts to crack."

I listened intently because someone like Uncle Nix knew the real reasons for victories or defeats.

The door swung open. "Sahib, dinner is served."

"Ah, good, come along, Edward."

In the dining room was a table that could seat at least forty, polished so that it reflected several golden candles. Tureens, china plates, and silver cutlery were set out in perfect order. We sat, and Kulbir splashed a bit of wine into the goblet in front of Uncle Nix, who tested it and nodded his approval. Kulbir filled our goblets.

"The gramophone, please, Kulbir."

Kulbir crossed the room and wound up the gramophone, and Clara Butt began to sing "Land of Hope and Glory." She sounded like an angel.

"Even when I was in Africa poor Kulbir had to lug my gramophone around." Kulbir lifted a silver lid to reveal a cooked bird. "I bagged this pheasant myself on Friday."

"Much better than what I'm used to!"

"An army marches on its stomach, Edward. Napoleon loved saying that."

"He certainly was right." It had been ages since I'd had to march anywhere.

We filled our plates and began to eat. "Why are we at war?" he asked.

"What do you mean?"

"I want your view on it."

"Well, they killed that duke, right? And the Germans invaded Belgium and France, so we had to defend our allies. It was our duty."

"Good. Good." I felt as if I'd passed a test. "That's part of it. The Germans think like clockwork, and we British are freethinkers. That's why we must triumph. Do you understand?"

"We think in better ways than them."

"Exactly! Picture the world as a hedge." He made a cutting motion with his knife. "Trimming the German branches was inevitable. A new order will grow out of this war."

"It needs doing." For a moment I thought of Paul and wished he could be here to listen. Uncle Nix would straighten him out.

"It's a heavy price we're paying," he admitted. "The Russians aren't holding up their end now, so that'll make it a close one. The Germans might even win."

"Win?" I nearly choked on some potato. "But how?"

"Sheer numbers. We need more advanced armaments, better plans, and more capital. Every man, woman, and child in the Empire has to dig in and give. The Americans may have arrived, but they're still far from having the manpower they really need to contribute properly. It'll take several months. Don't look so worried, Edward. Resolute men will win the day." He sipped from his goblet. "What do you think of our grand army?"

"It's grand!" I said, and immediately wanted to kick myself. "That is to say, it's well trained, and efficient, too."

"Are you happy in Remount?"

I paused. "I'm doing my job."

Hilts wagged his finger at me. "Ah, you're as reticent as your father. Do you enjoy what you're doing?"

"Yes, but I want to go to the front." Where had that come from? Just hours before, I hadn't wanted to transfer at all.

"I'm told you're an excellent horse breaker."

"I'm a better soldier, Uncle," I said with as much determination as I could muster.

He nodded and we ate silently for a time. I had to slow myself down; months of gobbling army food had ingrained the habit. In an effort to eat with some decorum, I sipped my wine between each bite, but soon suspected I was growing blotto.

Hilts emptied his goblet and set it down with a bang. "You obfuscated."

"Pardon me?" I said, suddenly very sober.

"You lied to your recruiters. You were ten when I visited your father's ranch. That was in 1910. So you had to be underage when you enlisted."

"Well, I'm not the only one!"

I'm sure the look on my face betrayed my guilt, because Uncle Nix laughed heartily and said, "Don't worry, your secret's safe with me. To be honest, I'm impressed by your eagerness. We need more men like you."

"But why Remount?" The wine had loosened my tongue. "It's—it's not fair!"

Kulbir refilled both our goblets. "There's no fairness in war," Uncle Nix said gently, "only calculations of cause and effect. And cost, always cost. I sent you to Remount because I wanted you under my watch, hoping you'd be as good as your father."

"Dad?"

"He was an excellent cavalryman and a damn fine sergeant. He was close to getting his commission when he resigned from the dragoons." Uncle Nix cut a large piece of pheasant. "He must be proud of you."

"Actually . . . he didn't want me to sign up."

"He'd already lost a son. Perfectly understandable." He gestured toward the bird and I nodded and sliced a piece. "How was his health when you last saw him?"

"He won't get out of bed."

Uncle Nix sipped his wine, studying me.

"So what was he like as a cavalryman?" I asked.

"The finest! He was brave, but he succumbed to mental strain. It can happen to the best."

"Strain?"

Hilts held up his hand. "First, have you had enough to eat?"

"Yes. It was delicious, Uncle!" It felt good to call him that.

"It's so much better when you bag it yourself." Hilts pushed his chair back from the table. Kulbir appeared with a pipe and a box of tobacco. Hilts lit his pipe, drew in smoke, and slowly let it out. "You know, sometimes surviving can be worse than dying."

"What do you mean?"

"Your father and I were in the battle for Colenso. The Boers had hidden on the other side of a bridge, waiting to open fire on our infantry. Blustery Colonel Long galloped his guns right over the bridge and pointed them at the Boers. Didn't even wait for infantry support! The Boers let loose before Long's guns could be unlimbered, killing nearly every gunner and all the horses."

Hilts looked out the window as if to avoid seeing the images in his mind. "Word of the loss came back to us. We were appalled. It's a dishonor to have one gun captured by the enemy, let alone a dozen! Your father immediately offered to retrieve them. Several of his men went with him. They galloped straight to the guns, under heavy fire. Wilfred's horse was hit but stayed on its feet. Men fell all around him. Even though he was wounded, they were able to bring back two guns. None of the other men who went with your father survived. And his horse died an hour after his return.

"Once he'd recovered, he reported to duty, but all he could think about were his dead men. Finally, he collapsed and returned to England."

Hilts let out more smoke and watched it roll across the room.

"Such loss can be a difficult thing to survive. And then to have your mother and Hector die, too . . . Perhaps his sickness is understandable."

I nodded. Ever since I was a child, I'd imagined Dad as a hero. And he was! He'd galloped into withering fire and brought back two guns. He deserved a Victoria Cross. But, sadly, he had lost his will. A sudden realization made me ask: "Are you worried that I'll break down, too?"

"You have the right stuff." I couldn't help feeling a little proud. He sipped from his goblet. "Have you ever considered the yeomanry?"

"Oh, that'd be perfect! I have infantry training just like them, and I can ride."

"The yeomanry will be needed when the breakthrough finally comes. You should keep applying for a transfer, but not back to your unit. There's been too much attrition in the infantry."

"I'll do that, Uncle Nix. Thank you!"

Hours later, when I was back at the barracks with my head on my pillow, I stared at the dark ceiling. I'd leave the breakers and become a yeomanry trooper, trained to fight on the ground as infantry or on a horse like cavalry. The dinner had been a test and I'd passed. He'd judged me fit for duty.

I thought of Dad's charge into almost certain death. Could I ever do that? But his breakdown had, unfortunately, cast a shadow across his glory. Bravery wasn't just one act; it was something you had to repeat again and again.

I wouldn't be like Father. Uncle Nix had seen the same things, been in the same battles, and hadn't lost his will. I'd have to be equally resolute.

I closed my eyes, and for the first time in weeks I felt a little happiness. My prayers had been answered.

12

A week later I lugged my kit to the door and stepped out into a bright day. I was done with Remount and I'd have to get used to marching now; the yeomanry practiced infantry along with horsemanship.

"Remove your regimental badges." Corporal Grimes stood in the alley between the barracks and the supply shack, a hand-rolled cigarette squished between two fingers.

"I'd rather wear them, Corporal."

"The troopers'll just look down their snooty noses at you."

"Then I'll pop 'em one and say, 'Here's a gift from Remount.'"

Grimes coughed out a hoarse chuckle. "You've got guts, Bathe. You're a little too uppity for my taste, but you did good work here."

"I'm proud of it."

"Good." Grimes took a drag on his cigarette, then ground the butt into the earth with his foot. "Show 'em what real horsemanship is all about, Breaker." And with that he walked away.

I carried on. Grimes wasn't such a bad fellow; perhaps we'd meet after the war and raise a drink to our Remount days. I liked that image of myself, older and wiser, the war just another job well done. By then I might have a stripe or three of my own.

The frost-covered hills stood between me and the yeomanry barracks, not much more than a few miles' walk. There'd be no breakers. No corporals. Just a new beginning.

I wasn't ever truly alone. I was part of a large and wondrous creation, with God leaning out of the heavens, shaping the day. What would he send me?

Since the dinner with Hilts I'd felt more alive. That night, I'd write father and tell him that I'd seen Uncle Nix, and that I was part of the local yeomanry.

I was about to pass the regimental aid post, halfway between Remount and the yeomanry barracks. If it was a perfect day, Emily would be standing on the veranda. *God*, I prayed, *please make her step outside.*

It was cheeky of me to ask him for a favor like that. He did bigger things, like flood the entire earth or part the Red Sea for Moses. He didn't make girls appear out of the blue.

Two men on crutches stood on the veranda, one with a bandage over his eye. He slowly lifted a hand and waved. I felt weak. My stomach lurched and my good mood vanished. I'd assumed that by now Paul had gone to another hospital.

If I were a good pal, I would have stopped, walked over, and talked to him. I would have told him about Kulbir's wooden foot, something that might give him hope. When the aid post was out of sight, I shook off the sense of dread I had about Paul. I reminded myself I was heading into a great opportunity. That was the way I should think of it.

A sign at the gates of the yeomanry camp said LINCOLNSHIRE YEOMANRY: HORSES FIRST, MEN SECOND, OFFICERS LAST. The wooden barracks were surrounded by twenty or so tents. Troopers lead horses across the courtyard.

A sergeant in the HQ hut glanced at my papers, looked me over twice, then grinned and said, "I'm Sergeant Applewhite. I'm sure you'll be bellyachin' about rations, so you might as well know me name. Your new regimental number is 2265. Quote it every time you go to the toilet. Only one bowel movement per trooper, per day."

"What?"

He laughed. "I'm just takin' the piss out of ya, mate."

He selected a uniform and dropped it on the counter. "That'll fit you. Got yer own boots, I see. Good!" He placed two regimental badges on the pile. "Drop your gear in tent seven, get settled in, then come back for your rifle and tack."

I found my tent and pushed aside the flap to discover two troopers inside, one looking in a mirror, combing his hair, the other on a cot reading a book. The bookworm was thin, pale as a ghost, his hair crow black. I guessed them to be nineteen or twenty.

"Hello," I said, "how are you? I'm—"

"A colonial," the bookworm interjected. "A Canuck, judging by your accent. How in hell did a Remount colonial get in our squadron?"

"They asked for me!"

"Who did?"

"Colonel Hilts." The men recognized the colonel's name.

"You must be good." The other man set down his comb, took a quick step, and shook my hand. He was an inch taller than me, with a craggy, handsome face, his hair streaked sandy blond. "I'm Will Cheevers. Welcome to the Lincolnshire Yeomanry. You five-bobbers aren't all that bad."

"What's a five-bobber?"

"Dominion boys make five times our pay," the other man said.

"I've been on the imperial payroll for months," I said. "Guess I'm just another one-bobber."

The sneering man stood and offered his hand. It was cold and his grip was firm. "Victor Blackburn." He wiped his hand on his trousers and sat back down.

"Ignore Vic," Cheevers said. "He was born with an iron rod up his backside." He flashed a grin that belonged in a film.

Blackburn shrugged. "As long as Billy Buffalo here can ride a horse and aim, he's fine and dandy with me. I do find it odd that they'd send a colonial here, though."

"I was born in these parts. My father had a farm near Aylesby."

"Aylesby!" Cheevers said. "I grew up there. We could've been chums. I guess instead of chiding you about your colonial ways we should be saying welcome home, mate."

Blackburn opened his book again, and Cheevers peppered me with chatter as I unpacked. "Does it really snow ten feet at a time in Canada?"

"We had twelve feet in the winter of '09. Train couldn't get through. But 1906 was the worst—not much snow, but so cold half our herd froze to death inside the barn."

"Impossible!" Cheevers said.

"God's truth. Of course, I don't remember it much. I was only six."

"Six?" Blackburn set down his book. "In 1906? Then you're underage."

Panic seized my heart. "Uh, I added wrong. I was born in 1899. I must've been seven then."

"Guess they don't teach mathematics in Dominion schools."

I ignored him, unfolded my new uniform and began to dress.

"Twelve feet of snow!" Cheevers said. "Twelve feet! You must be bucksome buggers! Did people drown in it?"

"We wore snowshoes."

"Of course! Of course! Uh . . . ol' ducky, I hate to break it to you, but you're tying your puttees all arserds."

"Arserds?"

"Arse backwards," Blackburn said without looking up from his book, "just like his accent."

Cheevers gave me a wink. " 'E's jealous o' me good looks. Now, let's get you all prim and proper."

I was halfway finished tying up my left leg. "But they're fine."

"Yeomanry tie their puttees counterclockwise," Cheevers explained. "I'm only trying to save you from looking clarted. You'd take it in the neck if Colonel Wilson saw that. He likes things spit and polish."

"Thanks."

"Troopers look out for one another."

I undid my puttees and wrapped them, awkwardly, in the opposite direction. That done, I put on my new collar badges: a white brass emblem of a king's crown over a shield with a cross, and the fleur-de-lys.

"Let's get you a gun and a horse."

I followed Cheevers to the quartermaster's storage shed. "Back again, are you, Bathe?" Applewhite dug around in the piles of equipment, leaving items on the counter. "Here's your tack: one saddle, a bridle, a halter, two blankets, two saddlebags, a rifle bucket, a picket rope, and a spare bandolier. The best of a bad lot."

He opened a large wooden box, removed a Lee Enfield rifle, and handed it to me. I held it as though it were a sword pulled from a stone.

I slipped the rifle into its bucket and slung it over my shoulder, then grabbed the saddle and blankets. Cheevers picked up the remaining tack.

Inside the stables were rows of horses, all combed perfectly. Several troopers were spreading straw through the stalls; others forked manure into the back of a wooden wagon. It was the neatest stable I'd ever seen.

"I'll introduce you to my Neddie," said Cheevers as he

opened a stall, and a tan gelding, fifteen hands high, turned his head, hay hanging out of his mouth. He chewed thoughtfully, watching us. "Hey, buddy. Hey, boy." Cheevers patted his side. "Look at the legs on him. When I say go, he's gone like the wind." At "go" Neddie raised his ears. "Take it easy, Ned. Tomorrow we'll ride."

"He's a fine horse!"

"Come hell or high water he'll get me through. That one there is Blackburn's nag." He pointed to a beautiful brown gelding. "Calls him Cromwell. What kind of name is that for a horse? Anyway, we'd better find Pitts. He's the ferrier. He'll have a horse for you." At the *ting ting* of a hammer tapping on steel, Cheevers turned his head. "There he is now."

Pitts was leaning over an anvil, hammering nails out of old horseshoes. He was built like a bull, and hair sprouted on his arms and neck; tufts peeked out where his uniform was unbuttoned. His head, however, was bald.

"Hey, Pitts, you have any gallant chargers for Trooper Bathe?"

"By! A couple went lame just yesterday, so I had to use our two good remounts. This last one, she's a clot-headed bumble-foot! Part donkey, if you ask me. You gotta give 'er the spurs."

I couldn't fight the war on a lazy horse!

Pitts led us to a pen where there stood a plump gray mare, her face burrowed in the trough. She didn't lift her head to look back at us, just moved her eyes. She was small compared to the black horse beside her.

"Back 'er out of there. Just beware the gelding. He's mad as a Stamford bull."

I set down my saddle and rifle. The mare's ears did look long—maybe she *was* part donkey. I'd be the laughingstock of the yeomanry. I grabbed a handful of oats from a pail, and as I walked between the two horses, the black one stomped his feet.

"Don't go near that one!" Pitts said. "We're sending him to the packers. Just get the mare."

I laughed and stepped up to the black charger. "Hey, how about some oats?"

"Are ya deaf! He's a biter!"

I reached out my hand. "He's a king. Right, fifty-eight? You're the king."

He turned his head, showing off the familiar white star on his brow. He licked the oats out of my hand, his chompers brushing my palm.

"By Christ!" Pitts said.

I patted fifty-eight's neck and he pulled back as if to nip me. "Gentle. Gentle. None of that." He'd grown in the last month. "This horse isn't meant for the packers."

"You trained him?" Cheevers asked.

I nodded.

"No wonder they kicked you out of Remount."

"When was he last ridden?" I asked.

"Him? Ha!" Cheevers slapped his leg. "I tried that bag o' bones a week ago and got dumped arse over 'ead. Still can't sit down properly!"

Fifty-eight accepted the bridle without much fuss. He shook when I threw the blanket across his back and tightened up the saddle. I led him out into the open corral.

"He's yours if you can ride him," Pitts said.

"Should we write your mom when you peg out?" Cheevers added.

I pulled myself into the saddle. Fifty-eight fidgeted and stamped but didn't try to buck.

"Now I've seen it all!" Pitts said.

"Let's go!" We shot out the gate across the barracks yard, dashed around a few barrels, and charged to the far side of camp. He loved galloping; that'd be handy in battle. Several troopers raised their heads to watch. After a few minutes we trotted back.

"Looks like you've got yourself a horse," Cheevers said.

"That's great!" I hopped off and patted fifty-eight's neck. "Hear that, buddy? We're a team! Has anyone named him?"

"Bone'ead had crossed me mind," Pitts said.

"Or son of a bitch," Cheevers added.

It came to me like a whisper in my ear. "Bucephalus." I'd always loved the stories of Alexander the Great, who conquered empires riding Bucephalus, the horse he'd tamed as a child. He built a city in the place where his horse had fallen. Fifty-eight seemed like that kind of horse.

Cheevers scratched the back of his head. "That's a long name to be shouting in the field."

"I'll shorten it to Buke. How do you like that?" I said quietly to the horse.

Buke whinnied softly.

13

"Closer," Cheevers whispered. "Hist! Come closer, Bathe."
I jerked the rein and gave Buke a nudge, but he shot a full step forward so that we were out of line with the rest of the squadron.

"Trooper Bathe, fall out!" Sergeant Applewhite shouted, his jowls shaking. I cringed. "Over here on the double!"

I spurred Buke toward him, knowing I was about to get a good going-over.

"Send that man here, Sergeant!" Captain Trollope shouted from the knoll where he and Lieutenant Rance were watching our maneuvers.

Oh, no, not the captain! "Go see the captain, now!" Applewhite commanded, pointing toward the brass.

I galloped up to Trollope and yanked back on the reins, and Buke snorted snot all over the captain's horse. I turned red, then, remembering myself, snapped a quick salute.

Trollope narrowed his eyes. He looked youthful but had his share of crow's-feet. "Hold your position, relax your grip on your reins, and calm your horse, Trooper." I watched with growing fear as he scribbled on a blank page in his tactical book. Lieutenant Rance glared at me while the captain wrote. I looked down, feeling as if I would melt. I wondered if it was a written reprimand or even a royal rebuke. After all, Trollope was Lord of Kesteven, wherever that was.

He tore the paper from the book, tied it with brown string, and shoved it into my hand. "Take this message to Captain Dickinson of A Squadron. They're camped near Aylesby. This is an urgent matter, so don't dawdle."

"Yes, sir!" I saluted again and placed the letter in my saddlebag. I charged down the road at a hard gallop. No reprimand or punishment; this was more like a reward. Captain Trollope was a damn fine fellow!

The more I pushed Buke, the faster he went and the smoother his gait became. At top speed it felt as if we were gliding over water. He loved racing; it was holding his position in line that he couldn't stomach. I let him run for several minutes, my identity disks banging against my chest. Then, fearing he'd tire, I switched to a canter.

For all I knew, I was riding right by my family's old farm. I'd seen a photograph of the buildings, but our place could be hidden in any of these green gullies.

I found A Squadron in a valley and watched as they galloped in an attack formation, lances aimed at an imaginary enemy. Half of them stopped and dismounted, ordered their horses to lie down, then used them as cover while firing at targets. The remaining sections wheeled about, roared their battle cries, and skewered the targets with lances. It was quite a sight.

When they were done I rode down and was soon led to Captain Dickinson, a thick-chested man with a drooping mustache and several scars on his face.

I saluted. "Urgent message for you, sir, from Captain Kesteven . . . I mean, Captain Trollope, sir, the Lord of Kesteven."

"Oh, and what does his lordship want?" Dickinson opened the message, read it, then looked at me oddly. "Are you Trooper Bathe?"

"Yes, sir."

"Do you know what this message says?"

"No, sir. It was private, sir." Was he accusing me of reading it?

"I'll share it with you, then: 'Good day, Captain Dickinson. Hope you've had time for tea. Trooper Bathe is keen as mustard, but he's green and needs a good workout. Tell him to ride back to his squadron on the double.' "

"That's what it says, sir?"

"Yes." He chuckled. "Trollope never misses a chance to play a joke. Now, ride hard back to your squadron. That's an order!"

"Yes, sir!" I saluted, smiling.

I kicked and Buke galloped across the hills. It had all been a joke! Captain Trollope was telling me that I belonged; I just had to work harder. I took a different route back, hoping it would be shorter.

We sped over a hill, kicking up mud. My smile grew even wider because the aid post was right below us. What a piece of luck! I charged up to the back of it and yanked on Buke's reins. A nurse sitting on a wicker chair stared with wide eyes. "What can I do for you, duck?"

"Will you kindly inform Emily Waters that Trooper Bathe is here to see her," I said, trying not to puff. "I mean, if she has time to chat, of course."

"I will."

I removed my helmet and hung it on my saddle, then ran my fingers through my hair and wiped the sweat from my forehead. I loosened my greatcoat to reveal more of my uniform. I was on top of Buke and we were on top of the world.

Emily stepped out and did a double take. "Edward? Is that you?"

"Of course!"

"You're in the yeomanry?"

"I transferred three days ago. It's been great fun!"

"Fun? You boys have odd ideas of fun." She held out her hand and let Buke have a couple sniffs before she stroked his forehead and said, "He's a marvelous horse!"

"He's Bucephalus, after Alexander the Great's horse. I call him Buke, though."

"Do you fancy yourself another Alexander?"

"Ha! He's just a good horse, that's all."

She ran her hand over his neck. How I wished those perfect hands were touching me instead. "You've been riding hard."

"He loves it. He's faster than the wind."

"I bet." She gave his shoulder a good pat. "When Vera announced your arrival I assumed you'd hurt yourself again. Why else would you be here?"

"Uh . . ." I was on top of my horse, in uniform; I felt unstoppable. "I wanted to ask you to a film or a show. Would you go with me?"

"How could a poor little waif refuse a knight in shining armor?"

My heart started beating rabbit fast. "You're not a waif."

"Well, I'm glad you think that. How about meet me here Saturday at six sharp? That'll give us time for dinner and a show."

"Saturday? Good! Good! I'll be here."

"You'd better be!" she said with a chuckle, and the cutest dimples dotted her ivory cheeks. "So how is yeomanry life?"

"Well, for one thing, there's a lot more action."

"Being bucked off a horse wasn't enough for you?"

"I'm trained for more than that."

The pop of rifles echoed across the hills and Emily crossed her arms. "You hear that target practice going on all day. They want you to get used to the sound so you forget how deadly bullets are."

"We have to know how to shoot."

"And to die, I guess. A trooper from A Squadron died last night. He fell off his horse and hit his head."

"That's terrible."

"Ordinary, that's what it was. No medals for him." She motioned toward France. "Every day men are dying in the trenches. It's all rather ordinary now."

"It'll be over soon," I said, trying to sound as if I believed my own words. I'd hoped to make her feel better.

"By Christmas, right? But which Christmas? It does feel

so pointless at times. Still, I've applied to go to Etaples. They need more nurses near the front."

"Just seeing you would make a guy heal faster," I gushed, my voice pitched a little too high.

She allowed a smile. "That's kind of you."

I struggled for something clever to say. I wanted to tell her she looked beautiful, even though she had black bags under her eyes. How come other men could banter so easily with girls?

"I was going to look you up," she said.

"You were? Why?"

"To thank you for helping us when we had all those wounded. You arrived at exactly the right time."

"It just seemed like the right thing to do."

"Your friend is still here. He asked after you."

My stomach churned. "Yes, he . . . I meant to visit him earlier. I've been busy with the transfer and the training. How is he?"

"He's healing. They'll send him to Lincoln any day now. Why not say hello? His cot is right inside the door."

I pulled on the reins and Buke took a step back. "Ahh, I can't. I have to get back to the barracks. I was supposed to ride directly there."

Emily frowned. "He's taking his wounds rather hard; he needs cheering up. Don't wait too long."

"I won't. I won't. It—it was good to talk to you."

"Yes, it was, wasn't it?" She grinned. "I kept hoping you'd hurt your arm again just so we could visit. Not proper thoughts for a nurse."

105

"If I stub my toe, I'll run blubbering to you. Otherwise, I'll be here Saturday at six sharp!"

"I'll be waiting for you, Mr. Knight in Khaki Armor," she said, laughing. I could have listened to that sound forever.

I strapped on my helmet and trotted away. Then, hoping she was still watching, I gave Buke a good kick and galloped toward the barracks.

14

Every night, bone weary from drills, I'd collapse on my cot, too tired to move. My mind would still be on the drill field, wheeling into different formations, waiting for the signal to charge. Every moment on Buke made me think of Dad's time in the dragoons; he might have trained on these very hills.

Partway through the week, I placed the ink jar on our small table and wrote:

Dear Father,

I am writing a quick letter between drills. I am in the Lincolnshire Yeomanry now. Imagine, I am part of your old county's yeomanry. I've even been to Aylesby, though I didn't see our home farm.

Uncle Nix arranged for my transfer. We had an

important talk about the war and Britain's part in it.
He sends his warmest wishes to you.

Remember when you made me ride with pennies
squeezed against the horse with both knees? Well, the
horsemanship you taught me has truly paid off.

I hope there isn't too much snow this year. I will
write again when I get a moment.

Faithfully, your son,
Edward

I sealed the envelope just as Cheevers arrived with a pink
gift-wrapped box.

"Spoils of war from one of my birds!" He fired several
sugar biscuits my way. I softened one in my tea and let it dis-
solve in my mouth. "Oh, and there was mail for you, Bathe."
He tossed a letter to me.

15/01/18
15th Canadian Batt
B.E.F.

Dear Edward,

First, forgive me for taking so long to write. I
received your letter asking about Hector in December
and am only now replying. I have no excuse, other than
the obvious one.

I often receive letters from family members who
want to know more about how and when their loved
one died, and I must admit I do write responses
intended to spare their feelings. I do not know exactly

what I wrote to you directly after your brother's death, but since you are in the service, I shall tell more of Hector's last hours. I shan't hold back, since you must already know what this war does to men.

First, Hector was always ready to fulfill his duty. On the day of his death he was unwell, but he refused to stay behind. We were to take a German position, and I'm afraid we didn't have as much artillery support as we'd hoped, but we charged on, through the trenches and into the muzzle of a machine gun shooting over the rim of a parapet. My lieutenant led a rush with a runner, the plan being to toss a Mills Bomb right into the gun crew. Both the lieutenant and the runner were killed outright. Hector was the second to run, and he was hit several times in the legs and stomach, but he lived. I'm afraid we couldn't do much for him at the time. He was left out in the open. It took us twenty minutes to dispose of the machine gunners and clear the area.

When I did get back to Hector he was quite pale and hadn't been moved, as it was judged the motion would kill him. You most likely know what a machine gun can do. He knew he was in for it, and he asked for water, but there is no point in giving water to a man with a gut wound. He did get rather delirious in those last minutes and called out for your mother. I find peace in that. He died shortly after.

Hector was a marvelous man and he had an infectious cheeriness that would often make the days that much easier to handle. He and I spoke longingly

of Canada and of going home and he mentioned you
several times. I do miss him.

I hope this letter has been of some help.

Sincerely,
Fred Gledhill

I leaned against the tent pole. It was so odd and terrible to know about Hector's last moments. He hadn't been shot through the heart but had had his legs and guts torn apart. To think he had lain there in excruciating pain for so long with none of us, his family, to comfort him. I ached to hug him.

"Bad news?" Cheevers asked. "You don't look so good."

"It's a letter about my brother, about how he died."

"You lost your brother?" Blackburn asked.

"Yes. Hector. Last September."

"Sorry to hear that, mate," Cheevers said. "We all know someone who's pegged out. Half the chums I went to school with have fallen." He gave me a soft tap on the arm. "Don't you worry. For every one of us, we'll kill five of them. I promise."

"We'll win this war," Blackburn said. "All these grievances will help us carry on."

"I hope so." I folded the letter and slid it into my rucksack.

Thoughts of Hector clouded my mind for the next few days. At times I'd even miss a command. Once, Sergeant Applewhite gave me a good going-over for being out of position, but I just couldn't get past the image of Hector in a pool of his own blood, his legs shattered. The vision of him being shot in the heart had become like a painting in my head. But this news from Gledhill changed all that. Now the painting was a lie. It was true that Hector had died a hero—he'd been rushing a machine gun—but his horrible death wasn't what he deserved at all.

On Saturday evening I walked to the aid post, each step tiring me out. It was hardly how I wanted to feel on my way to pick up Emily, so I told myself that Hector would want me to have a good time. In fact, I decided I would be like him that night, charming Emily from the get-go. I'd start off with something like "You outshine the sun," or "You're as pretty as a spring rose." That would get everything off on the right foot. I should have asked Cheevers's advice; he likely had a thousand romantic lines. I wanted my first date to be perfect.

Emily waited on the front veranda, wrapped in a long coat, a blue dress peeking out at the hem. The moment I saw her, all thoughts of Hector disappeared. She wore her hair down; her lips glistened. She looked simply gorgeous.

"H-hello." So much for my clever patter.

"You're shorter without your horse."

"I'm not short!"

She chuckled. "Don't worry; you're tall enough for me, Mr. Canada."

Was she being clever again? I was already feeling dizzy.

"Town will be jumping tonight!" Emily exclaimed. "Let's go to the Pickled Boar first, then catch the show at the Palace. All the nurses raved about it. You'll take me, right?"

111

"Of course! It sounds perfect. Smashing, in fact."

She pinched my cheek. "Don't try and sound English. Your colonial ways are what make you so interesting."

Interesting? As we walked to Grimsby I had an extra bounce in my step. "I cleaned all the windows in camp," I announced like a schoolboy. I wanted to punch myself.

"How exciting!" she said with a wry smile. I tried to think of something more heroic.

"At the rifle range, I scored the highest. The sergeant even gave me a pat on the back. I have a nickname now—the Canuck!"

"How original! May I call you the Canuck?"

"I'd prefer Edward."

"All right, my sweet Edward."

I grinned. "I like the sound of that."

Things were going well. I was keeping an older girl interested. There was a victory in that!

The sun was setting, casting long shadows over Grimsby. An oddly warm night had melted the skiffs of snow and drawn people out of their homes. The sidewalks grew crowded the closer we got to the market. Soldiers were drinking, belching, and backslapping on the street. Ladies from the munitions factory sat on benches, their faces yellowed from working with TNT.

"They call them canaries," Emily said. "Yellow skin is the price they pay for making bombs."

"It won't wash off?"

"It'll wear away after the war."

I hoped I'd see Cheevers so I could show off Emily,

but then thought better of it. One look from him might catch her in his web. Then again, she was too clever for him.

We ducked into the Pickled Boar and sat at a pockmarked table. Steak had been dropped from the menu because of rations, so at the counter I ordered eggs and chips for us. I took the plates back to Emily and returned for two mugs of beer.

An attractive girl wearing too much lipstick sauntered up to a nearby table. A trooper gave her a cigarette, and a few seconds later the two of them went arm in arm up the stairs.

"I like the seediness of this place," Emily said. "It's kind of dangerous, just like a place you'd find in an adventure novel."

"The food looks dangerous, too," I said, taking my seat. The boiled eggs were crumbling; the chips were cold. I'd expected Emily to be somewhat dainty about eating, but she appeared to be racing to finish first.

"You've got egg on your chin," she said, and wiped it with a napkin. "I feel like your mother."

That wasn't how I felt about her. I wanted to squeeze her against me, or even take her up to a room. If only . . . Of course, it was a sin before marriage.

"What are you thinking about?" she asked.

I blushed and she giggled, then patted my hand. "The thought of you going to the front frightens me."

"We'll be fine." I worked at keeping my voice deep, confident. "Our training will serve us well."

"Training won't stop a shell." She waved her hand. "I'm

being a worrywart. Let's have a toast." She raised her half-empty beer glass. "To our continued friendship." She clinked my glass.

Friendship?

"Aren't you going to drink?"

I drank, then tore off a chunk of bread. We looked briefly into one another's eyes. What would it be like to kiss her?

"So exactly how old are you?" she asked.

"Uh, old enough."

"To know better?" She laughed. "Really, you tell me your age and I'll tell you mine."

I was sweating. "You go first."

She licked her lips and was about to say something when from somewhere in the smoky haze a clock began to cuckoo. "We'll be late!" Emily said as she stood and hurried out. I followed, still chewing my last bite. Twice I lost her and she had to wait for me to catch up. Exasperated, she grabbed my hand and pulled me down the sidewalk behind her.

Two blocks later I looked up at the spires and rounded corners of the Palace Theatre, a castle in the middle of Grimsby. We joined the line. None of the girls I could see was as pretty as Emily. I wished I had the guts to tell her so. I paid for the tickets and we found our seats, which were covered with red velvet and made me think of royalty. I helped her remove her coat, revealing the blue dress.

"That's a lovely gown."

"Oh, what a kind thing to say."

We took our seats just as the lights dimmed. Already I was thinking about holding her hand, but I couldn't make myself do it; I was man enough to hold a gun, but not her hand. What was wrong with me?

The first act toddled out: an old comedian who burbled baby-talk songs. Emily leaned close and whispered, "He was probably quite funny fifty years ago." I laughed and caught a whiff of her flower scent.

The next performers were a song-and-dance troupe called the Sisters of Mercy. I couldn't keep from humming along. They were followed by a juggling gymnastic act. It ended with a musical about Faustus, a man who sold his soul for power. Every song was so unhappy. I stole glances at Emily, who was completely enthralled.

"I'd go every night!" she exclaimed later, when we were back on the street.

"I'd take you every night."

"That's sweet! You might get tired of me."

"Never!"

We walked along the docks and crossed a bridge. The brick dock tower, which was over three hundred feet tall, overlooked the pier. Lights appeared in the distance, and Emily ran ahead. "A ship is coming in!"

When I caught up with her she was shivering, so I offered my arm. "You are a gentleman," she said, and pressed herself against my side. "The stars are glorious tonight. I could almost believe there was peace on earth."

I certainly felt at peace.

"What did you do at home, Edward?"

"I rode my horse, played hockey and baseball. Farm work, of course. I read. I really enjoy reading."

"You aren't a budding poet, are you?"

"No! I'm not much for writing. Maybe letters. I do like history—Alexander the Great, the Roman Empire, and Kipling."

"What is it with boys and Kipling? I prefer Jane Austen myself."

I hadn't heard of her. "I sing, too."

"Sing?"

"At weddings and funerals. My mother was a good singer; I got it from her."

She poked me in the ribs. "You're only trying to impress me. You can't sing."

"I can!"

"Prove it!"

My throat was dry. "I just have to think of a song."

She was grinning at her little game. I thought of "Mademoiselle from Armentières," but I could only remember the racy version. Finally, I sang:

"By the light of the silvery moon
I want to spoon.
To my honey I'll croon love's tune.
Honey moon, keep a-shinin' in June.
Your silv'ry beams will bring love's dreams.
We'll be cuddling soon
By the silvery moon."

Her smile grew wider and I grew braver, finding my proper pitch. When I was done, she was momentarily speechless.

"You have a wonderful voice!" She took my hands. "No one has ever sung to me before. Sing it again."

I did. She gave me a kiss on the cheek, making my heart skip.

"This must be very odd for you." She took my arm again. "Being here, that is. Ships. The ocean. Not at all like home."

"Home is just grass and cows."

"I grew up on a farm, too, remember? We had two Lincolnshire reds, a bull, a milk cow, twelve chickens, and three pigs."

We settled on a bench that faced the ocean. A ship was passing by the tower.

"Your friend was transferred to Lincoln."

"Paul?" A sharp pain shot through my gut.

"He asked about you several times."

I pictured him in his cot. I was such a terrible friend. "I should have visited him."

"Why didn't you?"

I shrugged. "There wasn't time. And . . ." I decided to be truthful. "I—I don't know how to explain it. I just couldn't stand to look at him. He was such a go-getter and a very handsome man. Seeing him was . . . terrible . . ."

"He needed your company."

I nodded. I knew, I knew, I'd let a friend down.

She looked me in the eye. "But it's not just about him, is it? It's about what could happen to you, too. If you go to the front."

"No. Well . . . maybe. But Paul gave up. That's what I couldn't bear to see. Not Paul. And what will he do with his life now?"

"It's easier when we nurses don't know the men before they come in; then we can only imagine what may have been

117

lost. It's not that much easier, of course. And many good soldiers don't come back at all. Like my brother."

I turned to her in surprise. "Your brother?"

"Yes. Robert signed up with the Lincs Infantry and he died at Gallipoli." Her voice cracked a little. I didn't know much about Gallipoli, other than that it had been a hard campaign against the Turks, somewhere in the Mediterranean near Constantinople. "We were told a sniper got him, but that turned out to be a lie to save our feelings. One of his school chums gave us the truth. He died from dysentery. Dysentery! It certainly wasn't the heroic end he'd been promised by the recruiting posters." She seemed as if she were about to sob, but she got a hold of herself. "He had the thickest hair and softest hands; he always got blisters. He was a good poet. His grave is so far away from us I might never get to see it."

"My brother was murdered by the Huns." It came out angrier than I'd intended, my mind's eye offering up the image of his legs, torn apart by bullets, once again.

She put her hand on my shoulder. "How did it happen?"

I told her what I knew of his death. She shook her head. "It's really hard, isn't it? We're so alike. I knew that when I first saw you. Neither of us belongs here."

But I belong, I wanted to say.

She pressed herself lightly against me. " 'The war is killing our youth.' That's what Robert wrote in one of his poems. So true. The war kills our young and makes the rest of us old before our time. I feel like a crone."

"You're far from that!"

"Ah, Edward." She patted my hand, then held it tight. "I'm going to France, to Etaples, on Tuesday."

I was stunned. *Three* days! She was shipping out before me. I'd pictured her waving good-bye to me on the dock.

"Don't you have anything to say?" Emily asked.

"It's what you want."

"What I want is for the war to end. It's not that putting dressing on a soldier's wound will stop the war, but maybe it'll end it a little sooner. That night when all the wounded arrived was the first time I ever saw up close what happens. Not just broken bones, but injuries from shrapnel and bullets. They do terrible things to the body. I have to help."

"I know how you feel."

"Do you really want to go? It seems so horrid."

"We could lose the war, you know. I don't want Hector to have died for nothing."

She touched my cheek; her hand smelled like flowers. "I wish we'd been born forty years earlier. We could be sitting here together without thinking of the war."

I grabbed her hand. "I'll . . . I'll miss you, Emily."

"You don't even know me." She must've seen the look on my face. "I mean, well, these are strange days. Everything I feel is . . . heightened, somehow. I'll miss you, too, I know that. I know that. I'll write, I promise. Maybe you'll be in France soon and we'll meet again."

"I'll ask for leave every day."

"Ha! You'll come and see me off, won't you? At three on Tuesday."

"Nothing could keep me away."

That got a smile.

"Will you kiss me?" she asked.

"Wh-what?"

"It would be bad luck if you went to France and hadn't kissed a girl."

"I've kissed girls!" I lied.

"You haven't kissed me."

Emily leaned very close, her sweet rose scent tickling my nostrils. Her breath and mine mingled; then our lips touched. I closed my eyes. Was I supposed to move my lips? Hers were so soft.

"That was nice," she whispered moments later, leaning against me. "So nice." I put my arms around her and held her tight. I wanted to keep this moment safe in my heart no matter how long the war lasted.

15

The next day I brushed Buke. As I gently untangled the knots in his mane, his heavy odor reminded me of home.

"Emily is amazing," I whispered, glancing around to be sure no one was near.

I relived our evening a thousand times. Dining, talking, a show, and a first kiss. Thinking about it made my heart race. And now she was going to leave!

It was crazy to be daydreaming about her, especially during drill. Luckily, I'd made no boneheaded mistakes. Captain Trollope had even complimented me; Buke had again been fidgety and raring to go, but he'd stayed in his place in line.

I walked back to our tent, through slushy mud. At home now, it would be so cold you'd take your life in your hands just going outside. I pushed open the flap and Cheevers jumped right into my face, swinging a letter around like a flag. "My brother wrote me! We're missing everything! Listen up! 'Dear Mardy Sourpuss.'" Cheevers paused. "Isn't James funny? Anyway, he writes, 'Last night Sims, Adcock, Sidney, and me blackened our faces, climbed over the top, clipped the Hun wire, and crawled up to their trench. Quick as a wink Sidney jumped over and bayonetted their watchmen. The rest of us followed, tossing Mills Bombs ahead of us, then mopping up with bayonets. Stab! Twist! Wipe! Stab! Twist! Wipe! I got three; I'm up to five now. We dragged one scrawny, squob-eyed Hun back with us. Adcock pegged out just as we crawled back in—a damn fine shot in the forehead. I'll miss the bugger. Sergeant says we deserve medals, but we settled for an extra rum ration.'" He lowered the letter. "Stab! Twist! Wipe! Now, that's action, eh, Bathe? Eh, Blackburn?"

Jumping the bags! Hand-to-hand combat! All told as though it were just a stroll in the park.

"I doubt it really happened," Blackburn said. "You do come from a family of grandiose braggarts."

Cheevers glared. "It happened! Your brother's still picking his nose in Italy."

Blackburn shook his head. "I need some air." He marched out of the tent.

Cheevers gave me a wink. "The air in here's clearer now."

He poured himself a cup of tea from the camp stove and sat down at the small table. "Enough about war! Time to think of love." He laid out his paper, pen, and ink. "I've got to write another letter to my sweetheart. The problem is . . . which one?" He tapped his forehead. "I'll write my favorite, and when I'm done I'll send a copy to my other skirts. Changing the names, of course! Should I ask for gingerbread biscuits this time?"

I shook my head and laughed. Cheevers was doing wrong, but he did it with such relish it was hard to lecture him.

My back ached from all the riding we'd done, and I needed to take a walk, maybe even as far as the aid post. I pulled on my greatcoat and stepped outside.

"You shouldn't listen to Cheevers." Blackburn was a few steps away, a cigarette glowing in his hand. He let out the smoke. "He loves the glory a little too much."

"He's a good trooper."

"Oh, I know that. I'm just saying it's not all about charging like Indian braves. You have to keep a cool head, know when to charge and when to fall down flat. Cheevers is the type who's always charging."

I'd rather have him at my side than you, I felt like saying, but instead just replied: "He's my friend."

"Well, I don't need friends. I need dependable troopers next to me. We don't have to like each other, but I know tactics and I know my job." He flicked the cigarette skyward. It arced to the ground, scattering ashes across the road.

I tramped away. Blackburn was always reading manuals on fighting. But sometimes knowing or thinking too much could be a bad thing, like that time I read about how to properly swing a baseball bat, and didn't hit a single pitch for ages. Worse was thinking too much about what could happen to you. Every time I pictured Paul's broken body or

Hector's last moments, I got nervous. In battle, images like that could cause me to freeze in the middle of a charge over the trenches.

That was why Cheevers was so good. He wouldn't hesitate for a moment. Like Hector, he'd be a good man to follow.

16

Emily was trying to lug her trunk through the side door of the aid post. She was in her blue dress and had tied her hair back. "It's about time you got here!" Her cheeks were flushed as though she'd been running.

"I had to sneak over. I'm on stable duty, but a friend is covering for me. We'll both get field punishment if I'm caught."

"He must be a good friend."

Once I'd admitted to Cheevers that I had to see a girl, he'd said, "Get on over there and give her a kiss for me." I'd have about an hour before Sergeant Applewhite would notice I was out.

"Just one moment, Miss Waters." Major Purves, the regimental doctor, strode up. He was a tall man with warm eyes. "I couldn't let you go without saying good-bye." I was suddenly jealous at the way she smiled for him.

"That's kind of you."

"You're a marvelous nurse. I gave a glowing report to your superior. I'm sure you'll make a splash at Etaples." He shook her hand and a blush came to her cheeks.

"Thank you, sir! I learned so much from you."

"You'll do even better work there." He glanced at me. "You take care of her, Trooper. She's quite the catch."

"I will!"

Major Purves smiled at us and went back into the aid post.

"The lorry's waiting," Emily said. I lifted the trunk, surprised to find it so heavy. I imagined what was inside: books, combs, a hand mirror, dresses, and frilly underclothes—everything that helped make her Emily.

"Is there an anvil in here?" I asked.

"Two, just so I can see you sweat."

I lugged the trunk to the truck. The smoke from the driver's cigarette curled out the open cab. I heaved the trunk onto the back of it.

"How long until we go, mac?" she asked the driver.

"Just a bit more load-up to do, duck!"

She took my hand and led me around the side of the building, then folded both her hands over mine. I looked down at them, fascinated at how small they were next to my own. "You treated me well, Edward." She tightened her grip. "I truly appreciate that. You're a good boy . . . good man."

"Thank you." I'd rehearsed other words: *I really care about you. I think you're wonderful.* Nothing was big enough to express what I needed to say. "You're a good one, too . . . girl, that is." I bumbled hopelessly along. "More than that;

you're wonderful and . . ." Her eyes were so big I lost my train of thought.

"Chatty as always." Her smile made me flush with emotion. I likely wouldn't see it again for months, maybe even a year. Or longer. I wanted to hold her tight to me, but I was paralyzed.

The horn honked. "So soon," she said softly, and pulled her hands away, reaching into the pocket of her dress. She handed me a silver locket. I opened it, discovering a picture of her in her nurse's uniform. She wasn't smiling, but she looked poised and beautiful.

"It's what girls do, I guess—give pictures of themselves to boys."

"I'll keep it right next to my heart."

Emily reached out as if she were going to pull a coin from my ear. I jumped a little. "I'm not going to pinch you." She drew me toward her and we kissed gently. I tried to hold her but she'd already backed away. "That was our second kiss." She put her finger to my lips. "Your lips better not touch another girl or you won't get your third."

"I'll wait until kingdom come and longer."

"You won't have to wait that long, I promise."

I followed her to the back of the truck and helped her climb up. By then three other nurses had boarded, and Emily squeezed in next to them, straightening her skirt as she did. The truck gave a roar, then backfired and growled its way down the road. She waved, looking rather melancholy, and I waved back. My eyes were locked on her as she grew smaller and smaller and finally disappeared over a hill.

17

I checked my mail every day. A week after she left I received a postcard from Emily with a picture of a field camp hospital in Etaples, a coastal city in France. On the back she'd scribbled:

Dear Edward,

Kept quite busy! Not even time to breathe. Will write more later.

Yours truly,
Emily

Truly? Yours truly? Not even *Sweetly yours?* Still, she'd made it safely, and I was being selfish, expecting her to write more. Obviously, she was hard at work.

I wrote back to her immediately:

Jan. 30, 1918

Dear Emily,

Now that you're gone the sun has stopped shining. We have to train in the dark. It's really quite a nuisance. Could you please come back, if only to give us a little light by which to do our duty?

Wisecracks aside, I do hope things are going well there. I know you must be terribly busy, but if you get a moment, walk out to the ocean and look toward England. You'll see me on Buke, drilling and drilling and drilling. We trained in the lance this week. I felt like a knight. Next is the sword. It seems old-fashioned, charging machine guns with swords, but the higher-ups say they're effective. I'm not sure I want to test their theories.

Well, back to drills. I do wish I could drop by and see you, but I suppose that'll be months from now.

Very warmly yours,
Edward

Two weeks passed without news, though I checked the mail every day. Our squadron rode the twenty-five miles inland to Lincoln to join the entire regiment for further training. Townspeople gathered on the streets and cheered as we rode up the steep hill, past Lincoln Castle.

The barracks were three times the size of ours, with two flanking wings and a large courtyard. We drilled day and night—more than five hundred yeomanry galloping across the barracks' grounds or cutting through Rise-holme Park. I was astounded by the thudding of hooves and the sound of metal on metal as five hundred swords were drawn at once. Surely our enemy would wilt before us.

On the third day Sergeant Applewhite brought our mail. One letter for Blackburn, from his brother; three from girls for Cheevers; and one from Emily for me. She'd dabbed a bit of perfume on it, which made me sniff like a hound dog before I opened it.

Feb. 14, 1918

Dear Not-So-Bright Edward,

    I know. I know. You're wondering why such a cruel greeting. Well, you did say in your last letter that the sun wasn't shining without me.

    I'm sorry for not writing sooner. I do the work of ten nurses and there is no time to rest.

    All is well here according to the newspapers, but not judging by the wounded I see. We are kept busy "mending" (that's what we call it, as if we are stitching together shirts). I see a steady flow of men hit by shrapnel and bullets. Some look lifeless; others ask how soon they can go back to the front, as though they haven't yet had enough of fighting. Shrapnel is an evil invention that takes a terrible toll on a man's body. The guns are always firing. We hear them roar and we know another man, or ten,

*has lost his life. I am told this is actually the slow
season and the spring will bring a flood of patients.
Oh, joy!*

*Yesterday a German aeroplane flew over camp,
looking like a silver-white bird. Our anti-aircraft
guns got busy; then one of our own pilots appeared
on the hunt. They fought into the distance, so we
didn't get to see the end of the battle, but it was
terrifying nonetheless. We are so close to the front
here.*

*It's St. Valentine's Day today, so naturally I'm
thinking of you. I picture you on Buke, charging with a
sword. Please don't cut yourself! I know you want to do
your part, but I'm happy you're not in France right
now. I cringe every time I hear the big guns.*

*I miss our talks and I miss your singing. Do
you ever think of our evening in Grimsby? It was a
glorious time. I hope we can sit together on that bench
again.*

*Warmth and all best wishes,
Emily*

I folded the letter. Only forty-eight hours earlier this
paper had been in her warm, petite hands.

"Did your May Queen profess her everlasting love?"
Cheevers asked.

"She said they're very busy at Etaples looking after the
wounded."

"At least the poor sods have someone beautiful to care for

them," Cheevers said. "My girls all hinted they'd like a ring. I have to figure out a way to marry each of them, without the others finding out!"

"Good luck," I said, already setting out my writing paper.

Feb. 17, 1918

> *Dear So-Very-Bright Emily,*
>
> *I laughed at the first line of your letter. Clever! You sound hard at work.*
>
> *We drill and drill and drill. We know every maneuver inside, outside, and backwards. Sometimes we sit back and our horses do all the work. But we are a tight regiment now, ready for anything. Every one of us would gladly trade our comfy spots in the saddle to be in the trenches, and help get this war over and done with.*
>
> *It's not all drills, though; one day we had an intersquadron horse wrestling competition. We wrestle on horseback, in teams of three. Blackburn, Cheevers, and I did quite well, until three brutes from C Squadron got a hold of us and nearly broke our necks. Great fun, though!*
>
> > *Warmth and best wishes,*
> > *Edward*

I reread the letter. How stupid to end with wrestling!

> *P.S. Buke is doing well. In my humble opinion, he's the best horse in the regiment.*

Then I wrote what I was really thinking:

P.P.S. I do remember that park bench. I cannot count how many times I dream of being back on that bench with you. I wish I could sing to you right now.

P.P.P.S. Have I written enough P.S.'s yet?

18

The next letter I received had Reverend Ashford's address on it. My hand shook as I slit the envelope open, worried that Dad had passed on.

Jan. 19, 1918

Dear Edward,

I am writing to tell you about your father. I visited him recently and saw that a letter of yours remained unopened by his bedside. I must admit, I gave him a talking-to, opened it, read it to myself, and asked whether he wanted to know the contents, but he forbade me to talk about you. I am afraid I wasn't able to pass on your news, but I left the letter by his bedside. Perhaps when he gets over his stubborn streak

134

he will read it. At least he knows that you are still alive, but he seems to care little about the world around him, and I worry that his condition is worsening. He certainly is thin, even with the meals from the Empire Ladies. One cannot force a grown man to eat.

In part, his troubles are due to Hector's belongings having been returned: a few books, his regimental badges, his identity disk, and his cap. Seeing them hit your father hard. Also, Hector's last letter was included. It was unfinished, but he mentioned you and hoped all was well with the horses. It's a hard thing when we hear from someone who has already left us.

Judging by the reports in the papers, there is a long way to go before the end of this war. It's obvious you won't be home by spring, so the Somnerses will seed your land. Everyone here wishes you the best, and we pray for you.

I hope yeomanry life serves you well. I still remember the horse I rode in South Africa; he was a good friend. May God watch over you, and your horse.

Sincerely,

Rev. Robert Ashford

Hector had started a final letter? I wanted to read it so much. I wondered what his thoughts had been, what sorts of things had happened to him before he'd died. I wanted to hear his voice again, if only in print.

At least Dad was still alive, but what was going on in his

head? Was he reliving his mad dash for the guns in South Africa? Was he missing Mom? Where was the strength that had helped him cut our farm out of unbroken sod?

Maybe if I had taken his work clothes to him one more time, he would've found that strength. It might be that he just needed to lean on me, and I had abandoned him. I felt as though sand were filling my guts. I had tried for months to get him to walk out that door. I couldn't do everything on my own.

The following day the townspeople of Lincoln were invited to the barracks for Open Day, when we jumped barriers and careened our horses around barrels to the oohs and ahs of ladies and the polite clapping of old men in suits. We even performed a lance charge. Cheevers and I loved every moment of it.

Afterward, I stripped the saddle off Buke's sweating back. "Good boy," I gushed as I patted his side and brushed him down.

Sergeant Applewhite shoved his way through the stable door. "Inspection! Get a move on! Colonel Wilson is on his way!"

Cheevers threw a fork into my stall, nearly pinning my foot. "Quick-sticks, Bathe! Stop your lollin'!"

I rushed down to the pump and back, water splashing from the pail. The colonel must not think I was neglecting Buke. I tossed fresh green hay in the second trough.

I spit-polished my boots and straightened my puttees and my uniform. One middle button sagged, but there was no time to sew it. I dashed to the tiny mirror in the stable, jostling other troopers, and saw a dirty face, lined with streaks of straw dust and sweat. Oh, Lord! I ran to the trough, pushed Buke aside, splashed my cheeks, and dried myself on my spare horse blanket. Buke snorted angrily at me for the interruption.

"D Squadron! Attention!" Captain Trollope's voice cut through the din. "Stand to!" I rushed to my position outside the stall, joining a line of troopers, hands at their sides. The captain stood on one side of the stable door and Lieutenant Rance, the other.

Colonel Wilson strode in, medals arrayed across his chest, his hat under one arm, his gray hair short. He looked each man up and down; ran his fingers across the top of the gate, checking for dust; and moved on to the next stall. I watched out of the corner of my eye as he got closer. He had a reputation for choosing one man and berating him for his mistakes.

He stopped and looked me over, letting out a hiss. Then he stomped into my stall. Buke whickered. The colonel was back a moment later, so we were face to face. Wrinkles surrounded two stone-cold eyes. "Name?"

"Trooper Bathe, sir."

"Your stall is clean, Bathe, but your third button is loose."

"I'm sorry, sir."

"Good God, Trooper, sorry doesn't cut it with me! For the want of a nail the kingdom was lost. Do you understand?"

"Yes, sir," I replied. "I'll fix it immediately, sir."

"A little blot like that could change the course of your whole career. I won't have any shirkers under my command, especially since we'll be shipping out!"

I took a deep breath. The other troopers did, too. Finally, after all this waiting, it was going to happen.

"Are you men ready?" Wilson looked up and down the line.

"Yes, sir!" we replied in unison.

"You'd bloody well better be! There's a spot of trouble in the east and they need a hand cleaning it up. A month or two and everything will be tip-top, then we'll head back to France to show 'em all how it's done."

East? And then back to France? But France was east.

"Hard riding! Are you up to it, lads?"

"Yes, sir!"

"They'll be sorry the day they see the Lincolnshire Yeomanry riding down on them. We ship out Thursday. Don't miss the boat."

Everyone cheered.

"They're yours, Captain Holmes!" Wilson said.

Our regimental chaplain stepped up, a ruddy-faced man, impeccable in his uniform. His white collar seemed to glow. He stopped at a pail of water.

"I'm going to bless you and your mounts. Please bow your heads." We lowered our chins to our chests. "Almighty God, who didst send thy holy angel unto the pool of Bethesda, hear our prayers and be pleased to stretch out thy hand, and according to thy holy will grant restoration of health and the fulfillment of the good desires of all those men and horses who are about to be blessed with this water. Amen." He looked at the troopers. "Say Amen."

We echoed, "Amen."

The chaplain stood before the ferrier's horse, Brush Me,

and dabbed water first on the horse, then on Pitts's forehead. "May it please Almighty God of his great goodness to grant thee health and peace, according to his holy will, and fulfill all thy good desires for his honor and glory. The blessing of God Almighty, the Father, the Son, and the Holy Ghost, be upon thee now and always. Amen." The horse snorted.

It took a long time to bless us all, but when the water dribbled onto my forehead I felt as if God had placed an invisible suit of armor over me. Buke looked even stronger than before.

"Tomorrow we're going on an adventure, pal," I said, once the chaplain had moved on. I scratched Buke's ears. "We're going to see the world."

BOOK TWO

Will ye go to Flanders, my Mally-O?
And see the chief commanders, my Mally-O?
You'll see the bullets fly,
And the soldiers how they die
And the ladies loudly cry, oh, my Mally-O!

"Will Ye Go to Flanders"
(Traditional)

1

Our horses were stuffed into cattle cars, we soldiers were jammed into passenger cars, and then our train rattled south to Southampton. Within a few hours we stood before the HMT *Mercian*. One smokestack jutted above a deck cluttered with cargo booms, derrick masts, and piles of supplies.

"So that's our brave and valiant vessel," Cheevers said. "The perfect ship for a trip to hell."

"It's built to haul fruit, and it's not even armed," said Blackburn, frowning. "If we're spotted, we'll just pretend we're apples and oranges."

"Blackburn!" Cheevers clapped him on the back. "You made a joke—the end of the world is nigh!"

Blackburn snorted. "This 'fruit ship' ruse is the real laugh! The Germans tend to sink all ships, military or not. I wish we were part of a nice, safe convoy. They must want us out of here quick."

"Any idea where we're going?" I asked.

"Salonika!" Cheevers shouted. "That's what I heard from Pitts."

"The Italian front, is my guess." Blackburn thoughtfully scratched his chin, trying his best to look like officer material. "My brother said things are rough there."

I didn't know much about either place. I began to hum "I Don't Know Where I'm Going, but I'm on My Way." Cheevers laughed.

Soon we'd shuffled up the gangway to the deck and were led down a set of stairs to our sleeping quarters—a dimly lit cargo hold with several old, ugly tables and benches fixed to the floor. Hammock hooks stuck out of every post and along the walls. The room stank of rotting fruit and dead fish.

"Whoa!" Cheevers sniffed.

We were issued a printed card that read:

Somewhere in a British Port

Dear _____
    I arrived here safely and feel none the worse after the train journey. I am anticipating a pleasurable sea voyage, and will send another postcard upon arrival at our destination.
                    Address (Name and Rank) _____
                                No. _____
                    British Expeditionary Force

"Don't write anything else on the cards or I'll use them as bum wipe!" Sergeant Applewhite yelled.

144

I found an open spot at a table, addressed the card to Emily, and filled in the blanks. I wished I could add *I miss you.*

After six days of rough seas we docked in Gibraltar. The entire regiment crouched in the hold, either playing cards or Crown and Anchors or waiting in line to gawk out a porthole at the rockbound city. No soldier was to be spotted by the locals, since the Huns had spies everywhere.

Three hours after leaving port we were allowed on deck. We washed our uniforms and hung them on every open wire or post, where they flapped like a thousand khaki flags.

Dr. Purves had injected each of us with anticholera shots. I rubbed my aching shoulder, then checked my right front pocket; Mother's handkerchief and the locket from Emily were both safely buttoned inside. I also felt for the identification disks around my neck—still there. Patting for them had become a nervous habit.

"Any tinned fish?" Cheevers asked, looking out at the water.

"What?"

"Hun submarines. They're out there, mate, hiding in the water, watching with their beady little rat eyes. Cowards!"

"Don't we have submarines, too?"

"Of course! Sometimes you have to sink to their level." He paused. "Catch on? Sink to their level?"

"Funny," I said without smiling. "Very. Funny."

He chuckled. "Let's check the horses."

We walked toward the main stairwell, saluting Captain Trollope. "You troopers keeping out of mischief?" he said.

145

"Yes, sir!" I replied.

"Carry on, lads."

The moment we were out of earshot Cheevers whispered, "Officers! Eating steak and kidney pie with the ship's captain; sticking us with bully beef, tinned jam, and hardtack."

"Trollope is a fair man," I said.

"Well, if you like him so much, maybe you should kiss his lordship's bum next time you see him."

"You're a loudmouth rotter."

"I'll take that as a compliment!"

We clomped down into the hold, horse stink and flies clouding the humid air. Buke's ears perked up the moment I approached his timber stall and squeezed between him and the nearest horse. He snorted and rubbed against me as I backed him out into the aisle.

He looked thinner but was healthy and alert. We'd lost three horses in the first few days. One had slipped and choked on its halter; the other two had grown septic, perhaps from moldy hay.

We rounded the corner and nearly stepped on three men kneeling around a dead horse. I yanked Buke to a stop and he whickered his frustration.

"She was a good one." A trooper patted the horse's head. Her long pink tongue hung out, unblinking eyes glazed over.

"Hey, bring those nags up and help!" a corporal said to us. "This one's getting buried at sea." We pulled our horses past the corpse, Buke's eyes wide with fear. I whispered calming words, and soon we'd hitched him and Neddie to the dead horse and dragged it to the loading door. A burly trooper gave the door a shove, and bright light made us all squint.

A wind swept in, carrying the smell of the sea. The corporal hooked the corpse to a pulley, and the big trooper began cranking until the body reached the edge.

"Any last words, Trooper Sloan?" the corporal asked.

Sloan was a small guy, with spectacles and light brown hair. He wiped his eyes. "See you, Andy. See you, pal."

The horse was winched through the hatch and dropped into the water.

"Don't worry." The corporal patted Sloan's back. "There'll be another for you when we arrive."

"I want Andy. He was my horse."

He sounded like a child, but I knew I'd feel the same way if something happened to Buke.

As I inched closer to the door the *Mercian* swayed, and I had a panicky feeling that I might slip out. I clutched a post and sniffed the fresh air. They forked the manure out these doors at night so it would sink in the dark and submarines couldn't track us.

"Nice day for fishing," the corporal said. "Which squadron you boys from?"

"D Squadron, Corporal," Cheevers said.

"Yellow-bellied devils, the lot of you." He grinned, showing two buck teeth. "We're from A Squadron—the pride of the regiment. At least, that's what I tell me mum."

"She must be proud as a peacock!" Cheevers said. "Look at you all, the finest fighters in the King's army."

The corporal guffawed.

Cheevers could certainly make friends quickly, just like Hector. The two of them would probably have been great pals.

147

Seagulls flew low over the waves, which I guessed meant land was nearby. It reminded me of Noah waiting for the dove to return to the ark with an olive branch. I certainly was a long way from the dry prairie. I wanted to spot a dolphin, a shark, or a whale. The biggest fish I'd ever seen was a trout Dad had caught at Bone Creek.

A fin broke the surface. A whale! It was as if God were fulfilling my wish. The whale's blue body rose above the water; it was larger than Jonah's whale. Too large, I realized with a lurch of horror.

"A submarine," I said hoarsely.

"What's that?" the corporal asked.

I pointed. A submarine floated in the water, its dark hull glistening.

"Ah, Christ! It's the Germans!" The corporal slapped the burly trooper's shoulder. "Run, tell the colonel! Run, you bastard!" The man sped off.

"Why's it just sitting there?" Cheevers asked.

A hatch opened on the submarine's conning tower, and sailors in black uniforms climbed out and sauntered over to their gun. "We're sitting ducks, boys," the corporal said. "Close this hatch!" We slammed the door and latched it. "To the top deck, and don't forget your life belts!"

I reached to untie Buke. "Leave your horses!"

I gave Buke a pat. "Stay put, I'll be back for you." Cheevers and I ran down the aisle, with Trooper Sloan one step behind.

The ship's steam whistle screamed three times before we reached the stairs. Troopers were struggling up to the top deck as Sergeant Applewhite stood there shouting, "Orderly

148

now, boys! Use the right side of the stairway because there're lads coming down, so give 'em room. Orderly, I said! Remember, you're Lincolnshire Yeomanry."

I yanked a life vest out of the chest and fumbled with the knots as we climbed. A giant hammer struck the side of the ship, throwing me to my knees. Cheevers helped me up, saying, "That was damn close!"

We stumbled out of the hold into smoke and screaming men. A shell had struck amidships, blasting the wireless station apart; it'd be impossible to call for help now. A trooper was moaning in pain, and Dr. Purves bent over him.

We rushed to our boat stations and saw the submarine in the distance, a gray puff floating in front of its gun. The German sailors waved playfully at us.

"Did they fire a torpedo?" I asked.

"Why waste a torpedo?" Blackburn was looking paler than usual. "We can't even lob fruit at them."

The *Mercian* had picked up speed and leaned as we turned, making us a zigzagging target. Another shell went howling over the ship, and several men sent up a cheer. I even shook my fist at the Huns.

"Here we are, you bastards!" a trooper shouted. "Come and get us! Here we are!"

At first whispering, then louder, I began to sing:

"Here we are! Here we are! Here we are again!
There's Pat and Mac and Tommy and Jack and Joe."

Cheevers joined me; Blackburn, too, followed by Pitts. Several seconds later most of the regiment was singing or shouting the words:

149

"When there's trouble brewing,
When there's something doing
Are we downhearted?
NO! Let 'em all come!
Here we are! Here we are! Here we are again!"

At least we were fighting back with our voices. Maybe the Germans had stopped to listen to us.

The gun roared, and a screeching shell struck only thirty feet away, smacking several troopers off their feet. The heat of the explosion burned us; metal splinters whistled by. We cowered but held our position.

Many of the singers were moaning now. Dr. Purves, his orderlies, and the chaplain sifted through the wreckage of metal and men.

The section next to us was already in their boat, ready to be lowered.

"Did someone order abandon ship?" I asked.

"We're going too fast," Blackburn said. "They shouldn't be in the lifeboats."

A shell hissed through the air and cut the davit rope, and the lifeboat tipped and dumped the men into the water.

"Oh, God," I whispered. "Oh, God, save them. Save them."

They were bobbing in the sea, waving their hands, mouths open, but their yelling was drowned out by the noise of the ship. "Cut the davits!" Sergeant Applewhite commanded. "Let the boat drop!" I yanked out my knife and Cheevers and I hung over the edge, Blackburn and Pitts holding our legs. We hacked at the thick ropes until they snapped and the lifeboat fell. It smashed into the side of the ship and rolled in the air, miraculously landing upright. Who knew if the men could even reach it, let alone pull themselves aboard.

Captain Trollope walked by, his riding stick under his arm. "Hold your positions, and don't lower any more boats! Good lads! Look the Huns in the eye. Sing another song!"

Look and sing, that was all we could do.

Trollope carried on. "Hold the line! Hold—"

A flash filled my vision as something struck my temple and I collapsed. I struggled to open my eyes, but all I saw was blue sky and smoke. There was no sound and I couldn't feel my arms or legs. The sky shifted, and the deck of the ship and a face came into focus. I was being propped up by Blackburn. "Bathe! Bathe! Are you hurt?"

I could hear again, and see, so I still had eyes and ears. I sucked in a cloud of sooty smoke and coughed so hard I thought my chest would burst. "I'm all right." I sat up and counted my fingers. Ten. Shrapnel had torn a hole through my uniform and sliced my shoulder. I poked at it and found a trickle of blood. "Just a scratch!" Blackburn nodded and moved on. I was able to stand again on shaky legs.

Several troopers were facedown on the deck. The tongue of one hung out like a dead calf, and he was missing his lower jaw. Then I noticed his stripes and recognized the top half of his face—Sergeant Applewhite. My sergeant was dead.

I took a wobbly step and stumbled over a leg, reached down and picked it up. It was light; the puttees fluttered like banners. Whose leg was it? Dr. Purves could sew it back on.

It could be mine! I looked down, relieved to see both of

my legs in their proper places. I searched for the rest of the man because he could be put together again, like Humpty-Dumpty, but soon the leg felt heavy and I dropped it.

The ship rocked and I nearly stumbled into a broken winch pipe that was hissing steam. I wiped my eyes. Captain Trollope was sleeping on the deck, his orderly kneeling beside him. "Wake up, sir!"

Trollope opened his eyes, his face black as burned steak. The slightest smile appeared. "It has been a short life. . . ." He shuddered, and the orderly clung to Trollope's hand. I watched them, waiting for Trollope to move again.

I was spun around to face Lieutenant Rance. "Snap out of it, lad!" he shouted at me, spittle hitting my face. "Go give the machine gunners a hand. Now!"

I lurched my way over to three men unloading two Vickers machine guns from broken crates. "Bring those bullets!" a lance corporal commanded. I carried a belt box to the rear of the ship. This was work; something to keep my mind occupied.

Another blow rocked the deck and I nearly lost my footing.

"Quick, break it open!" the lance corporal said. Two troopers had set up the tripod and mounted the gun. I flipped the tin lid and pulled out a line of bullets.

"Let's give 'em hell!" the gunner said. He pulled the trigger, and then, about thirty yards from the submarine, water splashed up. The Germans shook their fists, but the submarine slowed until they were out of our range. Another shell screamed through the air overhead.

"We might as well be spitting wads of paper," a trooper hissed.

"At least we threw their aim off," the gunner said.

As I went back for another belt box I saw several of the ship's crew in a lifeboat, lowering themselves over the side. "Run for it, boys!" a seaman cried. "We're outgunned." He jumped over the side.

"Stick to your posts, men," Lieutenant Rance shouted. "A thousand tons of British guns and horses are not going to be sitting on the bottom of the ocean. Let the civvies go."

But who was running the ship? I hadn't seen the *Mercian*'s captain among the crewmen, so he must still be on board, but who was down in the stokehold?

A shell hit the water tank, splashing a wave across the deck. Men were blown to the side by the explosion; one fell down, down into the sea.

I struggled back to the machine guns, the deck now a mess of mangled metal and bodies. A shell tore through the staircase behind me but didn't explode.

Chaplain Holmes charged forward, grabbed the smoking shell, and threw it overboard toward the sub, yelling, "Get thee hence, Satan!" Several men clapped. Holmes examined his burned hands, then returned to the wounded.

I lowered the box. "Here's your bullets."

"You a Canuck?" the gunner asked.

"Yes!"

"Me too." The man sounded British. His voice was calm, as though we were just sitting down for tea. "My name's Herc—short for Hercules. I worked in the auto factories at

Oshawa. Good money. Okay, Pile, adjust the sights—let's give 'em another shot."

The gun rattled, spewing fire, smoke, and hot lead. Bullets sprayed three or four hundred feet from the sub. "They're still too far," Herc said.

I blocked the sun with my hand. "There's something else out there!" I said.

A shadow had appeared on the far horizon that was large enough to be one of our destroyers. The Huns saw it, too. The men stood around the gun, staring toward the ship. Then a German officer shouted from the conning tower and the Huns ran to it and climbed in. A few moments later the submarine dove.

We were silent, counting each second, staring out at the open sea. The ship on the horizon was gone, but so was the submarine. Muttering soon turned to jeering, and after about five minutes we began to cheer as if we'd just won a football match.

2

The *Mercian* raced over the waves as we gathered around our dead pals. All twenty-three of them had been wrapped in sheets and laid across the deck, glowing white in the dawn. They rocked with the ship, and it was hard not to imagine one or two standing up and saying, "See, I'm not hurt at all." But most of the sheets were stained red. It was just as well we couldn't see their faces.

Chaplain Holmes, his long robe snapping in the wind, said a few words about their bravery, their commitment to God and their country. Then several troopers carried the bodies one by one on stretchers and tipped the dead overboard as our bugler played "Last Post," followed by "The Dead March in Saul."

I shivered, wondering which bodies belonged to men I'd known. None of them would have dreamed they'd be buried at sea. When the last man was gone, the chaplain began a hymn:

"O God, our help in ages past,
Our hope for years to come,
Our shelter from the stormy blast,
And our eternal home."

I sang along, the familiar words a small comfort. When the song was over, we scrubbed the deck and cleaned up the destruction as well as we could. It was a blessing to have such a huge task; otherwise, I might have collapsed thinking of what I'd just witnessed.

Men had died, right in front of me. Captain Trollope. Sergeant Applewhite. Dead. They were gone. It wasn't like at home, watching an animal die. These men had had wives, children, brothers, sisters, mothers, fathers—and now their families would get letters telling them their boys had died bravely. There'd be no markers for their graves. No one would ever visit them.

Only one thought eased my grief, and I clung to it. Buke was safe in part because he'd been tied up alone. God had been kind enough to grant me that piece of luck. Nineteen horses had been crippled or killed just by falling onto one another. My injuries were scratches, a ringing in my ears, and an aching skull.

Cheevers leaned on his mop. "This is what happened down below. The crew had abandoned us, so good ol' Trooper Thompson grabbed the wheel and shouted to the ship's captain, 'You just tell me when to pull it right and left.' The Huns were aiming for him, but he stood tall.

Meanwhile, our boys in the boiler room kept up the steam!"

"What happens to the men in the rowboats?" I asked.

"Destroyers from Gibraltar will look for the survivors," Blackburn said.

"Poor guys! I hope a few made it."

"We survived, lads!" Cheevers grinned. "We even scared the Hun bastards away with our singing, thanks to you, mate. Good thinking on your part."

"Yes, good work," Blackburn said, giving me a soft pat on the shoulder.

A few minutes later roll call sounded and we gathered on the deck. Colonel Wilson stood on the remains of the wireless station. "Boys, we've been through the fire. Brave men have died this day—our friends, our brothers, our fellow yeomanry. I know you mourn them, and well you should. However, you must now remember your duty to your country, so that their deaths won't be in vain."

He waved a white paper. "I have a telegram from General Allenby himself, the commander in chief of the forces in Palestine. He wrote: *You are needed.* I replied: *We are coming.* I know every last one of you will be up to the task of giving Johnny Turk a good hiding."

What did Palestine have to do with us?

"The climate out there will test your limits, but you lads are made of stern stuff! You proved it just a few hours ago. Are you ready for your task, men?"

We forced out a tired cheer and were dismissed. I'd read about the battles for Gaza and knew the Suez Canal was important for transporting troops from India and Australia.

Our boys were in Jerusalem, which was probably where we would end up. I would be a million miles from Emily!

"You're looking glum, mate," Cheevers said.

"But why Palestine? Why not France?"

"Ah, who wants to be in a frosty trench? We'll be toasty warm in the Holy Land."

"But what do I know about Turks?"

"They're like Huns but uglier. Not sure why we haven't walked over them yet. Some daft boiled owl must be in charge."

"They'll fight hard to keep their empire together," Blackburn said. "Russia is on one side, eyeing up Constantinople. We're pushing through Palestine. No wonder they're taking money, troops, and guns from the Germans."

"The Turks will be pushovers!"

Blackburn snorted. "Remember Gallipoli? Hundreds of thousands of our troops thought they'd be in Constantinople in days. The Turks pushed *us* off there."

"The papers said it was a 'great and glorious retreat,'" I said, hearing Uncle Nix's voice: "When can a retreat be called great?"

"Ah, the Turks got lucky! They'll wilt when they see the Lincolnshire Lads riding at them. Don't be glum, chum!" Cheevers punched me in the shoulder.

I nodded, until he winked and gave me a grin. I faked a grin back. I felt heavy and tired, wishing I knew what the future held.

The *Mercian* sped on, leaving the dead deep in their watery grave.

3

We stood on the deck in full kit, rifles and all, gawking as we drew closer to Alexandria. The sun was so hot I felt like a boiled egg in a Tommy hat. I gazed at the tan stone buildings poking at the sky. It was as though the city hadn't changed since the times of the pharaohs.

We soon shuffled off the *Mercian*, glad to see the last of that tin piece of hell. I nearly broke into tears watching Buke trot down the livestock gangplank; he was thinner, but healthy, and he whickered the moment he saw me.

We saddled up and rode through the cramped streets, almost brushing against huts of stone and shells of wood and mud. The place smelled like charred meat and dead dogs. A few Egyptians stared, though others barely even raised their heads. They'd been here for thousands of years and would be here long after we were gone. I scratched at the lice biting my skin—the *Mercian*'s last laugh.

A troop of Australian Light Horsemen sat outside the train station, faces brown, weary, and wrinkled, slouch hats shielding their eyes from the sun. The Aussies had proven their worth at Gallipoli and were so feared that the Turks called them the white Gurkhas.

"They're tanned as dark as Turks," Cheevers whispered.

I nodded, though I wasn't sure what a Turk should look like.

"Hey, Tommies!" one Aussie shouted. "Welcome to Beelzebub's stronghold. If the Turks don't bite your arses off, the flies will."

Lieutenant Rance laughed, then shouted, "Ignore the Anzacs! They've all had a bit too much sun. We've got a train to catch!"

We loaded our horses in open cars. I climbed up the side, and Buke lowered his head enough so that I could scratch his nose. "It'll be hot, pal, but the sun'll go down, and you'll be the first to get water when we make camp." He gave a soft neigh and pressed against my hand.

Lieutenant Rance's whistle cut our visit short. I quickly bought a postcard of Alexandria from a one-eyed woman as old and weathered as the Sphinx. I scribbled: *Emily, Surprise! Will write more soon. Missing you!* I addressed it, dropped it in the mailbag, and got on the train, jammed between Cheevers and Blackburn in a stuffy passenger car.

We went from train to horseback to tent to train, officers constantly shouting at us to move faster. The sun threatened to cook us right off the backs of our horses. At some

160

point we crossed the Suez Canal on a pontoon bridge, then entrained again to cross the Sinai. For a farm boy, there was nothing more awe-inspiring and awful than the sight of endless desert.

Baked and rattled half to death, we passed the boundary pillars between Egypt and Palestine. We were in the Holy Land. I had expected to feel closer to God. Instead, I just felt tired.

Soon we spotted palm trees and, finally, the green-blue sweep of the Mediterranean. We stopped in Belah, a small village that had been a staging ground of the battles for Gaza. The train station was by far the largest building in the area. It was located next to a graveyard where wooden crosses poked out of the ground. Soldiers had fought and died for this chunk of sand.

"Everyone wants a Victoria Cross," Blackburn said, "but most of us just get a wooden one."

Cheevers smacked him on the back of the head. "Shut your gob! You'll bring bad luck."

We detrained, and watered from a well dug in the sand near the open sea. Buke gulped so much he began to cough. "Take it easy, boy," I said, and gently pulled his head back.

We set up our tents, and the sun forced us to stay inside them. I took out my writing paper and opened Emily's locket to gaze upon her photograph. Working on an empty cartridge box, I held the pen lightly because my fingers were so dry they had cracked and bled, and it hurt like blazes.

March 10, 1918

Dear Emily,

I am in Palestine now, only a short distance from the Mediterranean. It's a very romantic spot, except for the burning, boiling beast of a sun. Despite the heat, both Cheevers and Blackburn are sipping tea. You English and your tea! I'd do anything for lemonade. Or a new uniform. We are still in our heavy woolen khaki and Tommy helmets, so our travel has been quite a chore. Our lances were all left on the dock in Southampton. Army transport!

We had a terrible trip over. Our ship was attacked by a Hun U-boat, and several men died in front of me. The less said about it, the better. I'm just glad we didn't end up on the bottom of the sea.

Our general is somebody named Allenby, but they call him the Bull. Wonderful! We hear that a British officer named Lawrence has swayed the Arabs to our side. You may remember that he and his band of ruffians captured the port of Aqaba last year. Quite the surprise for the Turks! I guess they're blowing up railways left and right behind enemy lines, if the reports are to be believed.

I am exhausted. I do hope all is well.

Sincerely,
Edward

P.S. I wish I were in France, just so I could be closer to you.

I folded the letter and sealed it in an envelope, then closed the locket with her picture. I often wondered what she was doing at any given moment. Was she attending to the dressing on a wounded soldier? Or was she outside the hospital, lighting a cigarette, her thumbnail flicking the match?

I pictured her standing on a balcony, looking out over the ocean. I clearly saw the curve of her hips, the length of her legs. I hoped she was thinking of me.

I buttoned the locket into my breast pocket, next to my mother's handkerchief. Flies buzzed at me, bigger and ten times more determined than those at home. Out in the burning sun, I swatted them all the way to the quartermaster's tent.

4

We rode north into miles of brush and balding hills. The sun hadn't let up. We passed other yeomanry, tanned and smart-looking in their desert gear. They had a great laugh at our woolen uniforms and tin hats.

Blackburn kicked Cromwell until he was riding next to me. "We're almost at Jerusalem."

"How do you know?"

He tapped his head. "I memorized my map. The last village was Enab. Next stop: the Holy City."

We followed a steep road with hairpin bends. I tried not to look over the edge. Then, our horses ragged, we rode over a ridge and saw fifty or so bell tents, an ancient wall, and thousands of sand-colored buildings.

Jerusalem.

The city where Christ walked.

In the Bible, Jerusalem was like a crown upon the Lord's

head. I thought I'd be so stunned by the sight of it that I'd fall to my knees, but it looked fake, as if someone had painted it on a giant canvas.

We dismounted at an army camp, picketed our horses, and stood at attention in front of the largest of the tents. Inside was some bigwig for whom we stood at attention for nearly an hour, the sun blistering our skin. I blinked, my eyelids scraping bits of dirt across my eyes. My kit, rifle, and helmet were gaining weight every second; my uniform sponged up my sweat. We stank something fierce, and the lice were having a fabulous picnic under my clothes.

Whichever mighty officer we were waiting for was probably asleep, a plump general on a cot, his feet up, his boots polished to perfect glory, and an orderly waiting with a glass of water.

Water. Droplets slipping down the side of the glass. Cool water. I'd sweated all the water from my body. How was it possible that I was still standing? Droplets traced a path through Cheevers's dusty face. He gave me a grim little smile.

Loud laughter spilled out of the tent. Minutes passed. The cluster of white army tents blurred; so did Jerusalem. I blinked. The tents returned to straight lines, then blurred again.

Two orderlies strutted out of the tent and tied back the flaps. A colonel stomped out and stood to one side, and a major general in khakis appeared, wearing a sun helmet with a white plume. He commanded an entire division—thousands of men. He was just one step away from the commander in chief.

Colonel Wilson snapped a salute and said, "The Lincolnshire Yeomanry, reporting for duty, General Barrow."

"You're a day late!" The general rested his left hand on his sheathed saber. "Let's see what you brought me."

I peered over Blackburn's shoulder. The general was tanned, his scowling face scarred, his mustache bushy, like my father's. He wore a monocle in one eye. He swiftly inspected us, passing close enough that I caught a whiff of spicy cologne. He turned smartly and faced the regiment.

"You are now the property of the Fourth Cavalry Division." His voice was deep and strong, as if it belonged to a man three times his size. "You are *my* men. From here on, there are two things to remember." He pointed at the sky. "Number one: that is the sun. You will face no greater enemy. Johnny Turk is nothing compared to what the sun will do to you."

He motioned toward our mounts. "Two: your horses are more important than your mothers, your fathers, the men standing next to you. Good horsemanship is the backbone of this division. You will feed your mount, water it, brush it, be sure it is sleeping comfortably every night. If your horse gets sick or breaks its leg, we will shoot you."

"He's kidding, right?" Cheevers whispered.

"At the beginning of every day in the field you will be given a gallon of water. That is for you *and* your horse, so let your horse drink first. If your mount dies, then you are only half a soldier. Remember: it cost us more to ship your horse here than it did you."

I wasn't sure I liked this general.

Barrow pointed at the regiment. "I expect the best from

166

each and every one of you. You will begin your journey to your position tomorrow morning. Until then, you are dismissed." He saluted. Colonel Wilson returned the salute. Lieutenant Rance shouted, "Lincolnshire Yeomanry—about left!" and we turned in unison and began marching.

I glanced at the major general, who continued to glare as we passed. He said something to his staff sergeant, and the two men laughed. Perhaps the whole tirade had just been a cruel joke.

"Well, I guess we've been coddled up to this point," Blackburn said.

"Yep," I said. "Now it's for real."

5

Within twenty-four hours we held our own position at the front, surveying the moonlit hills. We had finally been given desert issue gear—tan cotton uniforms and sun helmets—so we all looked brand spanking new, clean, and green. Every few minutes one of our field guns roared, shaking the ground and my nerves. Somewhere in the distance the Turks waited, bayonets pointed in our direction.

"Saddle up, you worms!" our new sergeant shouted. "You've drawn night patrol duty, and you're going to have the pleasure of my company. Bring extra clips." Hargreaves was the toughest, meanest man I'd ever met. The army had shaved a badger and stuffed him into a uniform.

We assembled on the edge of camp—six troopers, a lance corporal, and the sergeant. Buke snorted and pawed at the ground, ready to go, but my hands were trembling. Any sort of ambush could be waiting in the darkness. Dad had charged into the Boers' fire; Hector had gone over the top; I could do this. I could.

"We'll be patrolling northeast. They're about three miles away." Hargreaves pointed. "The Turks'll be looking for us, so keep your cake-holes shut and follow my lead. If we're lucky we'll give the bastards a poke in the eye. Whatever you do, don't get taken prisoner; Abdul will castrate you."

I squeezed my legs together, and Cheevers, seeing me, let out a chuckle. An angry glare from Hargreaves silenced him.

We trotted down a valley and followed a wadi—an extra-large gully—navigating by moonlight. It had rained heavily a few nights earlier, and the bed of the wadi was thick with mud, so that Buke had to struggle with each sucking step.

Sergeant Hargreaves led us into another valley. The open space between the two armies was too rough for any major attack, but we were patrolling it just to keep their spies at bay. Sometimes the paths were so steep I thought we'd tumble down, head over horse.

With every step I took away from camp, my hands shook a little harder. I had to conquer my fear. Hector must have been scared, but somehow he had found the strength to say to his major, "Wherever you go, I will go, too."

Hargreaves seemed to know exactly where he was going, and knew the Turks inside and out. He had been with the Berkshire Yeomanry at Gallipoli and had the shrapnel scars to prove it. There was a rumor he'd killed eight Turks, three of them with a bayonet. Sticking close to him would be wise.

Buke snorted, Neddie replied, and Cheevers hissed his horse into silence. I was thankful for the soft ground that muffled their hooves.

We climbed a hill, and the moonlight glinted off my new buttons.

Crack!

Sergeant Hargreaves fell off his horse.

Crack!

A bullet whizzed past my head.

"Dismount!" Hargreaves ordered from the ground, holding his shoulder. Cheevers jumped down and grabbed the reins of the sergeant's horse.

I whirled Buke around in a circle, wondering if we should gallop back the way we'd come.

"Dismount, Bathe! Get off your goddamn horse!"

I slipped down, nearly getting caught in my stirrups. Two more shots whistled over my head.

"This way!" The sergeant led us into a wadi. "Woodward, you take the horses. Blackburn, tie up this stupid shoulder of mine." Blackburn pulled the medic pack from his saddlebag and began wrapping gauze around Hargreaves's wound. The sergeant was bleeding badly, but he paid it no mind, clutching his pistol in his left hand. "There can't be many of 'em; only four shots from the northeast. Cheevers, take a look."

Slowly Cheevers poked his head over the ridge. *Don't!* I wanted to yell, expecting a bullet to knock him backward.

"Somebody's moving about seventy yards away. . . . I see three of them, Sergeant."

Hargreaves motioned with his pistol. "Bathe, Cheevers. Go down the wadi, outflank 'em and pick 'em off or keep 'em pinned down. We'll move a bit to our right, so watch you don't hit us."

170

Cheevers hunched over and scrambled along the wadi. I followed, clutching my rifle so tightly my hands ached. Each step in the ditch created a noisy splash, and the mud sucked at my boots. We climbed a few feet up the ravine and peered over the edge.

They were Turkish cavalry, with *kabalaks* wrapped tightly around their heads. One Turk was holding the reins of three skinny ponies in one hand and a cigarette in the other, the red glow a perfect night target. The other two Turks were pointing their Mausers away from us.

Cheevers motioned with his head at the Turks and winked. I brought up my rifle; it felt twenty pounds heavier. My grip was still too tight, my shoulders corded knots. I worried that they'd see the steel glinting in the moonlight.

Crack! There was an explosion beside me.

The Turk with the ponies fell to the ground. "That found a billet!" Cheevers squawked.

I pulled my trigger but blinked at the last moment and hit the sand in front of the other Turks. They dove behind a ridge.

I yanked the bolt back, and my second shot hit a pony behind them. It let out a high neigh and ran around kicking, then fell over dead. The other two ponies fled.

One of the Turks peeped over the ridge, and Cheevers's next round caught him in the forehead. He slumped back down.

The last Turk stayed hidden.

The remaining troopers opened fire, and I shot twice toward where I thought the Turk was.

Pitts and Blackburn charged out of the wadi on their horses, galloping the seventy yards. They drew their swords and yelled, looking as if they were trying to scare rabbits out of a bush. At any moment I expected a bullet to knock one of them off his mount, but they jumped over the ridge.

I held my fire, waiting for a command or something to shoot at.

"It's clear!" Blackburn shouted. "The Turk is surrendering!"

We dashed over, rifles loaded and pointed at our enemy. The wounded Turk lay flat on his back, arms over his head. He'd been hit once in the side. His companions lay still on the ground nearby, blood pooling around them. Cheevers rolled one over. "Got him right in the heart!"

Hargreaves walked up and pointed his pistol at the survivor. "Get up, Turko! Up!" The Turk didn't move. Hargreaves put the muzzle of his gun on the Turk's forehead. "Up, or I'll blow your stinking brains out."

The Turk's eyes were wide, shining in the moonlight. He stood slowly and kept his hands high, babbling something we couldn't understand.

"Anyone speak Turk?" Hargreaves asked.

No one answered.

"Looks like he's just a trooper, Sergeant," Blackburn said.

"So he knows shit-all, just like you bastards." The sergeant motioned toward the two dead Turks. "Nice shooting, by the way."

"I got 'em both," Cheevers said.

Hargreaves gave me a squinty glance. "Guess you shot the horse so they couldn't get away."

"My sights seem to be off, Sergeant. I intended to hit the Turks."

Hargreaves chuckled. "You'll soon get the hang of firing on the fly." He pointed at the Turk. "We'll have to take him back, but he's got no horse."

"I don't want him riding with me," Cheevers said. "He's crawling with chits."

He did look half-starved, and smelled worse than we did. Since I'd shot his horse, I considered offering to take him, but before I could make up my mind Hargreaves said, "There's no point in taking him with us. He won't know anything. Eh, Turko? Speak up!"

The Turk looked back and forth, blinking slowly. "*Huuzur,*" he mumbled. "*Yarari.*"

"Well, he's certainly willing to talk now. You boys carry on; I'll interrogate Mr. Turko here."

Woodward approached with our horses. We mounted and began trotting south. I looked back at the pony I'd shot. It was much smaller than Buke and was still shuddering away its last moments of life. Poor, poor thing. I wasn't sure how I would have felt if it had been a Turk I'd killed.

"Now, that was action!" Cheevers whispered. "My heart's still pounding. To *see* those bullets hit home!"

I clenched my teeth. Any one of those Turk bullets could have found a home in me. And two of the enemy had died, right before my eyes. They would have killed me, given the chance, but it was still a sickening thing to have witnessed.

A shot rang out. We reined up and Hargreaves shouted,

"Just hold your positions, men." A moment later he came riding out of the darkness, holding his reins in his good hand. "Stupid bastard tried to escape."

All the way back to camp, I wondered if the sergeant was lying.

6

I didn't sleep a wink, even though we were given an extra hour of rest. I'd frozen on patrol; if Cheevers hadn't let loose those two good shots, my chums might have been dead now. I might have been dead.

But that wasn't the worst of it: the Turks kept me awake, too. I saw the blood spilling out of them, their slack-jawed faces. I'd heard the pleading of the one we'd captured, and I couldn't believe he had tried to run. I wanted to scream at Hargreaves, "We aren't Huns, we take prisoners!"

I rolled over. Cheevers snored peacefully, but Blackburn was peering at a book called *On War.*

"Trouble sleeping?" he asked.

"I keep thinking about our patrol."

"There's a lot to think about."

I sat up. Questioning the actions of a sergeant was a

quick ticket to field punishment, but I had to speak. "I think Hargreaves shot that Turk in cold blood."

Blackburn's face was dour. "I'm sure that has crossed everyone's mind."

"But did he do it?"

"The Turk was already wounded; I doubt he'd have struggled. Not that this is an excuse, but Hargreaves did fight at Gallipoli, and his section was decimated by the Turks. That could lead to a rather virulent hatred."

"But we're British! We don't shoot prisoners! That's not how we fight!"

"It's how some of us fight. You're not responsible for his actions, only your own."

"It's bloody simple, Bathe!" said Cheevers from his cot. "If that Turk had taken us prisoner, we'd be castrated and dead right now. Don't think about it any longer, mate. Just stop your yammering and let me sleep."

"But it was wrong! We should've brought the Turk back."

Cheevers rolled over and glared at me. "Don't be so daft. We wouldn't be talking about this now if you'd shot straight. Next time, don't miss!" He turned his back to me.

I was furious, mostly because he was right. I had missed. I had.

I stood up and Blackburn said, "Where are you going?"

"I have to tell the lieutenant about Hargreaves. Are you coming with me?"

Blackburn's eyes locked on mine. "Stop and think, Edward. You'll get no promotions, no thanks, and if Hargreaves finds out, he'll ride you into the dirt."

"Are you coming?"

"It's pointless. The deed is done."

I pushed open the flap into the cloudy morning. I thought of Reverend Ashford and was sure he'd agree with what I wanted to do. Hector, too. He wouldn't be as callous as Cheevers. That knowledge gave me the strength to walk right up to Lieutenant Rance's tent and announce myself.

"The lieutenant doesn't have time to chat," his orderly said.

"But I have something to tell him about the patrol last night."

"He's not—"

"Send him in," Rance commanded from inside the tent.

"Yes, sir." The orderly opened the flap, holding back the mosquito netting.

The tent was twice as large as ours, decked out with several chairs and a fluffy cot. Rance sat at a wooden table, leaning over a chessboard.

I saluted.

"Don't worry!" He motioned at the chessboard. "I'm not so batty that I've challenged myself to a game. I'm playing a friend through the post. He's got me in a tight corner. Anyway, you have a burning question, Trooper Bathe?"

"Last night, sir, we . . . uh . . . we were out on patrol."

"I am aware of that. Sergeant Hargreaves handed his report in promptly after your return. He wrote glowingly of both you and Trooper Cheevers."

"That's very kind of him, sir."

"What do you want to add?"

I locked my hands together to keep them from shaking. "I— It's just that there was a prisoner last night, sir. A Turk."

"Yes, Hargreaves also detailed that episode."

"He killed him, sir. In cold blood."

Rance's eyes cooled. "According to the report the prisoner attempted escape."

"I—I don't think it happened that way."

"Sergeant Hargreaves was wounded, correct?"

I nodded and began to sweat profusely.

"Is it not conceivable that the Turk wanted to take advantage of Hargreaves's debilitated state? He produced a knife and there was a struggle. Hargreaves simply subdued him."

"I . . . suppose . . ."

"Trooper, I want you to think very carefully about what you're saying. Did you see this struggle?"

"No."

"Then are you suggesting the sergeant's version of events is false? He's a fine NCO, and very experienced. We're lucky to have him in our regiment."

"I must have been mistaken, sir."

"Good. You are dismissed."

I saluted, but he'd already returned to his game of chess. I should've listened to Blackburn.

7

The Turk's sad, pleading eyes filled my thoughts, no matter what I was doing—feeding the horses, patrolling, trying to sleep. I imagined his body in the hills, torn apart by
vultures. We hadn't even considered burying him or his
companions.

I started a letter: *Dear Emily, I've seen something absolutely terrible,* but I ripped it up. I couldn't burden her
with it; she saw horrible things every day. Besides, one of
Hargreaves's duties was to censor every letter written by his
troopers. He'd crumple it up and stuff it down my throat.

Hargreaves returned from a hospital in Jerusalem the following week and treated me no differently, but I couldn't
look at him without feeling sick. He led us on several more
patrols, but we didn't encounter a single Turk. Nor did we
see the bodies of the ones we'd killed. Maybe a Turk patrol
had found them and given them a good resting place.

It was a while before I had the time, or the heart, to write to Emily. I couldn't pretend all was well, so I kept it short:

March 25, 1918

Dear Emily,

Only a quick note because we are at the front. The Palestine front, of course. It's nearly a hundred miles long! This is a quiet part of it and the Turks are a good distance away, so you don't have to worry about me. Our field guns tell them to back off every once in a while.

I've seen Jerusalem, but only from the outskirts. It was like seeing a city from a dream. Odd to think I am walking on the same ground that Christ once walked on. I keep looking for his footprints!

I do hope all is well there and that you are getting time to rest. I miss you and I miss you. Oh, did I say that twice?

> *All my warmest thoughts,*
> *Edward*

I sent it off, knowing she wouldn't get it for weeks. I might as well have been living in Antarctica!

I checked for mail every day but got nothing. We kept up our patrols and were moved up and down the line. At one point we were stationed so close to the Mediterranean we could actually glimpse it from the top of the hills.

One day at the beginning of April, Colonel Wilson climbed onto a large rock and the regiment gathered around.

This could have been one of the places where Jesus had preached.

"There's been some trouble in France!" Wilson shouted. Thankfully, it was a calm day and his words carried easily through the air. "The spineless, useless, turncoat Russians have signed a peace treaty! The Huns have turned all their guns and men toward the Eastern front. It will be a decisive battle; a true test of British mettle."

We're going to go to France! Colonel Wilson continued, but I was so excited I didn't even hear what he was saying. I'd have to survive another ship, but I'd gladly take that chance to see Emily. Maybe I could just pop by on leave and sweep her up in my arms! She'd be bowled over.

Perhaps I would take something . . . a ring . . . no, not a ring, it was too soon for that. I would buy her a fancy, glittering necklace from the hawkers in Jerusalem.

"Several regiments are going to be sent back to teach the Germans a lesson!" Wilson was shaking his riding crop. I paid attention again. "This is where we come in, boys! I know how desperately you would like to tour the French countryside, but we're staying put and finishing our job here. Someone has to look after the Turks! When we're done, we'll follow the others home."

I slumped. I was ready to go. I needed to see Emily and hold her again.

Within days, many of the original regiments broke camp and climbed onto the coastal trains. They would retrace the routes they'd spent the last eighteen months fighting to take. We heard that Indian regiments from France and Mesopotamia would soon arrive as replacements.

We were sent to the same part of the line where we'd killed the Turk patrol. The rain had let up, but the soil was so drenched it was hard to peg our tents. Several times I spotted British survey parties saddled with the task of measuring every inch of the mess. All was quiet on the front; the Turks could have been asleep in their trenches.

I wished we'd been moved to another sector altogether. I wondered if the Turks we had killed had chums who were itching for revenge.

I thought of Emily every day, mostly while I was brushing Buke, the only time I spent alone. I talked to him so much about her that he now looked bored whenever I mentioned her name.

Every night I closed my eyes and remembered her in that blue dress, then pictured what she would be like underneath it, her ivory skin, her breasts. It would be glorious to touch one. Every morning, I was ashamed of my lustful thoughts. I really did miss her, and my feelings for her kept growing stronger. If only there were some magical way to leap across all the miles between us and see her again. She wouldn't even recognize me now, my skin was so dark.

As the days passed, my legs and hips began to ache. I couldn't figure out the cause, until one morning it dawned on me: I needed to lengthen my stirrups. I'd grown! I dropped them an inch and the pain went away.

One evening, Pitts stuck his head into our tent. "Mail up! This un's for you, Bathe." He flipped a letter onto the table.

I reached out, but Cheevers snatched it and danced

around the hut, stirring dust and flies. He sniffed loudly at the envelope. "Ah, sacre bleu! Perfume! The scent of a smitten heart." He raised one eyebrow, pretending to read through the envelope. "Oh, Eddie! Oh, boy! How I miss your hairless chest and pine for your privates, Private!" He made as if to open the envelope.

"Cheevers!" I tried to keep my voice gruff. "It's mine."

"Just a peek."

"Give it to me!" I thrust out my hand.

"Don't be a toad, Cheevers," Blackburn said. "The joke's over. Open your own mail when it comes—if your mummy even knows how to write, that is."

Cheevers rolled his eyes and lowered himself to his knees. "You'll read us the naughty bits, won't you?"

I grabbed the letter. Emily's handwriting! I retreated to my bivvy blankets.

April 4, 1918

Dear Edward,

I am so relieved to hear from you! My two previous letters were returned to me, unopened and stamped undeliverable.

I received your note saying you were on a ship. I must admit I was frightened, and feared you had been sent to France and the very worst had happened. I didn't know what to do, or even who to contact to find out the truth. I was in quite a state. I couldn't sleep or do much more than worry. Imagine my surprise when I received a card with a picture of Alexandria, followed by a letter that said you were in Palestine! Now when I think of you, I see you crossing the desert, my brave Canuck of Arabia. It all sounds very romantic, except for the war, of course. I am so relieved to hear you are well and fine. I don't know how I would have carried on otherwise.

I am sorry and frightened to hear that your ship was attacked. It must have been terrible. A very brief report of the shelling appeared in the Grimsby Times this week, along with a list of the missing and dead. I knew several of the men, and will especially miss Sergeant Applewhite. He was a kind soul. I am so glad you are safe and sound. So glad. At dinner with the other nurses I said a toast to the brave Lincolnshire Yeomanry in Palestine. I felt proud.

It is dreary here, and the rain sets me in a foul mood. We are very busy. The Germans are pressing hard; no one really knows how close they will come. We are kept in the dark, of course, but judging by the lines of wounded, it is a terrible time for our armies. There are refugees streaming into Etaples. Even Paris was shelled by long-range guns.

The surgery wards are working night and day now. No two wounds are ever the same, Edward. They all look different on different bodies. I will never become accustomed to that. It makes every day new and terrible.

Ah, but I am not at the front, am I? I shouldn't

complain. The war will make me a bitter old maid
before my time.

As I reread this, I must apologize for how disjointed
it is. I'm happy to hear from you. I do wish I could see
you. Wouldn't it be grand if I could take a tram to
Jerusalem and we could go for a picnic in the hills
among the grapevines and olive trees? Imagine that,
Edward. I make wonderful cucumber sandwiches!

I must go. My shift begins in a few minutes. I shall
bundle up my other letters and send them to you soon.
If you see someone from the postal service, please give
them a good tongue-lashing. My heart was broken,
thinking you might be gone.

All my warmth, hugs and kisses,
Emily

P.S. Please write back. Or have you fallen for some
Arabian princess? If that is the case, I will be there in
a flash to scratch her eyes out.

I folded the letter. I wanted to read it all over again, but I
was shaking with emotion as it was. She'd worried about me;
obviously she cared deeply. If she had appeared before me at
that moment I would have dropped to one knee and pro-
posed.

"Did your skirt send any biscuits?" Cheevers asked.

"Not a one!"

"What good is she, then?" He laid down on his blanket
and covered his eyes with his sun helmet. "When you write

back to her don't forget to mention how the lice are makin' your balls itch."

I kicked his foot. Then, as he began to snore, I wrote my reply.

Apr. 25, 1918

Dear Emily,

It was so good to receive your wonderful letter. We are about to go on patrol, so I only have a few moments. The sooner I write, though, the sooner my letter will get to you. We are near the front line in support of the infantry.

We have heard how hard the fighting is in France. Many of the original regiments were sent back there, so we feel quite alone. Very little is happening here, though there are rumors of another big attack on the Turks.

I often think very fond thoughts of you. Oh, now that I reread that last sentence it sounds like I might sometimes think unfond thoughts of you! Not true! It's just that dreaming of you gets me all befuddled. I bet you're laughing right now! Sometimes when I'm brushing Buke, I tell him that you have a wonderful smile. And a quick wit—maybe too quick for me. Someday, I'd love to show you my father's farm. My home.

A picnic with you! I can taste the sandwiches, can hear your lovely voice. If we can't picnic for real, at least I can pretend.

*I must go. Don't be downhearted; you are doing
your job and saving lives. There will be an end to this
war. A good end.*

> *Warmly and thoughtfully and forever yours,*
> *Edward*

*P.S. There is no Arabian princess. I promise. Only a
Lincolnshire princess.*

I folded the letter and slid it into an envelope. Then, having ensured that no one was looking, I kissed it.

8

A week later we were sent to a rest camp outside Jerusalem, which meant more drills and parades to keep us in tip-top shape. At least we didn't have to go on patrol.

There was no mail for me, but Cheevers got a letter.

"See!" He waved it in front of Blackburn. "My mam can write!"

"It's a miracle!" Blackburn said.

Cheevers ripped open the letter. "She probably misses me. I am her favorite, after all." He read the first bit and his face went pale. "Oh, Lord."

"What is it?" I asked.

He was quiet for several seconds, still reading. "Nothing. Just a sick uncle . . . and my brother pegged out."

"What?" I said. "No!"

"That's terrible news," Blackburn said.

"Sniper got him. James always did have a big head." He chuckled a little too long.

"I'm so sorry. So sorry." I couldn't think of anything else to say.

Cheevers slumped down on his cot. After a moment he waved his hand, saying, "He wouldn't want mopin'. Least he took eight Huns with him. That's what his count was last time he wrote. God, I'll miss the bugger."

"Where did it happen?" I asked.

"I don't want to talk about it anymore." Cheevers's face was still pale. "It's done. I'm going to check on Neddie." He grabbed his sun helmet and left.

Blackburn tapped his fingers on a book. "You can't just shove these things under the carpet."

"No." I pictured Hector with his legs all shot up, calling out for Mom. The images were always there, waiting to pounce.

Cheevers returned an hour later, smiling, no sign of tears or anger. He cajoled us until we played a hand of poker, and later he slept like a log. It was as though nothing had happened.

The following afternoon when we were given leave he was his usual cheery self. It was our first chance to tour Jerusalem, despite having been camped outside for days now. I walked around with my eyes wide open, trying to keep my jaw from hitting the ground. Everything seemed so old and beautiful, especially the Dome of the Rock, a Mohammedan shrine. While gawking at it, we pitched a few rupees to a beggar with twelve toes and a gimp arm; then we went to the Wailing Wall, which was once part of Solomon's temple.

"That's a little odd!" I said, pointing at the old Jewish men with black coats, black felt hats, and long gray beards. They chanted and kissed the wall. It was as if a thousand years of kissing had chipped at the stones.

"Odd?" Cheevers tapped his skull. "Kissing walls is completely batty! God's our chum, he watches out for us Christians—he doesn't want us kissing walls."

I almost said that God hadn't watched out for his brother, but I bit my tongue. God didn't save everyone; Hector was proof of that.

As we walked under the heat of the sun, a few lines of a popular hymn came to me, and I sang them.

"I will not cease from mental fight,
Nor shall my sword sleep in my hand,
Till we have built Jerusalem
In England's green and pleasant land."

"It's a stirring song," Blackburn said. "Ol' Blake was certainly sentimental, but I'm not sure we want Jerusalem back home." He motioned at a row of beggars, some of them missing limbs. "It isn't so pretty up close."

Blackburn led us to a bazaar, its merchants packed into a thin lane. Stone walls were hung with red carpets, and shelves were lined with trinkets and multicolored plates. I stopped by a stall full of colorful silk. There was a beautiful green scarf for thirty piastres. I considered buying it for Emily but worried it would be stolen from the mail.

Several customers nudged me, and I kept my hand on my

wallet, fearing pickpockets. Next thing I knew, an Arab boy in a pillbox hat and a mud-stained robe grabbed my sleeve. "You Tommy! Tommies! I show you Mary." He had fawn eyes and looked half starved.

Cheevers was testing the sharpness of a curved sword with his thumb. "We're not looking for any blinkin' whore-house."

"Shoo!" Blackburn waved his hand.

"No! I show you Mother Mary, mother of Jesus. Bring very, very much luck. Good luck! You live through war. Five piastres."

"That's almost a shilling!" Blackburn exclaimed. "I'm not sure if Cheevers's life is worth it. I am curious as to how you'll show us Mother Mary, though."

"Maybe seeing her would cure your godlessness," I said.

"You're the one who needs curing. But I do want to see the Virgin Mary—I find religion an immensely interesting subject." He held out a bill and the boy grabbed for it, but Blackburn snapped it away before he touched it. "You'll get it when we've seen this Mary of yours."

"Come, come!" The boy led us down a long set of worn steps. We squeezed between hawkers who shouted, "Good wares . . . good wares!" "Vases!" "Gems!" "Eggs-a-cook!"

We made several turns through even narrower alleys. The sun was blocked by the sand-colored buildings, and I shivered. The boy took us into a dark room that stank of rotten fruit. I recoiled from the smell; it was too much like the *Mercian*.

"This could be a trap!" I said, keeping my hand on my knife.

191

"Be brave, Eddie, ol' boy," Cheevers said. "No one would dare ambush top-notch troopers like us."

We shuffled down a set of stone stairs and stopped in a lamp-lit hallway. "Here. Go in room. See Mother Mary. Pray."

The boy held out his hand, and Blackburn dropped the folded bill in his palm. Our guide bowed quickly to us and took the stairs two at a time.

"I always wanted to meet Mother Mary face to face," Cheevers said as he opened the door.

Candles flickered from chandeliers and hollowed spaces in the wall. Glittering and almost blinding, the Virgin Mary, made of gold, stood on a pedestal. She looked us in the eye, one arm extended in welcome.

I walked toward her, a little dazed. A nun was hunched in the back corner, her face hidden by a veil.

"Dear God," Cheevers whispered, "she's beautiful, she really is."

Medals, ribbons, and chain necklaces hung from Mary's hands like Christmas decorations. They were from Turk and German soldiers. Some had left pictures of their loved ones, and there was even a set of spurs. And in the center, hanging over the Virgin's neck, was a familiar medal.

"An Iron Cross," said Blackburn, touching it as though he couldn't believe it was real. The Iron Cross was the highest award for bravery a Hun could receive, earned on the field killing British soldiers. Some German had traded it for Mother Mary's protection.

Cheevers placed a bullet at her feet. "It's the one meant

for me. If I leave it here, my number won't come up." I knew he was thinking of his brother. I thought of mine.

"Poppycock!" Blackburn spouted. "It'll do nothing to alter your chances."

I reached in my pocket and found my mother's handkerchief. I couldn't leave that; Reverend Ashford had said it would bring me luck. I had to leave something, though. If I didn't, Mother Mary wouldn't smile on me and I'd surely die.

I jammed my hand in my breast pocket and found Emily's locket. I took one look at her; she was more beautiful than the statue. I closed the lid and returned it to my pocket. I couldn't survive without being able to look at her.

I reached inside my shirt and snapped off my green identity disk, the one that would be buried with my body. I placed it at Mary's feet, hoping she'd tell her son to watch over me.

"It's nothing but superstition," Blackburn hissed. "They'll probably sell everything after we're gone."

The nun turned her head, nodding rhythmically to herself. Her pupils were almost completely white, but she stared straight at us. I shuddered a bit. Was she somehow seeing our souls?

"Let's get out of here," Blackburn said. We followed him through the door and up into daylight.

9

A week of patrols passed. The weather was growing hotter, and both sides appeared to be happy playing one giant staring game. We knew it couldn't last. General Allenby was waiting for the Turks to blink.

One evening, Pitts, horseshoes clinking in a sack, poked his head into our tent. "Bathe, these came for you." He held out two letters.

"Thanks! Thanks!" My heart raced at the mere sight of them.

Cheevers didn't even lift his head. He just sat on his cot, spinning his saber.

One letter was from Emily and had been sent some time earlier. It had probably been gathering dust in a depot in Cairo. I could have had it weeks earlier! The other was addressed in another woman's handwriting. I panicked for a moment, thinking it might be from the Daughters of the

Empire regarding my father, but it had been stamped in Grimsby. I couldn't think of anyone I knew there.

I opened the envelope from Emily and caught a whiff of perfume.

"Why the sniffing, Bathe? Did you let one go?" Cheevers asked.

"Shut up, Cheevers!"

I unfolded the letter.

May 14, 1918

Dear Edward,

I have finally found time to write you! How are you? I miss you. As always, we are kept extremely busy and I wish I had more time to write, to rest, or to breathe, even. But the Germans are within shelling distance. Aeroplanes buzz like wasps. One patient grabbed me with his good arm and hissed, "There's thousands of them coming. Thousands!" As proof of their advance, there are always more ambulance trains, more wounded to sort from the dead, the near dead, and those with a spark of life. Hard choices have to be made about whom to give attention.

At night I stoke the fire in the patients' rooms, do rounds of bedpans, and prepare food on the beastly black oil stoves. But acute surgery, of which I have been doing more and more, is the hardest work. I have quick, sure hands, the doctors appreciate that, and I keep my wits about me, even though I am often staring down at some poor boy who has lost a leg, or his eyes, or who has been torn to shreds by shrapnel and become one large, living wound. Often, at the end of a night when we have only saved one or two men, I am wracked with despair. The cases of mustard gas are the worst, with their eyelids all stuck together, their lips blistered, their lungs fighting to breathe. Sometimes the only thing that keeps me sane is thinking of you.

I know how you long to be in France, but I am so glad you are in Palestine. It must be safer than this. The cases of septic wounds and trench foot are horrible. We would not put our cattle in such conditions, and yet we force men to live and fight there.

Please don't mistake me as completely downhearted. I do have hope. The day the guns finally stop will be a great one. Your letters have given me hope, too—hope that I will see you again, hope that the time when people just talk on benches about simple things will return. Like birthdays! You forgot mine; it was April 12. I guess I might have forgotten to tell you the date. I'll gladly accept a late present! I can't believe I'm . . . ha, I'm not telling you my age until I find out yours.

So you whisper to your horse about me. How sweet! As I hope you know by now, I do think of you often, and I wonder if we are perhaps falling in love, even though we are so far apart. I don't know, but I hope so. See, I have hope. I hope to hold you again; then I will know. I hope to go to your ranch, to look out across the

prairie and see the sun rise. There, I said it, or wrote it.
I have hope.

You are good, Edward. As simple as that. And in
this world we have to hang on to the things that are
good. I understand that more than ever now.

I miss you greatly,
Emily

I read the letter again and read the last paragraph three times. I wanted to write her back immediately, to say I was feeling the same way about us. I even considered shelling out the money for a cable. I had hope, too. And love.

Then I remembered the other letter. Still stunned and in bliss from Emily's words, I opened it and read:

May 23, 1918

Dear Edward,

You don't know me. I'm Vera Falls, and I used to
work with Emily in Grimsby and later at Etaples. I
know you were a good friend of hers. In fact, on a
number of occasions, she spoke of you as "my trooper"
or "that handsome colonial."

I have sad news. I don't know how to say this. There
is only one way, I guess. Emily died a week ago, on the
19th of May. She was attending to her duty in surgery,
operating on a wounded soldier. We were overcrowded
with patients; we always are. Our camp was bombed
by a Hun plane, and even though the bombs were

heard approaching, she refused to give up her post. I'm
afraid our ward was hit, and she, the doctor, and the
patient were killed outright. Her body was sent back to
Cleethorpes and she was buried near her family home.

I have no words to express how much I miss her. I
am sure you feel the same way. She worked very hard.
She was an excellent nurse. She made us laugh. I am
truly sorry to have to pass this news on to you. If there
is anything further I can do, please contact me.

Sincerely,
Vera Falls

I began to shake uncontrollably. The harder I tried to
stop it, the more I shook. I tried to wet my throat so that I
could cough, but to no avail.

Emily was dead. Dead. One bomb, falling out of the sky,
just like that. I knew about explosions now. I knew what they
did to the body. I'd seen it on the *Mercian*. Her face torn; her
arms shattered. Her beautiful legs. Gone.

Her eyes. Her lips. Her laugh. Gone, forever.

I shook and sobbed as quietly as I could. Flies landed on
me, sucking my sweat. She had died weeks earlier and I
hadn't felt it in my heart. How could that be?

"Edward." A whisper. I couldn't tell if it was Blackburn or
Cheevers. Tears stained my cheeks. I didn't want to face
them.

"Edward, are you all right?"

A hand touched my shoulder. I turned to find Blackburn
looking down at me. I lowered the letter.

Blackburn sat back down on his cot. Cheevers looked over

at me. I rubbed my arm across my eyes; my mother's face flashed inside my eyelids. How I longed for her to hold me.

"What is it?" Blackburn's voice was surprisingly gentle. "News from home?"

"She's dead. My girl."

"That's hard news." Cheevers reached out and patted my arm. "Really tough to hear. How'd it happen?"

"A bomb. A Hun bomb." It was so difficult to spit it out.

"Oh, I'm so sorry," Blackburn said. "I know . . . I know you were very enamored of her. She must've been a fine girl."

I folded the letter.

"If you need anything," Blackburn said, "just ask, Edward. Anything." I had never seen him so concerned. He always had his disdainful nose in a book. Not now.

"We'll get our revenge!" Cheevers promised.

The tent was too small. I rushed outside, not bothering to close the netting properly. The pitiless sun was finally setting. Some troopers were shoveling holes; others were hauling water. I walked to the picket line, my head down. When I found Buke, I wrapped my arms around his neck and sobbed, hoping no one would hear. He stood still, his heart beating, his neck warm, his familiar smell a comfort. "She's dead, Buke, she's dead."

I dabbed my eyes with my mother's handkerchief. I would never see Emily again; God had taken her, claimed her for his own. It was the cruelest thing I could imagine.

10

A month later, in July, I was sent to hell. Somewhere high above us General Allenby had uttered a command, and next thing we knew we were riding through the Judean hills toward the Jordan Valley.

"I 'ear no white man has ever made it through a summer there!" said Pitts, giving Brush Me a kick. His horse was already wasted in the sun.

"If we're there, it'll spread out the Turks' right flank," Blackburn explained, as though he were talking to schoolchildren.

"It'll roast our flanks," Cheevers said, trying to sound lighthearted. I couldn't even find the strength to chuckle.

We passed a Roman aqueduct that hadn't seen water in centuries. The sun blazed closer, brighter, and hotter. Heavy air hung over us like a shroud, forcing the sweat from our backs. Chaplain Holmes pointed toward Jericho, excited to see the city, but all I saw were waves of heat.

As the sun set, we trotted down a long ravine that led to the bottom of the valley. The air became chokingly hot. My uniform was a sweat rag. The trail became so narrow that we moved off the road, waiting by the ruins of a solitary stone house for the regiment we were replacing to pass. There was no sign of them in the darkness.

"Someone was jolter-headed enough to build a home here," Cheevers scoffed.

Blackburn laughed. "Wonder if they all died of sun-stroke?"

I sat on one of the stones, holding Buke's reins. A mosquito landed on my arm and I watched it suck my blood. I was too tired to give it a swat. How many had bitten me by then? A thousand?

Blackburn waved his hand at the swarm. "Our little winged pests will dictate our battle tactics."

Cheevers nudged me. "Ears up, Bathe! Blackburn is giving us another lecture."

"Don't get smart! I'm just saying it takes ten days or so for a trooper to succumb to malaria. Once we cross into the Turk trenches, hordes of mosquitoes will be waiting for us with new strains of malaria."

"Mosquitoes?" Cheevers gave me another nudge. "Oh, no!"

"Allenby is thinking about them. He's probably calculated he'll only have ten days or so to bust up the Turk lines because by that time, half his force will have malaria."

Watching several mosquitoes suck at my hand, I said, "Unless we all get it before the big push starts."

"He spoke!" Cheevers gave me another nudge, and I nearly smacked him. "Did you hear that, Blackburn? Bathe actually squeaked! He's been silent as a worm for weeks."

Before I could say anything the clopping of hundreds of hooves echoed from the trail. Riders in slouch hats appeared—Aussie Light Horsemen.

"What news from the Valley of Death?" Cheevers called out as they passed.

The Aussies stared ahead as though they might teeter off their horses if they took their eyes off the path. Their Walers, which stood taller than our mounts, were thin, the men even thinner. I'd never seen so many Aussies in such a dour mood.

"What outfit are you?" another trooper shouted.

Again, no reply. At the tail end of the column was a line of twelve ambulance wagons with three men per wagon laying squashed together, eyes closed. I couldn't tell if they were sick or dead. Finally, from the back of the last wagon, one lone voice could be heard, singing so terribly out of tune I nearly covered my ears:

> *"The bells of hell go ting-a-ling-a-ling*
> *For you but not for me;*
> *And the little devils, how they sing-a-ling-a-ling*
> *For you but not for me.*
> *O Death, where is thy sting-a-ling-a-ling,*
> *O Grave, thy victor-ee?*

The bells of hell go ting-a-ling-a-ling
For you but not for me."

As we lost sight of the men, the squeaking wheels and tuneless voice slowly faded away.

One last straggling Aussie on a pack mule clopped past us. "It's all yours, Tommies," he said hoarsely, "the land that God forgot."

With his words echoing in our ears, we mounted and followed the path into the valley. On the other side of the ruins, Dr. Purves and two orderlies tried to wake up a trooper who appeared to have fainted.

It was a long ride before the Jordan Valley opened around us, distant shadowy hills lit by moonlight. It was well past midnight, but still it grew hotter. I had to work to suck in the heavy air.

We found our camp of bell tents, and it dawned on me that the Aussies had left the place hours before. The Turks could have moved in while we were in the hills.

"Can't wait for daylight," Cheevers said. "I'm sure that'll bring a break from this heat."

We fed and watered our horses, working through the night because the day would be too hot for us to lift a finger. As the sun rose it revealed a desolation only the Devil could've dreamed up: a low, flat valley of white marl and salt, spotted with swamp, stony plain, patches of dense scrub, and a thin layer of dry grass. The land had never known rain. Lumps of dried flesh—dead camels—lay here and there as though dropped from the sky, a sky that had never seen a cloud. A hot breath of wind drove the salty dust into my eyes. Occasionally, a thirteen-pounder gun would roar just to let the Turks know that His Majesty's troops were still here.

Our section spent the morning oiling open water to kill the mosquito larvae. Flies and hornets attacked us, and under every stone lurked spiders, scorpions, or centipedes with huge pincers, the true rulers of this valley.

When we returned to our tents we learned that the man who had passed out in the valley had died. "Just gave up the ghost," Pitts said. "Bembridge from B Squadron. His constitution couldn't take it. They'll bury him at Jericho."

We were too sluggish to do much more than nod sadly. Had I known him? Trooper Bembridge. Poor sod.

It became so hot that we were ordered to rest in our tents. I stripped naked, but that only gave the sand flies more flesh to feast on. I tried to imagine playing hockey or making angels in the snow, to little effect. Even Cheevers couldn't get a wink in.

It didn't matter; whenever I closed my eyes I saw Emily, with a sad smile on her face. She'd been tattooed to my eyelids, to my thoughts. I couldn't escape the weight of my sorrow. I had often written letters to her in my head, but now I had no words for anyone, and no future to think about.

I recalled the moment I'd set my identification disk at Mother Mary's feet. I'd prayed for my safety, but why hadn't I prayed for Emily's? If I had, perhaps God would have tapped the bomb and turned it into a dud. It would have taken only the slightest effort for him to save her. Nothing more than a flick of the wrist. A bile filled my mouth.

Reveille sounded in the late afternoon, and I stumbled out into the oven, blinking away sweat. I passed a thermometer on a post. At the 115-degree mark someone had drawn an arrow and written: *This is where brains boil.* The thermometer read 132.

We layered three blankets on our horses' backs to prevent heatstroke. Buke's dark color sucked up every ounce of sweltering hotness, and he looked as though he'd been galloping for hours.

At lunch we had tea, which somehow seemed to cool my insides. When I opened my tin of bully beef I discovered that the meat had melted into a dripping soggy blob of fat. A mass of buzzing, fighting vermin attacked it, and I shook them off the tin, quickly forking two bites. The flies beat about inside my mouth, forcing me to spit it out.

"Don't waste food, Bathe." Hargreaves was standing over me, holding two halters. "You and Cheevers, come along. We have to get the lieutenant's horses."

I left my half-empty tin to the flies, and we trudged up a hill peppered with lava rock. Below us, troopers on horseback and lines of wagons trotted through the valley, raising a column of dust. "That's a ruse, to make the Turks think we're a battalion," Hargreaves explained. "Don't get on my bad side or you'll be eating dust with them." He laughed. It seemed as if ten years had passed since he'd killed that Turk.

We walked by a thousand or so horses made of reeds, complete with fake saddles and feed bags. It looked as though they were grazing on the hillside. The few Hun planes that spied on us would surely be fooled. Hargreaves kicked one of the horses over. "If the Turks have fallen for it, we'll be outnumbered three or four to one, but don't let that bother you."

"Bother me?" Cheevers said. "I'd welcome a tea party with Johnny Turk. We could stick bayonets in their bellies and use them as parasols."

Hargreaves clapped him on the back and handed across the halters. "We need more ugly buggers like you! Go get the horses."

Cheevers charged up the hill, and Hargreaves squinted toward the Turkish side of the valley. "Won't be long before we give 'em all a good pounding, Bathe. Then we can get out of this hell hole they call the Holy Land."

I wasn't sure if he was trying to begin a conversation or not, so I kept quiet.

"Are you gettin' on well these days?"

"Yes, Sergeant."

"Good. I want my men to be fightin' fit and ready to spit fire. If you have any complaints, come to me. Do you understand?" He put a hand on my shoulder and I cringed a little.

"I do, Sergeant. Thank you."

He tightened his grip, making me wince. "I know you whined to the lieutenant about that Turk."

A chill, impossible with the heat, crawled over my skin. How long had he known?

"You're soft, Bathe. In the head, the heart, and the guts. Soft men die out here, or their softness leads to good men getting it. You have no place in this war."

"I belong—"

"You don't have permission to speak!" He smacked me in

the stomach, shoved me onto the rocks, and put his boot on my chest. "If you go bellyaching behind my back again, I'll wring your neck. Just shut your gob and follow my orders, and you might survive."

The rocks poked into my spine, but I didn't move. He waved his boot near my nose, then lowered his foot to the ground. "Get up, Bathe."

I set my hand on the ground and felt a sharp pain on my wrist. "Ahhh!" I screamed. "Good God!"

A scorpion skittered away, tail raised. A pinprick on my hand bled freely and my fingers went numb. "I got bit!"

"Lordy me," Hargreaves said with a laugh. "For the life of me, I can't remember what to do for scorpion bites."

I yanked my knife from my belt and sliced a line across the sting, watching my blood flow out of the wound. I sucked and spat out blood and venom.

"What happened?" Cheevers yelled from above us. He was leading the horses down the path.

"Clumsy Bathe fell and was bit by a scorpion. You help him to the doc and I'll take the horses to Rance." Hargreaves grabbed the halters and left with the horses.

"Squeeze it out!" Cheevers said. I pinched droplets of blood onto the salty earth until my hand was stained red. "Harder, chum! You don't want to get poisoned. Harder!"

He helped me stand up and steered me onto the path. "I'll take you to Purves. How'd you fall?"

"I . . . tripped."

I felt woozy and began seeing double as we stumbled slowly down the hill. An angry line from a trooper's song stuck in my head:

Send him,
Oh, send him,
Oh, send our old sergeant to he-e-ll.

At the aid post, Dr. Purves greeted us. "You look like death warmed over, Trooper. What happened?"

"A scorpion bit me."

"Nasty business," he said, inspecting my hand. "You cut it open? Brave of you, but pointless. The next time you get bit, lower your arm and wipe the wound. We'd better get some Condy's into you." He opened a packet. "Crystal permanganate of potash. This will sting, but it'll get rid of the venom." He rubbed a handful into my wound. It stung worse than the scorpion had. I held still as Purves dressed the wound. "I would have given a seminar on snakebites and insect stings, but we left too quickly. You better take a cot."

"But I have to water the horses."

"Blackburn and I can do it," Cheevers said.

"No. It's only a bite, for heaven's sake." I said this even though I couldn't make a fist.

Dr. Purves pushed me toward a cot. "Lie down, Trooper Bathe. That's an order! You might start vomiting or having heavy heart palpitations."

"See ya, chum," Cheevers said, sweeping aside the tent flaps.

I lay back and a sudden bout of weakness washed over me. My arm was still on fire, and I was sweating. Still, I found the energy to chuckle.

"What's so funny, Trooper?" Dr. Purves asked.

"This is just our first day in the valley."

Dr. Purves took good care of me. He was the only other person in the regiment who had known Emily. When I told him the bad news, he said, "Such a damn waste. She was a fine, dependable nurse and a bloody good woman."

It was a week before I could use my hand properly again. By that time fifteen men had been taken with heatstroke and sickness. Another week passed and the count was over a hundred. The road became a train of medical wagons leaving every morning, dust trailing behind them.

I watched my back whenever I was around Hargreaves. "You're kind of a useless tit until that hand heals properly," he'd said, "so you've got dust duty."

I joined the columns riding up and down the valley creating dust. All day I breathed it in and at night I coughed it out.

At one point a German aeroplane flew over our column and dropped pamphlets that read: *Flies die in July, men in August, and we will bury you in September.*

"At least they have a sense of humor," Blackburn said.

After three long weeks, we were ordered out of the valley. Our numbers had been reduced from more than five hundred healthy men to a little more than a hundred and fifty. Thirteen had died. All we had left was enough to fill a squadron.

When night fell we rode back up the dusty path toward Jericho. As a joke, God sent a cloud our way that teased us with two or three raindrops. No one had the pep to talk. Halfway up the path yet another trooper fell off his horse and was tossed into a medical wagon.

The cloud spit on us some more; then the spit slowly turned into a warm shower, moonlight making the drops sparkle silver. We let out a ragged cheer and dismounted, taking off our sun helmets and opening our mouths to catch the rain. Then, as if a silent order had been given, we stripped naked. The officers watched from their horses and laughed. Rain washed off dust and sweat, revealing our young bodies, glistening white. We were barbarians about to charge naked into battle.

Chaplain Holmes rode up the line. "Cover thy nakedness!" he shouted, but he was grinning. "For shame! What would your mothers think?"

We mounted our horses again and rode on, wearing only our boots. As we passed our replacements, a regiment of Light Horsemen, the Aussies gaped at us.

"They've all gone barmy!" one shouted.

For the first time in months I felt completely clean. We left the Valley of Death behind us.

11

A week later, Lieutenant Rance led our motley squadron west toward the Mediterranean. He was now our highest-ranking officer, the only one still healthy enough to ride.

"Something's up," Blackburn said. "In every camp we passed, men are training. There'll be action soon."

We crested a hill to find a regiment of Indian lancers eyeing us from beneath their turbans. Most of their officers were British men who also wore turbans.

We dismounted next to them and picketed the horses. Giving Neddie's rope a good tug to be sure it was tight, Cheevers said indignantly, "We're not riding with cow-worshipping Indians, are we? The brass have gone daft."

"They're the Second Lancers," Blackburn replied. "I did a quick head count and they're short a couple hundred men."

Lieutenant Rance disappeared into a tent with officers from the Indian regiment. The Indians looked cunning and angry, with neatly trimmed little beards or smooth faces. They outnumbered us three to one, but we glared back. What did we have in common with Indians?

A dark-skinned NCO, grinning crazily, crossed over to our side and sat cross-legged in the grass next to us.

"Hello. My name is Ranjeet Singh. May I say what an extraordinarily great pleasure it is to meet you!" At first I thought he was making fun of us, using such formal-sounding words. "The regiment and I are extremely pleased you will be joining us."

Cheevers made a raspberry and rolled his eyes.

"You are not equally pleased?" Ranjeet narrowed his eyes. "Upon such an insult, I once ripped the intestines from my enemy and fed them to the baying jackals."

"You what?" Cheevers began to get up, but I pushed him back down. "He insulted me, Bathe. At least, I think he did."

Ranjeet made a raspberry, then winked.

I laughed out loud. I couldn't help myself. Cheevers gave me a hard look; then I hit him in the arm and he laughed, too. "You were only joking!"

"Absolutely yes! Yes!" Ranjeet exclaimed. "A real wise-cracker, wasn't it? All the sowars laugh at my splendid hu-mors."

"They have to," I said. "You're an NCO."

Ranjeet guffawed, showing a gold tooth. He waved and several Indian sowars approached, sitting across from other troopers, exchanging cigarettes.

"And what are you called?" Ranjeet asked.

212

"Edward Bathe."

"Edward Bathe, it is a very great pleasure!" He grabbed my hand and shook it warmly. He did the same to Cheevers and Blackburn. "What wonderful luck it is to have some Christians among us." He pointed at the gathered lancers. "We have good sowars here: Sikhs, Rajputs, Jats, and Hindustani Mussalmans. With you in our ranks, one can say with all honesty that God is truly on our side."

Cheevers whooped. "You are a funny man, Ranjeet."

"Ah, but you are being exceptionally kind, for I am not unaware of the tragedy of this situation. It must have been very difficult for you to leave your friends in the hospital and join us. We will put forth our greatest effort to live up to their heroism." He offered us a cigarette. Cheevers accepted. Several minutes later the officers came out of the tents and roll call was sounded.

"We shall be seeing you very soon, I am quite sure of it," Ranjeet said, and returned to his squadron.

Lieutenant Rance began to bellow, "From here on in, boys, we are going to be D Squadron, part of a composite regiment. We'll keep our colors, of course. They wanted to Indianize us completely, including making us wear their headdress, but I said, 'Lord, no! My Lincolnshire lads would never accept that.' So we'll start training here immediately."

Over the next week we fell into place, though it was a struggle to learn the new signals. The Indians were excellent horsemen, and their war cries as they did a lance charge would curdle the blood of any Turks. Our own lances never did arrive, so we used our swords for mock charges. We didn't seem anywhere near as threatening.

Hargreaves had recommended Cheevers to the higher-ups, so he received a stripe, making him a lance corporal. He sewed a chevron on each sleeve himself, then strutted about the tent all evening. "Now I'll be tip-top with the ladies. They can't resist an NCO."

"If you keep staring at your stripe like that you're going to get a kink in your neck," Blackburn said.

"Ha! At least I've risen a peg. If you work hard, you could, too."

Blackburn narrowed his eyes. "Well, look who's become Lord Muck."

"Careful, Trooper. Insubordination could lead to field punishment."

I wasn't sure if he was still kidding or not. "All you need is a parade to lead," I said, trying to keep things jovial.

Cheevers laughed and said, "It's a grave responsibility, Bathe. When you have a stripe, you'll understand."

At the end of the week we broke camp and rode close enough to the Mediterranean to catch the scent of the ocean. The land was growing flatter, and I found some relief in this. Having been raised on the prairie, I was never much for hills or mountains. We set up camp near the sea, but right after roll call the following morning we packed up and rode east again. It was as though Allenby didn't know exactly where he wanted us, and yet we knew we were close to a battle. We bivouacked halfway between Jerusalem and Jericho.

I was more than ready for it to end—all of it—so that my horse and I could go home.

We learned that our new major and new colonel had fallen sick. The command of the entire regiment now fell to Captain Davison from the Second Lancers.

"A captain, leading a whole regiment!" Blackburn said in disbelief.

"Davison seems right enough in the head," replied Cheevers, as though he had tea with Davison every day. "Don't worry, if he gets all gobsmacked, I'll straighten him out." He brushed the stripe on his shoulder.

"Ah, now I feel much safer," Blackburn said.

As the sun began to set, we were ordered to break camp and ride west, under the cover of night. The farther we traveled, the more congested the road became. We moved off to the side to let a row of trucks pulling howitzers rumble past, followed by Holt tractors hauling sixty-pounder guns, and artillery men marching in the rear.

If only we had one of those tractors on the ranch, harvest would be done lickety-split. I pictured Dad at the wheel, a big grin on his face. Right now Old Man Somners would probably be harvesting our fields. With any luck Dad would be out there, too. It had been over six months since Reverend Ashford had written. In the meantime, anything could've happened.

I hadn't thought about Dad much for quite a long time. What kind of son never thought of his father? And I hadn't thought very often about Hector, either. I was too tired to be angry at the Huns. I should have been struggling to remember every little detail about my brother. And about Emily, for that matter. But out here in Palestine there was nothing to

215

remind me of them or anything about my life as I'd once known it. The sun was burning away my memories.

We passed supply lines of pack-laden camels. There were more cavalry than I'd ever seen in one place. Horses whickered and stamped, but the men were mostly silent.

A crack of thunder echoed in the distance, and a second later came a reply. "Hear that?" Cheevers asked.

"We're near the front," I said, and wiped sweat from my forehead.

We continued to ride through the night, not stopping for sleep. The moment daylight stretched across the hills, Captain Davison ordered us to make camp in a grove of orange trees, where the leaves and bush would hide us from enemy airplanes. Other troopers had picked the bottom branches clean of fruit, so Cheevers climbed to the top, clinging like a monkey. He tossed down several oranges, and laughed when he hit me square in the head with one.

"Don't waste good oranges!" I shouted, stuffing a few into my saddlebags. Then I devoured one; it tasted heavenly.

Because we traveled at night, to the Turks it would appear as though nothing had changed. We watered our horses in the irrigation channels, fed them, and then crawled into our tents. The road we camped along was quiet; only the occasional truck or armored car motored by. I closed my eyes, but sleep was impossible; I scratched and sweated and cursed the hard ground. Not one trooper was snoring. Soon we would attack the front line. I couldn't help thinking of other charges I'd heard about that had ended in massacres.

What would a bullet in the arm feel like? Or one tearing

216

through my leg? My head? At least I wouldn't feel anything with a bullet through the head. The day he woke up and went into battle, did Hector know that death was waiting for him?

Hector, why didn't you stay in the trench? You were sick that day, but you always had to do the right thing, no matter the price: taking on bulls, bullies, or the Huns. If you had stayed you might be alive today, and I would be at home right now reading your letters. Damn you. Uncle Nix had said men had to be resolute, but our family had paid enough.

When night fell we were rousted out of our beds and set on the move again. There were even more cavalry now. The Dorset Yeomanry were to our left and the Thirty-eighth Central India Horse to our right, making up our brigade. With a simple wiggle of his pen, Allenby had set all this in motion.

But if we were all gathered here, then that could only mean that the rest of the front line stretching past Jerusalem and into the Jordan Valley was thin and weak. With any luck Lawrence and his Arabs were over to the east, swooping at the Turks like falcons. Keeping their attention from us.

When the sun rose, we camped under another grove of trees. I still couldn't sleep. The sun was too hot, the road too noisy with transport. Fear of the coming attack buzzed in my head like a trapped insect. I'd sleep for a minute, then wake, with a fading dream of home, a place where it rained and the grass grew.

"They're going to wear us out," Blackburn said, his head leaning against a rolled blanket. "Three days without a decent sleep, then they'll throw us at the Turks."

217

"That'll wake you up," Cheevers said, eyes closed.

The ground rumbled as a distant field gun lobbed a shell into the air. There was no way of knowing which side had fired the shot. The next day, I could die. I was surprised to find myself thinking that death might not be such a bad thing. I was too tired to care what happened to me. Who would miss me when I was gone, anyway?

Dad. Dad would miss me. Despite everything. It had been nearly a year since I'd left home. I pictured him in his bed. I was beginning to understand him. Each death of someone you loved weighed you down. If I could have gone to bed right then, never to get up again, I would have. But they'd shoot me for it. In fact, Hargreaves would be grinning as he did the job.

I gathered what little will I had and wrote Dad a letter:

Sept. 18, 1918

Dear Father,

I am writing from Palestine. I imagine you are surprised to hear from me, and from such a faraway place. We are up against the Turks, who are fine fighters. Tomorrow we will go into our first major front line attack, and this may be the last letter you get from me.

I have seen many things I wish I had not seen. Pals of mine have died, and so have Turks, of course. It's really terrible. I don't know what the censors will leave in this letter.

218

I paused. I wanted to tell him about Emily and that I now understood how terrible it must have been for him to lose Mother. But instead, I wrote,

> I do wonder if I should have left home. I miss it
> now. I wish I could be there to help you harvest, to feed
> the horses and the cattle. I wish I had been a better
> son, somehow. But I wanted to be a good brother, too.
>
> Faithfully yours,
> Edward Bathe

12

When night fell Lieutenant Rance approached our squadron; he was little more than a shadow in the moonlight, but his voice cut through the night and all hundred or so of us listened carefully. "Drop all excess weight—bivvies, blankets, greatcoats, and line gear. Pack it up and put your name and number on it." Bags of corn for the horses had been piled just outside the grove. "Each of you will carry one full bag and two nose bags. Put two blankets under the saddle. You'll need three days' rations including a day of iron rations."

"You eat the iron rations if you're surrounded," Cheevers said. "That'll finish you off."

"Shut your goddamn mouth, Lance Corporal!" Rance shouted, his eyes bulging with anger. Cheevers stiffened. "The next man who speaks out of line will find himself shackled to a gun wheel." The tan piece of paper—our orders—shook in his hand. It was seeing his hands tremble that woke the fear in me. "There are about five thousand entrenched Turks just over those hills. Zero hour for our artillery will be half past four hundred hours. There'll be a hell of a lot of banging; be ready for it. The infantry will then cut through the Turk lines and leave an opening for us. We're to proceed to the"—he consulted his paper—"brown line, our assembly point, by zero eight hundred hours. From there we'll be riding hard along the valley, maybe even as far as Bethlehem, to capture Turkish positions in the rear." He forced a smile. "We might have time for tea; then we'll have to mount up. I know you'll all do your best to bring honor to our regiment."

I packed my greatcoat and fingered my small bundle of letters, wishing I had time to read them all once more. I kept Emily's locket and mother's handkerchief in my breast pocket and placed all my other possessions in my haversack and left it in the pile behind us. It was only after I'd walked away that I realized I'd left my Bible in the bag. I considered going back, but I wouldn't need it where I was going.

I brushed Buke down, my hands shaking. "Good boy. You'll do well. Everything we've trained for, it's all going to happen now. I know you'll pull through." I saddled him with two blankets; we were going to ride hard! I checked my feed bags and made sure the pockets of my bandolier had clips, fifty rounds of ball ammunition in total. There'd be fewer by the time I was done.

Or I could be hit without firing a shot.

My legs buckled and I leaned against Buke. "I'll always have you, won't I, pal?"

Hargreaves ordered us to mount and we rode toward the front line. Supply wagons and marching infantry jammed the roads. I couldn't imagine heading into battle without my horse. Several transport columns rolled by, but there was a sense of order.

We crested a hill and thousands of glinting lances, guns, and helmets filled my vision—Indians, British yeomanry, French spahis, and hordes of Australian Light Horsemen had gathered in the valley. Cheevers looked back at Blackburn and me. "If the Turks could see us now they'd shit their britches."

Blackburn adjusted his sun helmet. "If they could see us now their field guns would grind us into mincemeat."

The front line was quiet now, and so were we—playing a giant game of hide-and-seek. The Turks on the other side of that wire and trenches would have no idea how many lances and bayonets were aimed at them.

At half past four the sky was torn by the thunder of our field guns. Hundreds of shells a minute were being lobbed at the enemy; it sounded as though all the British artillery in Palestine had let loose. Buke stutter-stepped and a constant deafening rumble shook the ground and rattled my bones. Turkish alarm rockets streaked skyward, lighting up the tops of the dark hills.

Cheevers yelled something at me that I couldn't make out, but his smile told me he was making a joke. Lieutenant Rance gave a hand signal and we broke into a canter.

"That way to the sausage machine!" Pitts shouted, his voice just penetrating the din. I was glad to be on Buke; I couldn't have walked on my own two legs toward the barrage.

We rode over the hill. Red artillery flares flashed and shells burst bright white in midair, spreading searing shrapnel across the Turks. Hundreds of them were trapped in their holes and getting hammered to pieces. Even God, if he'd wanted to, couldn't have stopped this battle.

We passed the lines of howitzers and sixty-pounder guns. Artillery men fed them, then jumped back as they roared. A haze of acrid smoke drifted over us, filling my lungs. The Turks didn't seem to have any guns left to make a reply: not one enemy shell landed among us.

Hargreaves urged our troop on with quick hand signals, his swearing lost in the noise.

We stopped after about ten minutes; apparently we had reached our assembly point. Lieutenant Rance squinted at his map. We were only a few thousand yards from the front line.

In the distance, by the glare of flare lights, figures could be seen scrambling through holes in the barbed wire, dozens of our infantry following one another into no-man's-land. It was clear they were well into the Turks' trenches.

I was already exhausted, my arms shaking. Unwittingly, I felt for my lucky handkerchief and locket. Still there.

"Blame the women!" Blackburn shouted.

I thought he was going mad. "What?"

He pointed at our exploding shells. "Every one of our shells was made by a British woman in a factory. Odd, isn't it?"

I had no answer. The world was upside down when mothers and girls made shells that killed.

Captain Davison checked his luminous-dial wristwatch every five seconds. Finally, he raised his hand and we rode in unison toward the front line. We picked our way over the British trenches on short wooden bridges that had been set in place for us.

The sun began to rise, glinting off the barbed wire. Lines of it had been cut by infantry, or by the shells. The openings were marked by red or blue flags. We followed the red ones.

The Turkish side was a mess of body parts—an arm here, a leg there, a head here, smaller parts everywhere, it seemed. They were scattered among their stores of weapons and food. A few half-starved, wounded Turks huddled under the watchful eye of an infantryman. Buke found his way through the debris and I turned to stare at the thousands of mounted horsemen behind me. It was a dream, as though the Bible had opened and armies were spilling from its pages into the Holy Land.

Soon we were on the Plain of Sharon, low hills swelling on either side of us. Australian Light Horsemen headed north; other riders turned east.

"Watch for wadis, men," Sergeant Hargreaves barked, "and the Turks, too!" We formed into three columns and rode on. The sound of shellfire faded behind us, and soon it seemed as if there were no battle going on at all. I searched for the enemy, my eyes so wide they began to hurt. Frankly, we were moving too fast to do any proper scouting. The Turks did pop up out of wadis, but the moment we came in sight, they surrendered.

"It's like rounding up cattle," I said after we'd ridden up to a group of Turks who threw down their guns and joined a line of prisoners.

Cheevers spat. "They're rolling over like whimpering dogs."

"They're delaying us," Blackburn said. "Every hour we spend gathering prisoners will give their reserves up ahead time to really dig in."

The day grew so hot, even the Indians looked out of their element. We rode hard, and just as the sun was setting over the hills, we stopped to water the horses at a deserted village. I let Buke drink, then swallowed a can of bully beef that sat like a hard lump in my guts.

Blackburn studied a little map he'd cut from one of his books. "Looks like we've covered about twenty miles already."

"And I haven't fired my gun once!" Cheevers complained.

I lay down on the ground and closed my eyes to nap. Moments later, a kick to my boots startled me awake. "You can forget your beauty sleep!" Sergeant Hargreaves grinned down in the semidark. "We want you ugly as the day you were born. We just got our orders; we're riding straight into Armageddon. Form squadron, on the double!"

Our regiment quickly carried on north. Two Rolls-Royce armored cars drove past us. A sandy-haired gunner in goggles stuck his head out the back and waved as though he were enjoying a Sunday drive.

Blackburn slapped at a mosquito. "The valley is too narrow. One machine gun could peg us like sitting ducks."

"Keep quiet," Cheevers said. "That's an order."

Blackburn fell silent, pouting. Our clomping, snorting horses would surely be heard for miles. The moon rose higher in the sky, bright enough to light our way and make our buttons glint. The advance scouts found groups of Turks cowering in ravines. They surrendered without a shot, sometimes without even exchanging a word. Soon the numbers swelled, and twenty or thirty at a time would be sent back with only one man on horseback as an escort.

We reached a crossroad and set up positions.

"Good God! Ride. Wait. Ride. Wait." Cheevers's teeth glowed in the moonlight.

I dismounted and stood staring out into the darkness of the deserted pass. Buke flicked his ears. A second later the rumble of an engine could be heard behind us. We turned to the sound as two headlights grew closer and brighter. The vehicle skidded to a halt, turning away from us so we could make out its shape: a long automobile with pennants flapping. Major General Barrow jumped out, shouting, "Davison! Davison! Where the hell are you?" I couldn't believe it; the commander of our entire division was at the front.

"Here, sir!" Captain Davison yelled, running to him.

Barrow's face was red. "You're an hour and a half late! Turks are already coming down from Nazareth to block the end of the pass." He pointed into the darkness. "You must get there first!"

Captain Davison nodded, gave a breathless "Yes, sir!" and ran to his horse. A minute later we were galloping down the valley, leaving General Barrow to wait for the rest of the brigade. I kicked Buke's sides, holding my place in line, my arms, legs, and spine aching. The path grew so narrow that we could barely push through two at a time.

Eventually we ascended one of the hills, following a steep ridge of jutting rocks, hooves hammering sparks. Buke stumbled, snorted, and found his footing, causing my heart to stop briefly. Just as we got close to the top, a scout came galloping out of the darkness, holding his rifle above his head.

"He's seen the enemy," Cheevers said.

Davison drew his sword and swung it from the rear to the front: advance! We kicked our horses into a hard gallop.

I clutched the reins, my ears roaring with the pounding of hooves and chugging breath of the horses. The armored cars on either flank bounced across the ground with their lights off. I couldn't see much farther than a few feet in front of me; I prayed there weren't any large stones. Or other surprises.

At the top of the rise, several lights appeared across from us—fires, blazing in the night, figures sitting around them. Davison signaled and, as one, the Second Lancers brought up their lances. Dust had jammed my sword in its scabbard, so it took a good hard tug to get it out. Davison swung his saber several times in a row: charge!

In the first moments of our approach I could see perhaps a hundred Turks around the fires, singing, of all things. It was obvious they were having a grand old time, their guns leaning against each other like stooks of wheat, out of their reach. They hadn't even bothered to post a watchman.

One Turk stood, turned, and dropped his coffee cup at the sight of us. They ran for their guns as the armored cars flicked on their lights and gave off a burst of machine-gun fire. The Turks fell to the ground, covering their heads. We thundered down on them, and in no time they were surrounded and taken prisoner.

Waiting for our next command, Cheevers and I stared down at our enemy.

"They weren't even watching for us!" I said.

"That's because this army is a total farce." Cheevers sheathed his sword. "We'll be sipping tea in Constantinople tomorrow."

I slipped my feet from the irons, got off, and warmed my hands by the enemy's blaze.

13

The Turks' fires died down and the rays of the moon out-lined a large hill beside us. Chaplain Holmes sat on his horse, contemplating the scene. For a padre, he'd ridden un-usually hard; his white collar and face were stained with dirt. "That's the city of Megiddo," he said.

"There's a city up there?" I asked.

"The ruins of King Solomon's city. This is where the armies of evil will mass: 'And he gathered them together into a place called in the Hebrew tongue Armageddon.' Then they'll march on Jerusalem. Armageddon will begin on the plains below."

"Maybe it just did," Cheevers said. "Not much of a bat-tle, was it?"

"This isn't Armageddon." Blackburn was cleaning dirt from under his nails with a knife. "Since we've taken Jerusalem and the Turks won't get it back. Ever."

"I can't imagine a war bigger than this one," Holmes said.

I opened up the corn bag, split what remained between the two feed bags, and hooked one to Buke's reins. When he'd eaten I sat down on the dried grass next to Cheevers. He ripped back the lid on a bully beef tin, and the raw salty smell made me salivate and feel sick at the same time. I wished I'd taken some more oranges. "An army marches on its stomach," I said.

Blackburn gave me a surprised look. "Napoleon devotee, are you?"

"Just something I heard once. What do you suppose is happening out there?"

"We're moving faster than they can react," Blackburn said. "Even a retreating army can't travel as quickly as we can."

"No point thinking too hard about it, lads." Cheevers leaned back, closed his eyes, and within moments was snoring lightly.

I lay on the ground wishing it were dawn and I could get a good look at Megiddo. How many armies had surrounded that pile of rock and been ground to death by chariots? And to think we had taken it without bloodshed. We'd made the big push and survived. I wanted to write Emily. I allowed myself to imagine what I would tell her, were she alive.

I considered writing another letter to Dad, but there was no time. It was September, and harvest would be in full swing. He used to fork stook after stook into the steam-driven threshing machine, amazing the crews with his tireless strength. Maybe, on the other side of the world, he was doing that right this moment. I closed my eyes.

Two seconds later I was kicked in the shin. "Get up, you clods," Sergeant Hargreaves commanded. "Prepare your horses." I'd have a nice bruise. If only I could kick the bastard back.

I pulled my watch out of my pocket. It was five a.m.

"Word is we're going to capture a town called Afuleh," Cheevers said. "The Turks we caught were just the advance party. Somewhere ahead of us is the rest of their regiment."

I tightened my saddle to the last notch, but it wasn't enough. Buke had sweated himself skinny in a matter of hours. "Pitts!" I called. "A belt plate and a punch!"

He came over, metal plate in hand. "Hold your horses, Canuck. You're not the only one." In seconds he'd punched another hole in the belt. "There ya be. You can't blame me now if you fall off."

We rounded the hill that the ruined city of Megiddo sat atop, the sun now rising behind it, lengthening its shadow through the mist. The city was overgrown; no one had lived there for a thousand years. Here and there I could pick out lines of ancient architecture. This was where the end of the world would begin.

"Can't imagine living on top of that," Cheevers said.

I flicked Buke's reins, urging him to speed up. "There's so much hullaballoo about it in the Bible, I thought it'd be bigger."

We rode through Megiddo's shadow and a chill ran up my spine. Maybe it was the ghosts of all the dead armies, their bodies buried beneath this soft soil. It was here that Satan would climb out of hell and gather his armies.

We rode down into a green valley, the mist still thick and

231

cold. The land we were trotting across was fertile; I could see it had been tilled recently. All the farmers were probably crouching in the hills waiting for us to leave. Funny, to think that many of us troopers were farmers, too. Shouldn't we all have just been growing things?

Vip! Vip! Bullets whined through the air, looking for a billet.

Captain Davison shouted orders, and the armored cars charged into the mist, returning fire. I was shocked to see a line of Turkish soldiers four hundred yards in front of us, their guns flaring. Where had they come from?

Lieutenant Rance shouted, "D Squadron, dismount! Form line!"

I was quickly down on one knee, firing back, surprised at how calmly and automatically I pulled the clips from my bandolier. I aimed wherever I saw a flash of light or a white dot—a Turkish head—never knowing for sure if my bullets were hitting home. The other squadrons were galloping to one side, hoping to outflank the enemy.

We kept up our volleys of fire for several minutes; then Rance barked out an order: "D Squadron! Stand to your horses!"

I stood and holstered my gun.

"Mount!"

I jumped onto Buke. We were going to charge into all that gunfire?

"Speed is armor!" Cheevers shouted. "The faster we ride, the harder it'll be for them to hit us."

Rance lifted his sword, his horse reared up, and he charged forward. From a canter we sped up to a gallop, riding knee to knee, excitement and fear threatening to make my heart explode. We broke through the mist. The soil was wet and soft; mud flicked off our horses' hooves, hitting us everywhere. Rance swung his sword again and again: charge!

Once again all I could hear was the pounding of hooves and Buke's labored breath. The flashes of rifle fire and the Turks behind the guns became clear. I drew my saber. This was insane! We were charging guns with swords in our hands. Guns!

A horse was hit and it rolled across the ground, legs splayed skyward, the rider thrown right in front of me. At the last second Buke jumped over him, but I didn't look back. We'd been trained to keep our eyes on the enemy. A few feet away another trooper let out a horrific scream and tumbled from his saddle.

The enemy's left flank became a chaotic mess of fleeing men as the lancer squadrons charged them, riding through the ranks, skewering anything that moved. The Turks didn't know where to turn. Many ran away, but a few kept shooting at us. I galloped into them, crashing through their first line and passing Ranjeet, who was dragging a dead Turk along the ground, trying to shake him off his lance. I charged straight for the second line of Turks, who were still manning their machine guns. Buke reared up. A Turk aimed his Mauser straight at my chest and pulled the trigger, but nothing happened. As I rode by, I thrust my sword into his shoulder, jarring my arm and knocking him to his knees.

Three Turks with bayonets had Cheevers surrounded, so he was swinging madly. I rushed toward him, but he spun Neddie, knocking two Turks to the ground. The third fell to his knees, and Cheevers stabbed at him, stopping an inch from his forehead. Cheevers laughed maliciously and wheeled Neddie away.

I made it through the second line and turned back to see that the Turks had thrown down their weapons and held up their hands.

I wiped my saber on my trousers, cleaning off the Turk's blood. I was proud I'd given him a poke, and a little sick about it, too. At least it wasn't my blood. I sheathed my sword and felt a rush of excitement unlike any I'd ever experienced. I was still alive!

Soon the bugle call rallied the squadron, and I took a moment to survey the land we'd taken. I expected to see lancers and yeomanry scattered across the plain. To my great and pleasant surprise, there were just a few horses on the ground, and one trooper down. He was being helped up by two others.

I lined up between Blackburn and Cheevers. "Only one man hit," Cheevers said. "Can you believe it? A full bloody blessed charge at over four hundred Turks and they only hit one of us."

"They were aiming too high," Blackburn said. "They weren't taught how to fight a cavalry charge."

We formed squadron and rode toward Afuleh. The Turkish prisoners began singing a happy song; they had wanted to be captured all along. Their war was over.

Lucky them.

14

At the gates of Afuleh there were several Turk soldiers who'd probably just recently given their comrades a terrific send-off. They fired a few shots at us, but when the entire regiment rode into view, they threw down their guns.

The town itself appeared deserted; the inhabitants were either hiding in their homes or had fled. We spent the next hour rounding up any Turks or Germans we could find. I observed the Huns closely in their gray uniforms. They were in better shape than the Turks; most had even shaved that morning. Several stared back at me, eyes fierce. I did my best to hate them for what they'd done to Hector and Emily and so many others.

Hargreaves led our troop to a storage camp on the east side of town. We rode right in, surprising a solitary Turk guard as he smoked his cigar. A trooper took the cigar, stuck it in his own mouth, puffed out some smoke, and led the Turk away.

In the camp we found three trucks with flat tires, and several wagons. One held something that looked like a pot-bellied stove.

"A goulash cannon!" Cheevers yelled, excited as a school-boy. He rushed over and touched the side. "It's warm, boys." He flipped the lid, and the smell of stew made my mouth water.

"It could be poisoned," I said.

"Bah, the guard wasn't even expecting us." Cheevers pulled a spoon from his kit bag. "All I need is my puggling stick." He stirred the stew and swallowed a mouthful. "It's goat stew! At least, I think it's goat."

Troopers crowded around and filled their plates; one even used his sun helmet. I got my share and followed Cheevers to a hut. He kicked open the door, stomped inside, and plopped down on a crate. I sat next to him, and we spooned the warm, peppery stew into our mouths, eating like pigs. Two bites left on his plate, Cheevers held up his hand.

"What?"

"We're missing something!"

He pried the lid off a crate; his eyes grew large, and, like a magician, he pulled out a bottle of champagne. "Fire in the hole!" He popped the cork and the bottle foamed. "Fizz! We're kings tonight!" He thumbed the cork off a second bot-tle and tossed it to me. I sipped from the bubbling fountain and coughed half of it back up. I'd never had champagne, but I liked it instantly. I finished the last of my stew, then washed it down with more warm champagne. It went straight to my head.

"We should tell the others," I said.

"Not yet." Cheevers dug around in a small wooden box and came up with cigars. "Where there's fizz, there's smoke!" He handed me a cigar and struck a match.

"I wouldn't change places with the King," I said, feeling full of myself. "Not even with General Allenby himself!"

Cheevers let out a belch and cloud of smoke. "We're on top of the world, Bathe. What a ride! What a ride!"

The door opened. Blackburn entered and his eyes nearly fell out of their sockets. "You sods! You dirty sods!

Cheevers blew him a cloud of smoke. "Finders keepers."

More troopers arrived to see what the joyful noises were all about, and soon the hut was jammed with yammering yeomanry grabbing bottles and lighting cigars. You'd have thought it was New Year's Eve.

For several minutes we forgot about all we had just seen and laughed like fools. And then there was a sudden hush. Cheevers and I stopped talking and looked up from our crates. There stood Hargreaves, his eyes squinched up in anger. "You useless worms are drinking Turk piss!" He grabbed a bottle from Blackburn. "Oh, it's German champagne." He took a swig and grinned. "The best hock there is!"

Cheevers jumped up to hand him a cigar and give him a light, and the celebration resumed.

My bottle was half empty. I knew if I stood up now I'd

wobble. We shouldn't have been drinking; we had to be ready to ride at a moment's notice. But we'd survived, hadn't we? We deserved a reward.

My eyelids grew heavy. I nodded once, twice. I wished I could share the champagne with Emily.

"How big is your farm, Bathe?" Cheevers asked, dropping down next to me again.

I struggled to remember. "Five hundred acres with fifty head of cattle."

"That's a kingdom! When we're done this little scrap, I'll come and wrangle cows. How does that sound? Me and you, chasing steers and chasing skirts. They do have girls there, right?"

"Of course!" I told him. "And you almost ride well enough to be a cowboy."

"I'll work on it!" He let a smoke ring waft to the ceiling. "We should go to 'stralia first, though."

"Why?"

"It seems like a cheery place. Good blokes. We could work on a kangaroo farm."

"They don't raise kangaroos."

"Edward, Edward, of course they do."

"I can't go to Australia." I took another swig from my bottle. "I have to get back to my farm. I don't know what kind of shape it'll be in. Someone else is looking after it."

"We'll go to Canada first, then." He released another smoke ring. "How many have you gotten?"

"How many what?"

"Turks. I'm at five now. Poor buggers keep getting in the

way of my bullets. Skewered one with my sword. How many did you say you got?"

"I—I don't know."

His red-rimmed eyes glowed. "It's a marvelous feeling, ain't it? Me against him, and I win. I always win. Edward, we're English gods."

My muscles tensed. "I'm not English."

"Close enough. I want to pot a Hun next; Turks are too easy."

My stomach lurched. Was it the food or the fizz or the look on his face?

"You sh-shouldn't enjoy k-killing." The words came out all jumbled.

"Speak up, mate. You're mumbling like a miserly mardy-cat."

"I've got to get out." I used the crates to pull myself up, knocking one over. Everything whirled.

"He's dancing, boys!" Hargreaves shouted, and clapped his hands in time with music none of us could hear. "The Canuck's putting on a girlie show."

I staggered to the door. Troopers laughed all around me, screeching like a bunch of crazed monkeys. I stumbled out into the endless heat.

I didn't want the food in my stomach. It had been made for men who were probably dead now. I heaved several times, then wiped my face. Thankfully, no one had followed me.

At the picket line I found Buke. I fell against him, grabbing his mane for balance.

Cheevers liked killing. He truly did. He was the perfect trooper.

Buke made a soft whinnying sound, switching his tail at flies. He was so solid, and he smelled like home. I didn't want to ever let go. "I can lean on you, boy. I can always, always lean on you."

15

I ran my hand along the inside of my sun helmet, wiping sweat and grit from my forehead. I looked back over the Jordan Valley. Eight hours of hard riding had taken us only three-quarters of the way across, the sun watching us closely. A swarm of flies followed us everywhere, landing on the hands of officers trying to read their maps.

This was an ugly, stupid place. How could the Jews, Arabs, and Turks live here? One moment you could eat an orange or a grape; the next you were caught in a burning desert. Palestine couldn't decide whether it wanted to be heaven or hell.

Buke trotted along, his mane damp. I explored my cheeks with a dry tongue and reached for my water bottle, then remembered I'd drained it an hour earlier. We didn't stop to rest. It was no wonder we kept losing troopers to malaria.

We'd spent the last few days rounding up Turks as we

rode farther east. Thousands of Turk soldiers were streaming up from the south, herded toward us by the infantry. We had them surrounded and were pulling the noose tighter, cutting off their escape routes. Soon they, too, would be prisoners.

We'd been assigned to a new CO, but I couldn't remember his name. Our next objective would be to capture the railway station at Deraa. I didn't know where the hell that was.

Blackburn began to cough, sounding like he was hacking up a lung. He spat a wad of gunk into the sand and waved off our inquiries about his health. I watched him, though, as his head began to bob with the motion of his horse. Asleep in the saddle.

"Hey, Blackburn," I said.

As if in answer, he fell off Cromwell without putting his arms out, smacked into the ground, and lay there like a broken doll. Cromwell stopped and sniffed his master.

I jumped down and knelt beside Blackburn. "Victor, can you hear me?" I rolled him over. His face was shockingly pale, one eye open and rolled back, the other closed.

Cheevers was off his horse in a flash. "Hey, no sleeping on duty, Blackburn."

"T-t-tell Hannibal to mind the trumpets," Blackburn mumbled. "Obtain superiority of fire and enfilade!"

His forehead was cool; malaria had conquered another one of us.

"Medic carts are several hours behind." Hargreaves was looking down from his horse, no pity on his face. "You play mommy, Bathe. Prop up a blanket so he's out of the sun and whisper sweet nothings in his ear."

A few troopers rasped with laughter.

"I'll look after him, Sergeant!" Chaplain Holmes dismounted. "No sense being one gun short."

"Good, then, sir." Hargreaves spat. "We're always happy to have the colonial along. He's such a good shot. Mount up, Bathe."

"I'll take good care of your friend," Holmes promised. "I'll quote the Bible to him."

I coughed out a chuckle. "That'll keep him awake."

"I know, son. I know. I'm sure he and I will have plenty to discuss."

As if to answer, Blackburn groaned.

Getting back on Buke was like climbing a mountain. I finally pulled myself over and kicked his side, urging him to catch up.

"Blackburn didn't even complain," Cheevers said. "He's tougher than he looks." He thought a moment. "At least we'll be spared his lectures."

"Frankly, Cheevers," I said coldly, "he was the only one who knew what was really going on."

Cheevers tapped the chevron on his left arm. "You forget I'm a lance corporal. The major consults with me before he farts."

I didn't laugh. "You're a piece of work," I said. He actually liked to kill. I couldn't get that out of my head.

Cheevers pointed east. "As we speak, Colonel Lawrence and his Arabs are somewhere out there giving the Turks a good beating. He's six feet tall and can ride a camel a thousand miles through the desert. Jolly good English pluck, if you ask me, outplaying the Arabs at their own game."

"Do you think we'll join him?"

"Ah, that's classified information, mate. Now who knows what's really going on? Hmmm?"

We halted at a deep gorge and looked across it toward several huts guarded by three pitiful date palms. Goats wandered about, but otherwise, the place seemed deserted.

Two shots rang out and our major dropped his map. He stared angrily toward the village as his orderly dismounted to retrieve it.

"Bloody Turks!" The major snatched the map from his orderly, raised it in the air as if it were a flag, and charged.

We followed him down a narrow path into the gorge, the way so steep that I jabbed my feet into my stirrups and leaned forward on Buke's neck. On the other side of the gorge we climbed an equally treacherous path to the top and then galloped to the huts. We found three Turks crouching behind a well, holding rifles. When our regiment thundered down on them, they dropped their guns and raised their arms.

The well was so small it would take days to water the regiment. An old Arab man in dirty white robes sat near it, a goat rubbing against his knees. He patted its head and grinned.

"Bring that Arab here," the major said, pointing to Cheevers and me. We rode over and tried to speak to the man in English, but he only shook his head.

"*Aasif. Aasif.*"

We motioned for him to come and he followed, the goat bumping the back of his legs.

244

"Does he speak English?" the major asked.

"No, sir," I said.

The major looked down at his orderly, a short man with round-lensed glasses. "Ask him how many Turks are at Irbid."

The orderly spoke in Arabic and the old man appeared confused, but kept nodding. "*Aasif.*"

The orderly repeated his questions and the Arab yammered, pointing several times.

"What's he say, Gibbons?"

"That's Irbid over there, sir. There are about two thousand Turks, exhausted and ready to surrender."

"He said that?"

"Well, he said they lacked will. So I believe that's what he means."

"Good show. Give him a couple piastres. We can't wait for our field guns and the rest of the battalion. We'll need the water in Irbid before dark."

We formed squadron. Our regiment had lost more than a hundred men to malaria during the previous few days, which left us with about four hundred riders to fight against two thousand Turks.

Don't think of the number, I told myself. *They've been weakened. The Turks have been bombed by aeroplanes, harassed by Lawrence and his Arabs, and marched double time for days on empty stomachs. They'll probably beg to surrender.*

We rode in formation toward the enemy. C and B Squadrons broke off and galloped past us, planning to attack from the flanks, while A Squadron dismounted to give covering fire. Our squadron wheeled about, aiming straight at Irbid. The village had been built partly on a ridge, the huts and stone houses spilling onto the flat ground below it.

The major had somehow decided that our squadron would be the ones to charge. I looked across our ranks. There were only about fifty of us, half yeomanry and half Indian lancers, riding on thirsty horses. Captain Davison, who had lead the whole regiment for the last few days, was our squadron commander now.

The Turks began to shoot, their bullets hitting the ground in front of us, spraying dirt as they found their range. The setting sun was to our right, lighting us perfectly for their target practice.

"D Squadron, form ranks!" Davison commanded. Several troopers kicked their tired horses, trying to get them into position. "Form ranks, I said!" He raised his sword and directed us to move ahead at a trot. After a couple of hundred feet he signaled us to gallop. Heavy stones were scattered across the plain, and Buke stumbled on them several times. I kept my eye on Cheevers, the troop leader, trying to keep the line straight. Twice I had to break formation just to get around a large stone.

It wasn't long before the trooper beside me was hit and thrown from his saddle. "Close up that section!" Hargreaves roared a few feet away. A moment later his horse took a bullet to the head and the blood spattered across me. Hargreaves managed to jump clear of the beast as it fell to the ground. I glanced back to catch Hargreaves swearing as he kicked his mount.

Captain Davison swung his sword in an arc and I dug in my spurs. It took all my strength to hold on to Buke and aim, arrow straight, for the village.

To my left another man fell. Then a third. A high-pitched *Vip! Vip! Vip!* filled the air. The entrenched ridge was higher than it had appeared from a distance; I couldn't even see the Turks, only the smoke from their guns. They had probably set their sights long before our arrival. Fear twisted in my guts.

An Indian trooper fell and was crushed under his rolling horse. We broke through the outskirts of the village, past a few small sandstone houses and down several narrow streets. The Turks above us no longer bothered to hide their heads. They leaned over the sandbags, found their marks, and shot.

Davison raised his sword and pointed left. The remains of the squadron wheeled in that direction, but the advance troops didn't see the signal or hear the captain's whistle. All twelve of them climbed the steep hill of the ridge straight into the enemy guns, riderless horses following. Three sowars fell over at once; then another, and a fifth, rolling back down the ridge. Their leader made it right to the top and raised his sword to strike, but a bullet knocked his head back and he fell out of the saddle onto the sandbags.

I followed Cheevers into the village, our flanks open— making us perfect targets. Ahead of us Davison screamed out in pain, dropping his whistle. We halted behind a building in the town square, breathing hard.

The captain's horse slipped down onto its front knees as

if bowing, then fell over. Davison tumbled to the ground and got to his knees to inspect his horse. It was breathing slowly, blood bubbling from its nostrils, its white chest crimson.

"Oh, dear." He looked as rough as his horse, his puttees stained a dark red. He struggled to get to his feet, but when he put weight on his right leg it collapsed. His Indian orderly rushed to his side and helped him stand up again. "Thank you," he said, fumbling for his pistol.

When he had shot his horse, Davison let out a loud, sad sigh, then turned to the eight of us. Cheevers and I were the only ones with horses.

Davison looked us up and down. "You two will have to ride—"

Neddie collapsed and Cheevers somehow landed on his feet. "Aw, Neddie, Christ almighty!" His horse was bleeding from a wound in his neck. "They got you! Goddamn Turk bastards." He yanked his rifle out of its bucket, stuck his head around the corner of the building, and let off three quick shots toward the ridge. "Bastards!" They returned fire, knocking chunks of stone off the walls. Cheevers kept pulling the trigger and recycling the bolt.

"Lance corporal!" the captain snapped. "Hold your fire!"

Cheevers shot once more. "They got my horse, Captain!"

"Well, mine, too." A resolute grin lit Davison's face. "And they even shot me. No sense just firing back wildly, though. Kheri, Basti, check those streets." The two sowars went to the opposite end of the building and peered around it, only to be met with a hail of machine-gun fire.

Davison was now leaning on his orderly. "The attack has failed, and the other squadrons obviously haven't made any

248

progress. We'll have to retreat." He pointed at me. "Trooper Bathe, you've got the only good horse now. You ride hell bent for leather down that alley—use the buildings for cover—then head west. Circle back to the regiment and let them know what happened."

"But I can't just leave you here!"

"Not your problem, Trooper Bathe. Now, prepare to mount."

"Ride hard!" Cheevers said, rubbing his hand through Neddie's mane. "In the morning we'll kill every Turk rat up there."

I tightened my saddle and climbed onto Buke. I almost said a prayer but caught myself in time. What would be the use? I dug my spurs into Buke and yelled, *"Heeyah!"* We charged straight down the street, the *Rap! Rap! Rap!* of the machine guns following us. We galloped behind another building before the Turks could adjust their sights, then turned sharply, racing out of the village. "Go! Go!" I shouted, and Buke found the strength to speed up. The stones in front of me chipped as bullets struck them.

If I'm meant to be hit, I hope it'll be in the head, I thought, remembering Hector's long, painful death. I passed the last building of the village and burst into the open, feeling the Turks' sights trained on my back. I clung tightly as Buke jumped a boulder. Then we were across the stony plain and over a rise. We'd finally made it!

Pain flashed across the right side of my head and blood spattered my arm. I reached up and fingered what was left of my ear. A bullet had come that close! I rode down into the ravine, out of the Turks' sight.

A man popped up in front of me and I tugged at my sword just as he waved. I noticed his turban; he was an Indian. I yanked on the reins and Buke stopped, snorting hard.

"That was an excellent ride!" the sowar said, grinning. "Really quite marvelously excellent!"

He led me to his captain so I could report what had happened. Then, as night fell, he took me to a medical cart. A rotund, tired doctor jammed a metal cup into my hand, saying, "Drink this." I gulped the rum, then lay down on the back of the cart, where he splashed iodine onto the wound. It might as well have been acid, it hurt so much. He stitched the dangling pieces of my ear together. Lines of fire crisscrossed my head. "You're missing most of your lower ear." It felt as if he was trying to yank the rest of it off, too. "Close shave, though. Lady Luck was with you today." He applied the dressing.

An inch. That was how close I'd come to having my brains splattered all over the sand. I thought about Cheevers and the others. How could they possibly survive?

I stumbled out of the tent, one side of my head still on fire. The sowar handed Buke's reins to me and offered his water bottle. I took it gratefully, poured a handful, and let Buke lick it up with his dry tongue.

"You really love your horse," the sowar said, smiling broadly. "What a fine horseman you are."

I nodded and gave Buke a few more handfuls. The Turks were sitting on the wells in Irbid, so we wouldn't get any more tonight. I handed the bottle back to the Indian, but he refused it until I'd had a drink.

I tied Buke to a wagon and collapsed on the dead grass. A

250

few minutes later our field guns roared. They'd finally arrived. I closed my eyes and prayed that they'd blast the Turks to hell.

No sooner had I dropped off than I was shaken awake again. The sowar was standing over me.

"Rejoice! Praise Almighty God! Your captain lives!"

"What about the others?" I absently brushed my wounded ear and grimaced.

"Yes! Yes! Come please!"

I followed him to the medical cart.

"Hey, Bathe!" Cheevers sauntered up as though he'd just been to the opera.

"Look at you, not a scratch!" I said as we hugged. It was so great to see him alive and well.

"Actually, I thought my number was up several times. Had my hair parted twice by bullets."

"How'd you get out?"

"Over the rooftops and down through the buildings. Sit, sit." I sat down. "There were bullets flying everywhere, so we ran like hell. The captain was hit in the arm and the leg, so his orderly carried him the rest of the way. These bloody Indians got guts, I tell you! I've never been so happy to hear our guns. You must've had a nailing good gallop!" He stopped. "What happened to your head?"

"I was winged. Lost half my ear. It hurts like hell."

"Ah, buck up! Your ears were too big, anyway."

I lay back on the dry grass and laughed.

16

In the morning the village of Irbid was silent. The first rays
of the rising sun cast long shadows over the fallen troopers
and their horses, strewn across the ground. Scouts returned
to us with the news that the Turks had fled.

Twelve men had been killed in our charge, and twenty-
nine wounded. Lieutenant Rance and Frank Pitts were
among the dead. I didn't want to see their bodies; there
wasn't time to mourn anyway. Hargreaves had survived,
proof that God really did work in mysterious ways.

Cheevers was given a dead trooper's horse; others got
ragged remounts, and we watered and pushed on. What was
left of our regiment was kept in reserve, so we were at the
back of the column when our brigade reached our objective:
the train station at Deraa.

The town was already burning. We stood a distance away,

watching plumes of smoke rise from the station. Rifle shots echoed through the hills. We sat listening for an hour before news trickled back that Lawrence and his Arabs had already taken the town and forced a column of Turk troops to flee down the road to Damascus. A few of the Dorset Yeomanry were quite excited that they'd seen the man Lawrence himself but didn't have a kind word for his Arabs. Apparently they'd slit the throats of every Turk they'd gotten their hands on, even the ones who were loaded on a hospital train. I was relieved not to have witnessed any of that, but I would have liked to glimpse Lawrence with my own eyes.

Our brigade went after the column of Turks, speeding up now that we had their scent. Hargreaves had our troop leave the road and ride into the open land, in case there were smaller groups of devious Turks trying to hide from us.

The land was just more rock and tamarisk bush. Each step made my helmet rub against the dressing on my ear, so that drops of blood slowly stained my neck curtain red. The flies loved feasting on my blood. I'd given up slapping at them. Eventually the dressing fell off and they had full access to my wound.

Cheevers rode up to me. "You look wretched, Bathe! You should've had Purves give it another go."

"He didn't have time." I shrugged, not really caring.

Two hours later Hargreaves stopped to consult his map.

"We might be a little lost," Cheevers whispered, wiping sweat from his brow. "We should have been back with the regiment by now."

The sun stared down from the middle of the sky. We had

twisted through several wadis, and I no longer knew which way was which. Hargreaves cleared his throat, then drank from his water bottle and replaced the stopper with a flourish. The bass *Thump! Wump!* of field guns echoed through the hills. The sound could have come from any direction.

"This way!" Hargreaves turned his horse. "Give your nags a kick, boys!"

We rode faster, the thunder of battle growing louder.

"There's someone over there!" Cheevers yelled, pointing at several troops of men climbing a hill, feathers bobbing in their slouch hats.

"Aussies," Hargreaves said. A moment later an Aussie scout popped up out of the bush.

" 'Oo are you?" he asked, his dusty face covered with several days' growth.

"Lincolnshire Yeomanry," Hargreaves replied. "With Fourth Cavalry Division."

"Well, you're in time for a spot of action, then. The Barada Gorge is just over that ridge. And so are the Turks."

"I assumed that." Hargreaves pulled on his reins. We dismounted and tied our horses in twos, head to tail. I yanked my rifle out of its bucket and followed the Aussies up the hillside, climbing through brush, the way sometimes so steep that I had to use my hands to crawl. A clump of French soldiers were above us, their blue uniforms stained with sweat. Behind us teams of New Zealanders lugged up their machine guns.

An Aussie captain commanded, "Fire at will!"

I peered over the edge of the hill. The gorge was only a hundred yards wide, split by a shallow river. The engine of a

254

train had been blown off its tracks, and the cars were burning. A mass of Turkish troops struggled to get through the mess and run to Damascus, but the head of their column had been devastated by gunfire from both sides of the valley. They were trapped like pigs in a slaughterhouse.

"You heard the man, lads," Hargreaves said. Cheevers shot into the mass of Turks. Then I fired. The man I aimed at fell, followed by another. Some Turks dove into the shallow river and were hit, and their bodies floated to the surface.

Horses keeled over, wagons flipping to further block the gorge. A German troop quickly set up their machine guns and let a blast go from the top of a truck, but the height of the cliffs made it impossible for them to see us. Only once did a bullet strike anywhere near me. In no time, the Germans were all dead.

I stopped shooting. No one had ordered me to, but I couldn't do it anymore. The Germans weren't surrendering, nor were the Turks, even though they had no hope of escape. The rain of bullets poured into the valley from both sides. Why didn't anyone wave a white flag? It had become a massacre.

Cheevers was firing with what seemed like a smile. He pulled a clip from his bandolier and slid it into place. Hargreaves was next to him, a cruel grimace on his gob. If he had been made in God's image, then God was a twisted, bloodlusting animal.

Our machine guns opened up, and cries of anguish filled the hot air, a confused chorus of voices and neighing horses.

Stop it, God. *Stop it.*

A German tried to ram his truck through the bodies, flames, and wagons, but the windshield was shattered by bullets and he slumped out the window. Turks dove for cover under the truck, and it exploded a moment later. I couldn't even begin to count the number of dead.

Without any signal from an officer, the gunfire petered out. Everyone peered over the edge of the cliff at the hell we had created. The Turks and Germans who were still alive had their hands up. All around them were countless bodies and wounded men, twisted together in agony, blood and guts painting the bottom of the gorge.

I closed my eyes but could still hear the screams; I would never hear the end of them.

17

At dusk, we stumbled down the hill; my rifle was still warm in my hand. Hargreaves seemed to be in a hurry now. We mounted up and struck out to join our division. No one spoke until Hargreaves said, "It's the luck of the draw, ain't it? I actually felt sorry for the damn Turks."

There was no response from those within earshot. Perhaps, like me, their brains were numb. Buke struck a stone and stumbled, then corrected himself, but he trotted with a bit of a limp for a while. An hour passed. My ear ached with each heartbeat.

"Cheevers," Sergeant Hargreaves said. "You and the Canuck scout ahead. Give Bathe a smack in the head if he lags behind."

I was glad to oblige. Anything to put more distance between me and the sergeant. Cheevers and I trotted on ahead, with me in the lead. We rode silently, alert, watching for the enemy.

After a while Cheevers rode up next to me. "You seem pensive, Eddie ol' boy."

"I'm tired."

"Aren't we all?" He paused. "You worried about that tiff in the gorge?"

My hands tightened on the reins. "Why didn't someone stop it?"

"Stupid Turks didn't raise a white flag, did they, now?"

"We could've stopped. What's the bloody difference between us and the Huns?"

He chuckled. "We've got bigger balls." When I didn't laugh, he said, "And we're just . . . well . . . better." The tone of his voice had changed. He was dead serious.

"Better? We're no better. And you . . . you *enjoy* shooting them."

Cheevers yanked his horse to the left so it bashed against Buke. We were riding knee to knee. "You spoiled weak runt!" His spit hit my face. "They started it! Remember? Get that through your thick head! *They* started it! And now we have to do the dirty work to fix everything, so toughen up! If we weren't here, they'd be burning down our homes and raping our women." He took several deep breaths. "Every day I think of the lads who died on the *Mercian*. My pals! The Huns and the Turks killed them. And my brother. Wouldn't you like to shoot the bastard who murdered your girl?"

"Don't mention her!"

Cheevers slumped a bit in the saddle. We rode silently, and it occurred to me how foolish we were being, taking our eyes off the terrain. "I . . . I'm sorry I got so miserly, mate," he said. "I'm sorry. I hate Palestine just as much as you. And I don't like killing. Really, I don't. I just have to make it a game or I'll go all moffled."

But he'd been grinning as he fired down into that gorge. Grinning.

He patted my shoulder. "Cheer up! Tonight we'll find a nice patch of ground, clear out the snakes and scorpions, and sleep like babies."

As the sun was setting, we rode to the top of a rise and looked down on the road to Damascus. We could just make out a column of men on horseback. The yeomanry regiment trotted slowly, horse heads lolling, troopers asleep in the saddle. "It looks like the Dorsets!" said Cheevers. "I can taste the tea already."

Just then, on another low hill a distance from us, I caught a flash of silver. "Look over there," I whispered. Several soldiers were moving down into a small gulley. The shape of their helmets was unmistakable.

"Germans!" Cheevers hissed. "At least four of them, with machine guns. They're setting up right under our noses! They'll have the Dorsets dead to rights."

The Germans were already partly hidden, but I saw another flash as they began setting up their guns.

Cheevers glanced over his shoulder. "Hargreaves is dilly-dallying—I can't even see him and the rest of our troop." He drew his sword. "We'll have to gallop the Huns down ourselves."

"What?"

"If we come at them from the flank, they won't be able to

259

turn their machine guns on us. They've been running for days. They'll put up their hands like good little Huns."

"But—"

He waved his sword. "We go! That's an order, Trooper Bathe. Now!"

With that he kicked his horse and didn't look back. Cursing, I spurred Buke into a gallop, drew my sword, and gained on Cheevers.

A Hun turned, shouted, and jumped behind a boulder, positioning his rifle. Two others joined him. I expected Cheevers to stop—it was obvious they weren't going to surrender—but he kept riding. Bullets hissed past us. Cheevers's horse was hit and it crumpled, throwing him from the saddle. He rolled along the ground, his sword flying into the shrubs.

I sheathed my sword, yanked on Buke's reins, wheeled around, and turned back to get Cheevers. He was struggling to pull his rifle out of its bucket, but it was pinned under his horse.

I galloped up to him. "Get on! Get on!" I shouted, staying low to Buke's back to avoid bullets. Cheevers gave a frustrated yank, retrieved the gun, and grabbed my hand. As I pulled him onto Buke, he shouted, "The daft bastards have more guts than I thought!"

I gave Buke a good kick, but before he could take a step he let out a soft whinny and fell to his knees. "Buke!" I yelled as we jumped to the ground. Blood was running down his side and he let out a long wheezing breath. His eyes were wide with pain and fear, reflecting the moon. Blood bubbled in his nostrils. "Oh, Jesus. Don't die, Buke."

260

Then another bullet hit his chest and we crouched behind him. His eyes closed and he stopped breathing. I grabbed his mane and pulled on it as if it would somehow keep him from leaving this world. "Get up, boy, get up! You're the king! C'mon, get up!" I slapped his side hard, but to no avail.

Now he was just another carcass, like all the carcasses I'd seen over the last few months. The flies were already landing on him, planting their maggoty eggs. I waved my hands at them. "Get away!"

"Pipe down!" Cheevers said. "Have you gone daft?"

Bullets struck the ground near us. My chest flared with pain, but I ignored it. Cheevers let off a few rounds, only attracting more gunfire.

"We have to move," he shouted. "There's a wadi right over there. Let's go!" I got my gun and fired back, standing in the open, daring them to hit me.

Cheevers grabbed my shoulder and pulled me into the wadi, where we splashed through the runny muck. Water! I hadn't seen this much water in weeks.

"We have to circle around them." Cheevers dragged me about twenty more feet. There were shots, but nowhere near us. Perhaps they were still shooting at Buke.

Finally Cheevers leaned me up against the wall of the wadi. Buke was dead. My horse was dead.

Cheevers patted my shoulder. "Sit tight! I'm just going to take a quick look-see."

He peered over the edge of the wadi. "They're just over—"

Vip!

261

Cheevers slumped down in front of me, kneeling silently. He had a small hole in the middle of his forehead. He fell to one side, and I could see that the back of his skull had been shattered like an egg. Blood and brains glistened in the moonlight.

Just like that, he was gone.

I crossed his arms over his chest and tried to close his eyelids, but they wouldn't stay shut. His eyes were dull, his face emotionless. It took everything I had not to vomit, to find the will to get on with my job.

I crawled through the mud another twenty yards, then lifted my head above the edge of the wadi, praying that a bullet wouldn't find me. The Hun machine gun was now firing, and the Dorsets returned fire. The Huns had their backs to me, but I didn't have a clear shot, so I crawled across the ground, now in danger of taking a bullet from my own troops. Covered in mud, I dragged myself over the sharp rocks, getting close enough to hear the Hun commander growling orders. Either they expected reinforcements, or they were fools for having launched the attack with so few men.

I crawled to the top of the gulley and saw three Huns below me. I fired. A dark spot appeared in the back of one man, and he fell over. I shot again and another collapsed. The third, a stocky hulk of an officer, turned, and I got him in the throat. He slumped over the ammunition boxes, his life gurgling out of him.

There! I thought. *That's for Hector! For Cheevers! For Buke!*

I dropped into the gulley and turned. A German, no

older than I was, cowered near some brush. He showed me his empty hands.

"Don't move!" I shouted.

He was shaking. "*Eesh capeetuleeruh.*"

"Shut up! Shut up!"

Rifle fire hit the lip of the gulley, spraying dirt over us. I reached in my pocket, fastened my mother's handkerchief to the top of my gun, and waved it in the air. A bullet shot through the cloth. I held it higher, keeping my hands below the line of fire.

The shooting stopped.

I turned to see that the German was reaching into his belt.

"Don't!" I yelled, but the German mumbled, "*Eesh haba shocolahdah.*" He looked at me, earnestly. "*Shocolahda,*" he repeated softly; then something metallic flashed in his hand.

I fired. A red rose formed on his chest. He staggered back, his helmet tumbling to the ground. Without it he looked younger, so young that I doubted he had ever shaved.

The silver thing had fallen to the sandy earth. It was a piece of chocolate, wrapped in foil. He had been offering me candy, for heaven's sake.

Somehow the boy was still upright, gawking at his chest. There was so much blood gushing out of a hole near his heart.

"*Ess toot meer vay.*" His hand clutched the wound and he collapsed. "*Mutuh.*"

I felt as though I were floating over us both, looking down, watching him and watching me.

"*Mutuh. Mutuh.*"

He was going to die. All he wanted to do was share a piece of chocolate, and now he would die.

He shivered, his face pale. He reached for me in a daze, as if greeting an old friend. *"Ess toot meer vay."*

"You'll live." I tore the ragged handkerchief from my gun and held it against the wound and felt his heart beating.

"Mutuh," he whispered.

"Mother," I echoed. "You want your mother."

"Mutuh."

I held him up against me and began to weep for the terrible thing I'd done. Like Hector in his last moments, this boy was calling for his mother. "She's here, my friend. She's with you now. Can you hear her?" I hummed a lullaby my mother used to sing.

"Hushaby, bairnie, my bonnie wee laddie,
When ye're a man ye shall follow your daddie."

The boy's face dripped with tears. I'd forgotten how to sing; my voice was husky, my throat dry. His eyes glazed over. The bullet was working its evil, threatening to take him from this world. And then I felt a presence, as though my mother were with me as I sang, her lilting tone in my ears, the lyrics transforming me. Us.

"Lullaby, lullaby, bonnie wee dearie,
Sleep! Come and close the e'en, heavy and weary."

This boy could have grown up on a farm, been issued a gun, and sent down here to the Holy Land.

"Got. Mutuh."

He had probably prayed a thousand times, and now God

264

wouldn't lift a finger to save him. "You won't die," I promised.

My right shoulder felt broken, but somehow I carried him to the top of the ridge. Several yeomanry approached with their rifles pointed at me. I stumbled down the embankment.

"Bloody good job!" a trooper shouted. "You'll get the VC for this." I staggered on. The Victoria Cross. That wasn't what I wanted. I was looking for a different cross. Someone had to live. I lugged the boy past the first line of yeomanry. Several troopers spoke to me, one getting in my way, so I pushed by him, cradling the German. He seemed to be growing lighter.

The medical carts were next to a tent. I pushed through the flaps and laid the boy on the only empty cot. There were wounded men on the others.

"Fix him," I said to an orderly.

"Are you mad! You carried a Hun in here?" I blinked. Perhaps I was mad. I had no idea what I looked like anymore; my head was dirty, bleeding from cuts.

"Save him." My voice was still hoarse.

"He's dead. Look at him. He's dead, mate."

"Heal him," I said, pulling out my knife. "Do it now."

Someone touched my shoulder and I whirled to face Dr. Purves. "Stand down, Trooper Bathe," he said softly. My muscles tightened for a moment; then I dropped the knife. He gently pushed me aside and leaned over the German. "He's still breathing." I couldn't see any sign of life, but then the boy let out the softest wheeze.

"You better lie down, too, trooper," Purves said.

"No. I must go. My horse, Cheevers, I . . ."

"You've been wounded."

"It's not my blood."

But then, as though his words had somehow given me permission, I felt the pain shooting through my lower chest and right shoulder. I looked down. There were two holes in my uniform.

"Someone has to live," I whispered. My knees gave out and everything went black.

Later, I came to, lying on my back, Dr. Purves's face floating above me. He looked angelic. "Sleep, Trooper Bathe. You've done enough. You'll be happy to know we found some Turk anaesthetic."

The orderly lowered a white cotton cloth over my face.

"Breathe," Purves said, "slow and easy, son."

I saw the glint of a scalpel.

"No, no," I whispered, "the German first."

But the orderly pressed the cotton tight against my nose and I soon felt nothing at all.

BOOK THREE

There's a long, long trail a-winding
Into the land of my dreams,
Where the nightingales are
*   singing,*
And a white moon beams . . .

"The Long, Long Trail,"
lyrics by Stoddard King

1

"Mom." Her face, in a shadow, was almost within reach. "Mom. Mom." She opened her arms and drew me to her, stroking my hair, her hands so soft.

"There, there," she whispered. It was so wonderful to hear her voice and to be held against her. And then, too soon, I began to drift away from her.

I awoke on a cot, sweating. It had been a dream. Nothing more. And now I ached. Every muscle and ligament hurt, and my spine seemed twisted in a knot.

Slowly I turned my head and saw that I was in a large room lit by a dim electric chandelier. Cots were lined up against the wall; wounded and sick soldiers hacked and moaned.

I remembered jumbled images of traveling into Damascus in a wagon, but little else. Ten days could have passed since then. Or ten years.

269

My wounds still stung, felt fresh and itchy. I struggled to pull back the sheet, my arms stiff. Bloodstained dressing was wrapped around my right shoulder and lower chest. Every pore on my body dripped sweat. I shivered even though I knew the room was hot.

More images came into my memory. I'd shot someone. A German? A Turk? More than one man.

Hours passed without my seeing a doctor or nurse anywhere. Some hospital. A man screamed down the hall, but I couldn't lift my head to see what was bothering him.

Then a nurse appeared beside me, as if out of nowhere. Her gray hair was tied back, and she had bags under her eyes.

"So you're awake again."

"Again?" Even speaking hurt.

"Yes. Several hours ago you were awake for a spell. How do you feel?"

"I'm shaking. Was the operation a . . . a success?"

"You asked me that last time," she said, smiling. "Yes. You may have some stiffness in your shoulder for a while. Luckily, that bullet passed right through and nothing important was damaged. The other bullet was embedded in a rib. Your regimental doctor got it out."

She held a cup to my lips and I sipped. The water was the most delicious I'd ever tasted.

"Oh, and you have malaria," she added, as if she were talking about a slight sniffle.

"Malaria?"

"Yes, that's why you're sweating. You'll pull through; we've put enough quinine in you to cure a horse."

A horse. Buke. The memory came back so suddenly, I almost wept.

"Are you all right, Trooper?" the nurse asked. "Do you feel like you're going to be sick?"

I shook my head. "How long have I been here?"

"Four days."

I nodded. "May I have more water, please?"

She put the cup to my lips again and I drank.

It was two weeks before I was able to walk on my own. My ribs and chest still ached, and the damage to my left shoulder made it impossible to lift anything.

Several patients suffered horrible deaths, first coughing lightly, then harder and harder. Within a couple of hours, they began to hack up blood until they drowned in their own froth. I sat helplessly as the nurses worked on them. An influenza was sweeping over soldiers and civilians alike. It seemed the Four Horsemen had been loosed upon the world.

Every night I waited for the pestilence to strike me. I deserved it. I had killed. I would never forget the way the holes had appeared in those men after I pulled my trigger. I deserved to grow sick and die.

Instead, I grew stronger.

At the end of the third week Dr. Purves came to my bedside. "Trooper Bathe, I'm sorry if I left a few scars on you. How is the movement in your arm?"

"It's stiff. Very stiff."

"There's been some nerve damage. Funny thing, bodies aren't meant to have holes in them."

271

"I couldn't agree more," I told him.

"You know, you saved a lot of lives by taking out that machine gun. You did a good thing."

"It had to be done, that's all." I'd killed three Germans and shot a fourth. Was it a fair trade for the deaths that had hurt me so deeply? "What about that boy I brought back?"

Purves shrugged. "He survived my operation, but I didn't see him after that. I don't know where he was sent to convalesce."

He'd survived. I had thought I would feel happy at such news, but instead, I just felt dull.

"You take good care of yourself, now," Dr. Purves said. "You've done Lincolnshire proud."

"I'm sure they'll write songs about me," I said.

Purves narrowed his eyes, surprised by my answer. "They should, son."

I spent as much time as possible in the courtyard, sitting in a wicker chair under a palm tree, dressed in my bathrobe and loose blue pajamas. The sun warmed the malaria chill, and at least I could see part of the sky. Yeomanry officers played croquet several feet away, pipes jutting out of their mouths.

Another week passed. Every morning when the sun rose a muezzin crouched in a nearby mosque and called the faithful to prayer. His song was mystical and beautiful and as old as time. Dogs barked and roosters crowed in answer.

I learned from the nurse that the Turks were being pursued farther north and that whole regiments had been knocked out by malaria and influenza. It was all happening far, far away from this pleasant little courtyard.

"Daydreaming, are you, colonial?"

I looked up. "Blackburn!" He was dressed in a new uniform, his buttons shiny, but he had dark bags under his eyes. There was a stripe on his shoulder. "So good to see you, Blackburn—or should I say, Lance Corporal?"

He shrugged. "Anyone left standing has a chevron now. It took quite the effort to find you, Bathe. Heard you deserve a VC."

"I don't."

He looked a little surprised at how adamant I was. "Well, apparently you were mentioned in dispatches. They'll hear about that back in your hometown. The brass are chintzy with their medals as the end of the war nears." He wiped under his left eye. "I was sorry to hear about Cheevers."

"Yes. It was horrible to see him die. His time was up, I guess."

"He was a cheeky bastard, but he had a good heart. He'll be missed."

"Yes, he likely will," I agreed.

A moment or two passed, but I was too tired to feel awkward. Blackburn cleared his throat. "You're looking well. How long before you're out?"

"I go back to England on Monday."

"It'll be a shame to lose you."

"Can't fight if you can't aim a gun," I said, then recalled how he'd fallen off his horse sick with malaria. "You seem loads healthier than last time I saw you."

"It took a long time, but I eventually got better. Missed all the action, though; I joined our regiment just as everyone else was struck down with malaria. They had to call a halt to the advance after Aleppo." He paused. "The Turks signed an armistice that goes into effect today. Had you heard that?"

"No." They just signed a paper and the fighting stopped? Was it that easy? "What happens now?"

"Now?"

"To Palestine. To all those places we rode through."

"It'll all have to be put in good order."

"Good order?" He sounded like Uncle Nix.

"Yes, it needs to be organized. Arabs! Jews! The French! They'll all want some part of it, too, I suppose. Who knows what the heads have promised them; a promise during a war isn't worth much."

They could have it all. It wasn't an Eden. No heaven on earth here. Just date palms and desert.

"We've finally made the big push against the Germans in France. No more trench warfare; it's a war of movement again."

"It's about time." More men were dying over there, waiting for papers to be signed.

"I was happy to ride beside you, Edward. When my job is done here I want to travel. I'd like to look you up in Canada."

"Of course. You're always welcome at my home, Blackburn," I said, and I truly meant it. "Always."

2

I returned to England on the *Nevisian*, a bucket of a ship crowded with wounded soldiers, nurses, and a few civilians. I spent my time in the open air quietly staring out at the sea. We stopped at Gibraltar, but I remained on board.

As we approached Portugal, the sun came out and the clouds vanished. Most everyone, even some of the sailors, basked in the heat. A few nurses held parasols over the weaker patients.

There was a sudden cheer at one end of the deck, and I wondered if someone had seen a whale. Soon dozens of people were on the deck, hooting and clapping and letting out hurrahs. One soldier, who couldn't have been all that sick, dipped a nurse and kissed her hard.

A one-armed infantryman came up to me, grinning ear to ear. "Germany has surrendered!" he roared as he patted me on the back with his good hand, sending sparks of pain through my wounds. "How about that! The war is over."

"That's great news," I said, gritting my teeth against the pain.

He began charging around the deck, shouting, "The war is over!" like a town crier. Several men threw their hats into the air, where they were caught by the wind and tossed onto the ocean.

We'd won. With the arrival of the Americans and the failure of Germany's big push, it had been inevitable. Finally all those deaths had been avenged; maybe the pilot who had dropped the bomb on Emily was dead now. I should have been dancing, but I didn't have the will. He'd just been doing his duty. All of us had.

By the time we arrived in England we'd been hit by sleet and snow. I watched it gather on the deck, not quite believing it was real.

I was officially discharged from the yeomanry at Grimsby barracks. Several of the draft troopers watched me with nervous curiosity and a little awe. They knew I'd been over there with their brothers, uncles, or pals. I'd seen war.

"Thank you for your service," the regimental sergeant major said as I signed my papers.

I couldn't bring myself to say *You're welcome*. I walked into Grimsby, found a clothing store near City Hall, and dressed in civilian clothes for the first time since signing up. I packed my badges and my uniform neatly in my kit bag and walked out onto the street.

It was odd not to feel the uniform chafing me. I kept

looking at my shoulders, feeling naked without my regimental insignia. The only lice I scratched at were imaginary.

I briefly thought of visiting Uncle Nix, but in my heart I didn't want to see him. I had no idea what we would have to talk about now. He'd be happy that all the calculations he'd made with other officers had paid off.

I booked passage on the next civilian boat from Liverpool to Canada, then spent a full day finding Emily's home in Cleethorpes. It was a cottage on the outskirts of the town, surrounded by a stone fence and crowded by a small barn. That was where she had milked the cow.

It took me several minutes before I mustered enough courage to walk up to the door. Finally, heart beating hard, my guts queasy, I knocked.

Her mother answered. "Hello?" she said. She was so much like Emily my knees began to quake. "May I help you?"

"I—I was a friend of Emily's," I muttered.

Her face grew sad. "What's your name?"

"Edward Bathe. She was a very good friend."

Her mother stared at me suspiciously; then her face softened. "Edward. Edward. She spoke of you." She opened the door wider. "Would you like to come in? I could make tea."

I glanced inside, where there would be books, pictures of Emily, and her room. I feared I'd fall apart if I saw it any more closely.

"Please," her mother said.

I stood, frozen, trying not to burst into tears. Finally I blurted out, "I'm sorry, but I just want to see her grave, please. I have to say good-bye."

She stepped toward me, and I worried momentarily that she was going to open her arms and hug me. Then I would surely be lost. Instead, she moved by me and pointed toward the road, giving me directions.

"She was really important to me," I said.

"I know. Thank you for coming and putting a face to the name."

I nodded and backed away. I walked over a hill to a small, flint-walled Anglican church. It had been worn by hundreds of years of endless English rain. Behind it, the graveyard was filled with rows of rounded headstones. Some had fallen over; others were from as far back as the 1700s, encrusted with frozen moss. I went to where the earth was freshly turned and the headstones had sharper edges.

EMILY WATSON

BELOVED

APRIL 12, 1897–MAY 19, 1918

I stared at the mound of earth, not yet grown over with grass. She was twenty-one. I finally knew her age.

"I loved you." I tried not to fall to my knees. "I loved you, Emily."

Like a fool, I hadn't brought any flowers, so I reached into my kit bag. My Lincs Yeomanry cap badge was all I had. If I left that on top someone would steal it. I dug into the earth next to her headstone, the gesture reminding me of my father looking for moisture in the soil. When I'd buried it there, I stood up. The shadow of the church was working its way over the graves. I wanted to say so many things, to tell her about Buke, about Cheevers, about everything I'd seen, but I was mute. It began to snow, large flakes sticking to my coat.

Sensing I was being watched, I turned slowly. Someone stood behind me on the path, hidden in the shadows of the church wall. I allowed myself to believe it was Emily; I saw the familiar slant of her nose, the shape of her eyes. For a moment I let my spirit soar.

But the woman took a step out of the shadow and I saw that it was Emily's mother. Crying.

"I'm sorry!" She dabbed at her eyes. "I wanted you to have your time alone with her, but I—I need to talk to someone who knew her. I really miss her."

"I do, too."

She moved hesitantly toward me. "I can see why she fell in love with you."

She held me and I put my arms around her. "She was so pretty," her mother said, "so pretty." Her sobs were muffled by my shoulder. I wanted to say I didn't deserve to be held like this, I had marched off to war and killed men, but I thought of Emily and a fleeting sense of sad peace came over me.

3

The voyage to Halifax was long and tiring. I spent my days wandering the deck of the *Orduna* or lying in my third-class bunk, not once feeling seasick. Whenever the ship shook, I wondered if it was a shell.

Soon I was on a train, chugging through the provinces, and traveling deeper and deeper into winter. The car grew colder with each passing hour, and I was glad for the thickness of my greatcoat. I shared the car with several young soldiers, their hair freshly cut and their eyes full of life. They laughed and sang, relieved that the war was over. They hadn't had to leave the country.

I was one of the few without a uniform, though my greatcoat was an obvious military issue. I was thankful no one spoke to me. I stared out the window, watching the snow fall.

"Hey, mate!" I looked up to see Cheevers lurching forward, a red hole in his head. I gasped and grabbed the armrest, then blinked. One of the soldiers had taken Cheevers's place, leaning forward so his friend could light his cigarette.

The train stopped in Moose Jaw. The recruiting car was long gone, and the train station, where we'd stood and saluted Sergeant Billings, was nearly deserted. I thought of Paul; he would be in one of the houses somewhere nearby. I hoped he was warm, his family close around him. I promised myself I'd look him up one day, then swore it on Emily's grave, to be sure I would do it.

In the early evening the train pulled up to the Tompkins station, and I was the only passenger to detrain. I walked across the wooden platform, my kit bag over my shoulder. Though my wounds were mostly healed, the scars throbbed with each step.

I walked down Main Street, past the outdoor rink where I'd played hockey, and over the fields. The wind jabbed cold fingers through the holes in my greatcoat. There were no leaves on the trees, and my footprints were fresh and clean. Years earlier, whenever snow fell so perfectly, Dad would hook up the horse to the sleigh and take us out under the stars, the reins in one hand, the other arm around my mom's shoulders. The thought of it put a lump in my throat.

The gate to New Aylesby Farms was open, and a shutter on the house banged occasionally. Dad had always insisted a lamp be left lit in the window during winter nights in case there was a storm. That way we would be able to find our way home. Tonight there wasn't a light to be seen.

I walked in the front door and set my rucksack down. My heart beat heavily and my palms sweated. "Hello!" I called, my voice hoarse. "Hello?"

I climbed the stairs and paused to look at my mother's picture. She would always be the same age, staring back at me. I ached, seeing how much I looked like her. The ache continued as I glanced at the photograph of Hector and me; we were just children.

I stood outside the master bedroom and gently pushed on the heavy door.

"Father?"

The bed was empty. In fact, it had been made! I hurried down the stairs and into the living room. I'd left the front door ajar, the cold seeping in. I peered out at the yard. There was nothing moving around the barn and there were no cattle in the pen. Just as I closed the door, at the edge of my vision, I caught a movement in the den.

I crossed the foyer and looked in. Dad sat in his chair, wearing his coat, melting snow dripping from his boots. He glared at me.

"I told you not to go," he said quietly.

"I know, Dad."

"All this time. Waiting. Worrying."

"I wrote."

He grimaced. "I know. But you left me here alone. With all this work to do. Alone."

"I'm sorry."

"How can I be sure you're real? Whenever the floorboards creak, I think it's one of you boys sneaking up the stairs. Or your mom bringing lemon tea."

282

"I'm home, Dad. It's me."

Anger and doubt lurked in his eyes. I stepped into the den and he got up slowly, as if it was a great effort. I was surprised to discover that we now stood eye to eye. In the year I'd been away I had grown.

He moved toward me suddenly, and I stepped back, thinking he wanted to strike me. But instead, he opened his arms and held me so tight against his chest that my ribs and shoulder ached, but I didn't care. I hugged him back, tears in my eyes, as he said, "Don't you ever go away again."

4

Dad put together a meal for me: leftover roast from one of our steers, and garden potatoes. He'd received the official telegram about my being mentioned in dispatches, and told me how proud he was but didn't press for details. I didn't want to discuss it further anyway.

Later, too tired to talk, I climbed into my own sweet bed. The pillow was so familiar and soft, a luxury I'd long forgotten. The room was as undisturbed as an Egyptian tomb. My Kipling books were on the shelves, the stack of *Boy's Own Papers* sat on the side table, and the African spear from Hilts still hung on my wall.

I was home. I closed my eyes, hoping for my first good night's sleep in weeks. I was just nicely drifting off when I heard the wind, and it reminded me of the strange, god-awful punctured-lung wheezing of Buke in his last moments. Then I worried that Emily had made the same sound as her life had been torn from her, her beautiful body shattered by the bomb.

My eyes snapped open and I stared into the dark, and still the images remained, impossible to shake. Each one had been etched into my memory forever.

Why had I lived? So many were dead, but I still breathed the air. *Why me?*

I tossed and turned, unable to leave the war behind. Frustrated, I sat up and decided to go for a walk. Downstairs, I pulled on my greatcoat, expecting Dad to appear any second to tell me to get back up to bed. He had left the lamp burning in the window.

The beauty of the front yard, its white carpet of snow and frosted trees, was something from a fairy tale. The Jordan Valley and its terrible heat had made me believe I'd never see such a sight again.

I opened the barn door with a good tug, stepped inside, and began to gag. The air was warm and moist and heavy with the smell of horses. One neighed as though asking a question. Buke! His wonderful face flashed before me. I stumbled back out and leaned against the fence, taking deep, ragged breaths, the cold cutting into my lungs. I cleared my throat and spat. After several minutes, I found the strength to carry on.

I trudged out of the pen and into the pasture. It was unusually mild. The stars were small and distant, a sliver of the moon scarring the sky. I wandered until I found myself in front of the church. I looked at the door for a long time and finally went in. The stained-glass windows were barely visible, but as a child I'd memorized them. Back then the mere sight of them would fill me with the fear of God and longing for the warmth and love of Jesus. And now I felt nothing.

At the altar I stared up at the carving of Jesus on the cross. Eternally in agony, he looked blissfully heavenward. I'd seen that same agony in the faces of the wounded on the battered *Mercian*, heard it in the Barada Gorge, smelled it in the aid post. I had imagined it on the faces of the people I had loved. For all that, Jesus wouldn't even look me in the eye. He was too busy gazing at his Father in heaven.

"I walked everywhere you walked," I whispered, "and I didn't see you anywhere."

He had died for us; died so that we might live. Live for what? To fire bullets through one another's brains? To drop bombs? Where was his almighty Father in all of that? He hadn't lifted a holy finger to stop it.

"You weren't anywhere!" I yelled, and picked up a psalm-book, slamming it on the altar. I whacked at the altar again, then stood there, shaking uncontrollably. I wanted to pitch the book through one of the stained-glass windows, but instead, I flung it to the floor and looked for something larger to throw. With a sweep of my hand, I knocked away the candles and they clunked across the floor.

"Stop that!" a gruff voice yelled from the back of the church. I turned to face Reverend Ashford.

"Who are you?" He charged down the aisle, dressed in his black robe. "What are you doing?"

"I've come to pay my respects!"

"Respects?" Ashford stopped a few feet away, and the anger in his eyes matched mine. Then he raised his eyebrows. "Edward? Is it you?"

286

I glared at him, breathing hard, not sure what to do next. "Edward?"

"It was all a lie."

"What was?"

"All of it. Everything." Then finally the words I most needed to say. "There is no God. And no Son of God. There can't be."

I expected an argument, but he only nodded, as though I'd answered a question. "Let it go, then. Don't believe."

"What?"

"If your faith is meant to be, it'll come back."

"Are you mad? I said I don't believe anymore."

"God forgives all. I think he would understand."

I wanted to hit him in the gut. "What's to understand? He watches us and does nothing. He's a blackguard. To let all those people die. Hector. Cheevers. And . . . Emily."

"We don't know why these things are allowed to happen, Edward. We aren't meant to know. But God is here, whether you believe in him or not."

A horrible feeling was growing inside me, a sense that I was cracking apart. Ashford went on.

"He didn't send you to war. You chose to go. You stood in this very spot and told me you wanted to go."

The reverend placed his huge hand on the top of my head. I wanted to lash out at him for daring to touch me, for making me believe that God was good, that Christ cared.

He removed his hand and said softly, "You're allowed to mourn, Edward. It's your duty."

"Duty?" I said, and then I wept, tears spilling to the floor. My heart, my soul, had pointed toward God, and toward

Hector, as a compass points north. Now there was no north. I was lost.

Ashford pulled me closer, pressed me to his chest. "No man was made strong enough to hold the weight of the world on his shoulders."

I wept for some time, drawing in deep, sobbing breaths. Then I pulled away, unable to look at him.

"There's no shame, Edward. You did everything you could. In the end we are all just men."

I walked home through the fields. Soft falling snow shrouded the land. In the spring it would melt and fill the creeks. But for now it was winter. The light in the front window of our home glowed warm in the distance, beckoning me back to my bed.

Author's Note

With any historical novel, readers naturally wonder what is real and what is fiction. The answer is: the emotions are real, and the rest of the story is inspired by history. The primary inspiration for this novel was my grandfather, Arthur Hercules Slade, who left Canada in 1914 to join the Lincolnshire Yeomanry in England. He was sent to fight in Egypt and Palestine. His father and three of his brothers also enlisted in the army, and the youngest brother, Percy, died in France. The letter detailing Percy's death hangs on my parents' wall today and is quoted almost word for word at the beginning of this novel.

The book is based loosely on the experience of the Lincolnshire Yeomanry and the Second Lancers. Their stories can be found in many of the histories of the British cavalry. To learn the story of the fighting Slades, visit www.arthurslade.com.

Many individuals and organizations helped me in the writing of this novel. I am extremely thankful for the funding provided to me by the Saskatchewan Arts Board and the Canada Council. I am indebted to the staff at the following places: the Lincolnshire Life Museum, the Imperial War Museum Archives, the Canadian Archives, the British National Archives, and the Saskatoon Nutana Legion. The Internet was, of course, a great help, but I raise my cap to the always eager British Regiments listserv and the World War One listserv. Finally, I owe thanks to Scott Treimel, Wendy Lamb, Lynne Missen, Dr. Shawn Grimes, T. F. Mills, Jim Parker, Jack Flaherty, Captain Gordon Kozroski (ret.), HLCol Geordie Beal, Kenneth Oppel, Alan Cumyn, Sara Jane Boyers, Philip Kashap, John Wilson, Karleen Bradford, Kevin Major, Vincent Sakowski, Nicky Singer, Jarret Olson, Dora Nasser, James Romanow, and finally, my wife, Brenda Baker.

About the Author

Arthur Slade was born in Moose Jaw, raised on a ranch in the Cypress Hills, and educated at the University of Saskatchewan. He now writes full-time from Saskatoon, Saskatchewan, Canada. He is the author of six novels for young adults and has won several prizes, including the Governor General's Award for Children's Literature. Arthur Slade can be visited virtually at www.arthurslade.com.